### *Kelly moved closer to him.*

Suddenly, looking at her seemed silly—he could be holding her.

Ben opened his arms, and Kelly stepped into them, resting her head against his chest. This was the best. He could stand here, holding her, and close his eyes to the shabby reminders of where he was, of who he was now. He could concentrate on the softness he held, the joy that had come so unexpectedly into his life.

"You know," he said softly, "I was thinking about our friendship."

"Oh?"

"We never said friends couldn't kiss."

"No, we didn't," she admitted.

Ben looked down at her, at her eyes so vibrant and inviting. At her hair, glowing with a fire that had to be echoed in her heart. He lowered his lips to hers, and the sweet, wild touch brought hope to his soul.

Everything was magic, just for this moment. The darkness of the past and the shadows of the future receded with Kelly in his arms, bringing back the dreams that life used to hold.

Dear Reader,

Welcome to the Silhouette **Special Edition** experience! With your search for consistently satisfying reading in mind, every month the authors and editors of Silhouette **Special Edition** aim to offer you a stimulating blend of deep emotions and high romance.

The name Silhouette **Special Edition** and the distinctive arch on the cover represent a commitment—a commitment to bring you six sensitive, substantial novels each month. In the pages of a Silhouette **Special Edition**, compelling true-to-life characters face riveting emotional issues—and come out winners. All the authors in the series strive for depth, vividness and warmth in writing these stories of living and loving in today's world.

The result, we hope, is romance you can believe in. Deeply emotional, richly romantic, infinitely rewarding—that's the Silhouette **Special Edition** experience. Come share it with us—six times a month! With this month's distinguished roster of gifted contemporary writers—Bay Matthews, Karen Keast, Barbara Faith, Madelyn Dohrn, Dawn Flindt and Andrea Edwards—you won't want to miss a single volume.

Best wishes,

Leslie Kazanjian,
Senior Editor

# ANDREA EDWARDS
# Make Room for Daddy

*Silhouette Special Edition*

Published by Silhouette Books New York

**America's Publisher of Contemporary Romance**

**SILHOUETTE BOOKS**
300 East 42nd St., New York, N.Y. 10017

ISBN: 0-373-09618-6

First Silhouette Books printing August 1990

**Books by Andrea Edwards**

Silhouette Special Edition

*Rose in Bloom* #363
*Say It with Flowers* #428
*Ghost of a Chance* #490
*Violets Are Blue* #550
*Places in the Heart* #591
*Make Room for Daddy* #618

Silhouette Intimate Moments

*Above Suspicion* #291

## ANDREA EDWARDS

is the pseudonym for Anne and Ed Kolaczyk, a husband-and-wife writing team who concentrate on women's fiction. ''Andrea'' is a former elementary school teacher, while ''Edwards'' is a refugee from corporate America, having spent almost twenty-five years selling computers before becoming a full-time writer. They have four children, two dogs and four cats, and live in South Bend, Indiana.

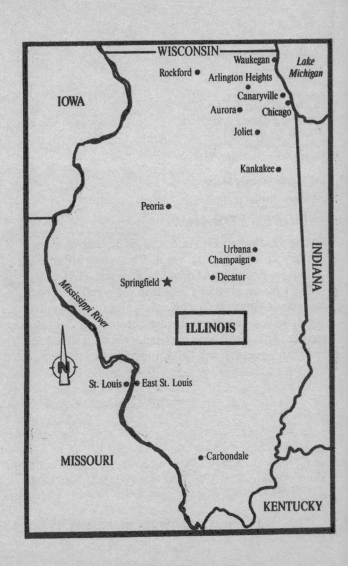

## Chapter One

The front-door bell tinkled its welcome, and Kelly Farrell put aside the shaker of candy sprinkles. "I'll get it, Mom," she called across the back room to her mother, who was packaging cupcakes for the senior citizens' luncheon at St. Pat's.

Kelly wiped the stray bits of icing from her hands and pushed back her auburn curls as she walked into the bakery salesroom. She had centuries of Irish lineage behind her, and her hair was as unruly as any colonial boy's. Trying the current styles would have required axle grease and industrial strength staples though, and Kelly was never one for trends. Keeping her hair out of her eyes was challenge enough. A white-haired old lady stood peering into the glass case displaying the sweet rolls and doughnuts.

"Hello, Mrs. O'Brien," Kelly said. "Isn't it a beautiful morning?"

"It is that," the old woman agreed, keeping her eyes on the rows of pastries.

Kelly's grandfather, Michael James Farrell, had landed in Boston at the turn of the century, carrying only his strong back and an eagerness to see all of this great new land called America. He became a journeyman baker and took to wandering, picking up jobs as he moved west. On reaching Chicago, he'd met Maureen O'Flaherty and he wandered no more.

"The jelly bismarcks are still warm," Kelly said. "I just dusted some sugar on them."

Mrs. O'Brien nodded her head and grunted a reply as she continued to study shelf after shelf before her. The old woman always bought two apricot sweet rolls, but before every purchase, she carefully examined all of the bakery's wares. Kelly smiled fondly at her neighbor and let her mind drift back into her familial past.

Michael and Maureen had set up house in the Canary-ville neighborhood of Chicago, then a new neighborhood filling with their countrymen from the old country. They'd moved into an apartment above the bakery where Michael worked. As the years passed, Michael purchased the bakery and six children joined them in that snug little set of rooms above the store. One boy went to the Lord soon after birth. The remaining four girls and the remaining boy grew to adulthood.

That boy was Kelly's father, Patrick, who had taken over the bakery when Grandpa Michael had grown old. Kelly and her brother, Michael, like their father and aunts before them, had been born at St. Bridgit's and had grown to adulthood in that same little apartment above the family bakery.

"I do believe I'll treat myself to two apricot sweet rolls, dear."

"That's a good choice," Kelly agreed. "The sweet rolls came out especially good today."

"Give me those two at the end," Mrs. O'Brien said, pointing toward her right. "They seem a touch fuller than the rest, and the doctor wants me to have more fruit."

Smiling, Kelly put the woman's two rolls in a small bag and patiently waited while Mrs. O'Brien rummaged her purse for the correct change.

"How is Moira?" Kelly asked as she rang up the sale and put the coins in their proper slots. "Are she and Joey Sheehan still going together?"

"Oh, yes," Mrs. O'Brien replied. "And if gambling weren't a sin, I'd bet that they'll soon be making their union a permanent one."

"That's wonderful," Kelly said, a smile warming her cheeks and heart. "Moira's such a sweetheart."

"But as shy as those little babies she teaches," Mrs. O'Brien said with a sigh. "I'll never know how you ever got her and Joey together."

Kelly just laughed. "It wasn't that hard." Joey was a tough, aggressive cop, but he had been smitten immediately with the quiet, gentle Moira. Though it had taken some hard work on Kelly's part to get Moira to consider dating him.

"She's a little worried about marrying a policeman," Mrs. O'Brien continued. "But I told her that in today's world, being an accountant is just as dangerous. Besides, that Sheehan boy is a smart one. He's attending law school, you know."

"Yes," Kelly said with a nod. "DePaul."

"That's where his honor, the mayor went," Mrs. O'Brien said, crossing herself. She was referring to the father of Chicago's present mayor, who'd died almost fifteen years ago after running Chicago for twenty-two years. "That Sheehan boy is going to make superintendent one day, mark my words."

"He certainly might," Kelly agreed.

Mrs. O'Brien picked up her bag, shifted her purse and started for the door, only to stop. Her smile had a touch of sadness in it. "Now, don't let all the good ones get away, Kelly," she said. "Your own sweet mother is praying for grandchildren, just like all the rest of us."

"I know, Mrs. O'Brien," Kelly assured her. "You have a nice day and give Moira and Joey my best."

She watched Mrs. O'Brien step out into the street and pause twice to exchange greetings with others on the street. Twice, and she still wasn't past the bakery's large front windows yet. That was what Kelly liked about Canaryville—it was like a small town where everyone knew everyone else. People looked out for each other and their children.

Of course, that also meant that everyone knew everyone else's business. Who was having trouble making ends meet, who wasn't feeling well and who didn't have a man in her life at the moment. But Kelly's "moment" had lasted more than a year now, and she was getting expert at changing the subject and deflecting comments. Her heart no longer hid in the closet each time the idea of love was approached. Acting cool and unattached had once been pretense—now it was a state of being.

"Did Mrs. O'Brien have her usual apricot sweet?" Kelly's mother asked as she came into the front of the store.

"Two," Kelly replied.

Anna Farrell chuckled as she put the tray of cupcakes back onto the glass shelves in the display case. "I think the last time she'd had something different was in 1945. When we'd heard that the Germans surrendered, she had a fudge-filled bismarck along with her apricot sweets."

Kelly reached for a loaf of rye bread awaiting slicing. "It looks like Moira and Joey Sheehan are getting serious," she said.

"That's nice," her mother grunted. "You certainly can pick them." There was a long moment's pause. "For others."

Kelly's jaw tightened ever so slightly as she fitted the bread into the slicing machine. "I like fixing people up."

"You do a lot of it," Mrs. Farrell replied.

"I can feel when two people are right for each other," Kelly said, and turned the slicer on. "And lots of times they're both so shy and concerned that they won't accept each other without a little nudge."

"I've noticed," her mother said dryly.

This discussion was on a straight track to nowhere, with short stops at arguments and hurt feelings. Kelly slid the sliced loaf into a bag and twisted the end shut as she forced a smile on her lips and a lilt into her voice. "I almost forgot that I planned to drop in on our new neighbor this morning. You can manage here all right for a few minutes, can't you?"

"I could manage better if I weren't always weeping at the thought of you growing old alone," Anna muttered.

Kelly said nothing, knowing by now that some remarks were in a mother's blood and she was going to speak her mind. She took off her apron and hung it on the hook just inside the back room.

"So, who you going to fix him up with?" her mother asked as Kelly went around the counters toward the door. "Better be careful. He might be a hard sell. Mrs. Callahan thinks it's only a year since his wife died."

Kelly went outside, letting the warm summer air melt any traces of a frown from her forehead. She had no intention of forcing someone on the man, certainly not if he was still grieving, but she could help him get acquainted with more people in the neighborhood. That's all she ever did—just helped friends meet new ones. If one of those persons found somebody special among one of those new acquaintances, then that was a wonderful bonus. She liked to help people.

Not that Ben Peterson looked as though he was in need of her help. With his ruggedly Nordic good looks, the man was almost enough to make her own heart race a bit, and she wasn't looking for anyone at all. He appeared to be in his late thirties, seemed intelligent, sensitive and thoughtful. And then there was his little daughter, cute as the proverbial bug's ear. The man would have lots of friends—female ones especially—once he got settled into the neighborhood.

Kelly pulled open the door and stepped inside. The sandwich shop was deserted except for Ben along the far wall, wiping empty tables. He was reasonably tall, built like a linebacker with muscle to spare. "Good morning," she said, then added, "I'm Kelly Farrell from next door."

He glanced up at her briefly, treating her to a hint of a smile that would have been enough to flutter the hearts of any of a half dozen ladies she could think of. Rather than find someone special for him, she was going to have to help fight them off.

"Hi," he said, then wiped off the last table. "I remember you. The bakery lady."

He had a voice that was smoother and richer than milk chocolate. Kelly shifted from one leg to the other as she sampled the silence, watching him work. He picked up a tray of napkin dispensers and began to distribute them, one to each table. His presence seemed to fill the room to overflowing, though he wasn't big enough to be in the overweight category. There was just something that made you notice him. He just seemed so in control, which was a weird way to describe someone distributing napkin dispensers around a diner. Kelly took a deep breath and sat down at the counter.

"I thought I'd come over to see how you're doing," she said. "You know—see if you need a tour of the neighborhood or anything."

He finished with the napkins and put the tray on the counter before he really smiled at her. "Debbie and I took a walk after dinner yesterday. I think Rand McNally can take a vacation."

"Found everything, did you?"

He squinted off into the distance with a thoughtful crease to his forehead. "An ice-cream parlor, the neighborhood branch of the library and a park with swings."

Kelly laughed. "Right. Everything."

He smiled at her, a pleasant lifting of his lips that brought an echo to her own mouth until she noticed the bleakness in his deep blue eyes. They seemed to convey a soul-wrenching depth—trouble was lurking. Not trouble for others, but the memory of it for him. Pain resided in his heart. Pain and something else she couldn't quite put a name to. Clouds seemed to cover the hot summer sun.

She hated to see someone hurting, even though she knew that suffering was an inevitable part of life. Still, if there was any way that someone around her could learn to smile again, she would find it. She'd done it by befriending Bertha Witte in sixth grade, by going to the homecoming dance with Jerome Kuhn in her sophomore year of high school and by fixing up couples in the neighborhood. It might be harder with a stranger, but she was up to the challenge.

"So, if you don't need a mapmaker, how about if I fill you in on the social events of the upcoming season?" she said.

"Are there many?"

"Sure. Ice-cream socials, concerts, chess in the park. Canaryville offers everything and anything you could possibly want."

The bleakness returned, as if a wound had been re-opened, and he turned to slide the empty tray under the counter. "I'm afraid I'm not much of a social butterfly."

Her heart wanted to ache with his pain, but she was here to show him that Canaryville was a healing place. She put a wall around her soft-touch nature. "Somehow I can't picture you as any kind of 'butterfly,'" she told him. "Social or antisocial."

His laughter came back, and like the return of the sun after a storm, it was strong and doubly blessed. "Can I get you anything? Some iced tea?" he asked.

"Sure," she replied.

Ben filled two mugs with iced tea and brought them out to a table. They sat down across from each other. Up close she was even more aware of his strength, the sense of power kept at bay, and strangely enough, the sense that danger might lurk under that calm surface.

"I'm sorry if I seem a little unfriendly," he said.

"No problem," Kelly quickly replied.

He looked off into the distance for a moment, and it was as if she were watching a runner gathering strength for a race. His eyes came back to her, their blue depths calm.

"I'm new to the area," he said. "I have my daughter to take care of and—" He paused for a long moment to study the street scene outside. "And I have a lot of things to sort out."

Kelly sipped at her tea. "Mrs. Callahan said that your wife died last year," she ventured. "It must be hard to be alone with a child to raise."

He stared next into his glass, moving it slightly in an ever-widening circle of condensation on the tabletop. "At times it can be."

"Sometimes being with friends can help," she told him gently. "And, as your neighbors, we're also your friends, even if you don't know us yet."

He smiled and nodded, but it was such a sad smile that Kelly wanted to reach out and brush his locks back. But she kept her hands to herself and just finished her tea. She had to move slowly.

"Well, I'd better get back. I've got bread in the oven that should be almost done. What do I owe you for the tea?"

"My treat. Thanks for stopping by," he said, and followed her to the door.

"See you around." She stopped at the door, wanting to do or say something that would turn that cloudiness in his eyes to sunshine, but what words could ease the pain of losing a loved one? In time, she'd find him someone to bring smiles into his life. In time.

The late-afternoon sun had slipped down behind the Callahans' two-flat when Kelly came out of the bakery to roll the awning back up. The creaking old mechanism was drowned out by the lumbering clatter of a bus coming to a stop at the corner.

"Hi, Kelly," Moira O'Brien called out.

Kelly waited a moment as Moira walked down from the bus stop, carrying an armload of books. "I thought you were on vacation," Kelly said. "School closed last week, didn't it?"

"I'm taking a graduate course in child psychology at the U. of I.," Moira said. "Mom thinks I should just take the summer off, but Joey thinks it's great that I'm going for my masters degree." A faint but telling blush captured her cheeks.

"Joey, huh?" Kelly teased. "Now whose opinion counts for more?"

Moira's blush deepened and her eyes grew dreamy with love. "He's so nice. I can't believe how happy I am with him." The dreaminess faded a touch, and she took on a scolding frown. "What I can't believe is that you didn't snatch him up for yourself. By the time you've noticed that you're lonely, all the good guys will be gone.''

"Hardly.'' Kelly laughed. "Or maybe I've got some good ones stashed away.''

But Moira wasn't fooled. She squeezed Kelly's hand. "Hey, you should be over that jerk Randy by now. Don't let him turn you off from guys forever.''

"No chance of that,'' Kelly vowed as, with a wave, Moira continued down the block.

She was over Randy, Kelly assured herself. She'd been over him the moment he'd left. What she wasn't over was her financial debacle, which had resulted from her own stupidity.

She bent over to pick up a candy wrapper on the side-walk and straightened up, staring at the sandwich shop next door. It was dark inside, except for the lighted cola clock on the far wall, which cast a cheery glow over the empty tables and chairs.

Somehow the emptiness of the place saddened her. Not that it ought to be open now—this was not a neighborhood for dinner restaurants, just lunch and breakfast places. But still, the lighted clock, turning the shadows into brightness, somehow seemed representative of Ben's efforts to start a new life with his daughter. Though all it took to light up the sandwich shop was a flick of a switch, Ben didn't have an easy way to turn off his grief. No, friends were going to have to do that. And that was something she was good at—being a friend.

Stuffing the candy wrapper in her pocket, Kelly went back into the bakery, locking the door behind her and turning the sign to read Closed. She turned off the main lights and went through the back room to drag her weary body up the stairs to their apartment. Her feet felt as if they were encased in heavy bread dough. The day had started at its usual 4 a.m. for her and ended at six-thirty. A little dinner would perk her up, though, and give her the energy to tackle the challenge of getting Ben Peterson's eyes to smile.

A yawn escaped Kelly's control, and she thought it might take more than a little dinner to keep her eyes open. Maybe a lot of dinner and a gallon or so of coffee. She didn't usually work this late, but her brother, Michael, who usually spelled her in the afternoon, had had a meeting with the adviser in his engineering department regarding a scholarship for the coming year. Aware of the importance of the meeting, Kelly simply covered for him. Her mother had objected, saying she'd fill in, but Mrs. Farrell needed her afternoon naps. She was fine now, but that flu bug back in the early spring had really taken a lot out of her.

Pausing at the top landing, Kelly took a deep breath to smother another approaching yawn. Besides, it didn't matter how her mother felt. Kelly owed them. If it hadn't been for her gullibility, no one would be in the straits they were in now, working their fingers to the bone. Mom would be down in Florida with the rest of her retired friends, and Mike would be a full-time student, worrying only about his studies.

Kelly hung a smile on her lips, opened the door and threw herself into the apartment. "Hi, guys," she called out. "I'm home."

"We're in the kitchen, honey," her mother called out.

Where else? Kelly's smile took on a life of its own. They were always in the kitchen. That was the heart of their home. She remembered doing her homework at the heavy old round table along with Mike, while Mom made dinner. Then her father would come up about this time, yell that he was home and they'd all yell back that they were in the kitchen.

"Sit down," her mother ordered as Kelly stepped into the kitchen. "You look tired."

"I'm fine," Kelly protested.

"I'm sorry about running out on you, sis."

"You didn't run out on me," Kelly replied. "You were taking care of your future."

"That's right, Michael," their mother said. "Besides, Miss Ironlady didn't have to stay down in the store. I wasn't doing anything this afternoon."

"Mom, I'm younger."

"Oh, so now I'm an old lady." Mrs. Farrell looked at Michael and rolled her eyes heavenward. "Someone you can push aside and leave in a corner."

Kelly moved to the stove and lifted the pot's cover. A stronger dose of the wondrous smells that filled the kitchen leaped out at her. "If you were working in the store, you wouldn't be able to make this delicious stew," Kelly told her mother.

"She got you there, Mom," Michael said with a laugh as he looked up from his job of setting the table.

"Don't get smart, or I'll whack both of you." Her mother handed Kelly the bowl of salad. "Put this on the table, please."

"Anything interesting in the mail?" Kelly asked as she passed the pile on the kitchen counter.

"A letter from Sara," her mother replied.

"How does she like Florida?"

Mrs. Farrell shrugged. "She says it's real hot and muggy. Even worse than here."

"Maybe that's why they invented air conditioning," Kelly pointed out.

She put the salad on the table and went back to the counter to check the pile of envelopes. Mrs. Farrell was always so negative when the subject of Florida was brought up. It had to be because so many of her friends had moved there, and her mother wished she could, too. But since Kelly had mortgaged their future by loaning money to that loathsome creep, her mom was stuck up here in Chicago. Rather than admit to her feelings, she dressed the subject in negativism so that she wouldn't feel as bad. More than just a twinge of guilt pinched at Kelly's conscience, and she grabbed up the letter addressed to her.

Her heart sank though as she recognized the name of the law firm printed on the envelope. Damn, wouldn't they ever give up? She stuffed the letter in her jeans pocket.

"How did your meeting with the adviser go this afternoon?" she asked Mike as he took three glasses out of the cabinet.

"Real good," her brother replied. "He says I'm almost sure to get another two grand in aid for this coming school year."

"Great," Kelly exclaimed. "That should really help."

He shrugged. "I'll need it. I'll have three lab classes all year. So I won't be able to work as many hours as I did before."

Kelly clenched her jaws momentarily. Money, money, money. Damn, why had she been such a ninny? She'd lost fifteen thousand to that flimflam artist. Money that would have made life so much easier for all of them. And it didn't help to know that they had all agreed to lend Randy the money. The real decision had been hers.

"They're talking about less rain this month," Mike said. "So it looks like I should get a lot more hours before school starts. That will help."

She stared at her brother's deeply tanned arms as he poured iced tea for the three of them. Her brother was night clerk at one of the downtown hotels during the school year, but when summer came he took another job with a landscape crew. Kelly sometimes wondered where he got all his energy from.

He turned to carry the glasses to the table and winked at her. "I'll do fine, sis. Then, once I graduate, I'll design some new ovens for you that'll never break down."

Her heart was what was threatening to break down at the moment, and she turned quickly. "I'm going to wash my hands before dinner," Kelly said.

"Okay, dear," her mother replied. "Don't be long."

Once in the bathroom, Kelly blinked away the tears that were threatening and pulled the envelope from her pocket, opening it. Just as she suspected. The video chain had upped their offer for the property.

Kelly stared at the letter until the words blurred. Maybe she should take their money. Then Mom could go to Florida with her friends and Mike could go to school full-time. Their money worries would be over.

But what about her father and grandfather and all the years they'd put into this place? Had it all been to finance some con artist's scheme? No, it had been to provide security for their future, for the future of all the Farrells to come. Selling out would really mean that Randy had beaten her, and she would never let that happen. The bakery would stay in the family, and those lovely cabinets that Grandpa built himself would get polished with love every morning. Sighing, Kelly folded the letter and put it back in her pocket.

Ben Peterson lowered his bulk into the slatted wooden chair and let the warm evening breezes blow his tensions away. The front of their second-floor apartment looked out over the street, but the back porch was fairly quiet. It didn't exactly give them much of a view, as it overlooked the small backyards and the alley, but it was away from the street and prying eyes. Debbie could play without his worrying over every car that passed by.

Ben stared at the porch railing's long shadows reaching across his legs. Funny the twists and turns a man's life took. He'd been in the top ten percent of his mechanical engineering class at M.I.T. Several Fortune 500 companies had wanted him, but he'd gone to work for a small, high-tech firm out on Route 128 in Boston to be close to Sheila. Then, before he knew it, Debbie had been there, also. A tiny little mite who hadn't even hit seven pounds when she was born. Now eight years old and still on the petite side, the kid had a stranglehold on his heart and life. And the world couldn't find a happier prisoner. Now they were both prisoners of another kind.

"Daddy."

Debbie's hair was in a ponytail that whipped the shoulders of her T-shirt as she bounced out onto the porch in bare feet. She leaned against him, and he put an arm around her shoulders.

"Do you know how to play jacks?" Debbie asked.

Ben frowned. "Afraid not, honey." His daughter gave him a fierce scowl and he grinned. "Okay, say it. I'm a failure."

"No, that's okay," she said with a sigh, and pushed herself away from him.

"Weren't there any instructions in the package?" Ben asked.

She shook her head and knelt down on the porch with her newly purchased package of jacks on the wooden floor in front of her. She stared at them as if they'd come to life by watching them long enough.

"How about an ice-cream cone?" Ben asked.

"Later." Face set in determination, Debbie was concentrating on the ball and the little jacks, setting the jacks in patterns and rolling the ball between them. Ben let his attention drift into guilt.

Playing with a dollar set of jacks, when she could be riding a horse or swimming in her own private pool. Ben set his jaw and shoved all negative thoughts out of his mind. This place wasn't so bad. The porch here was spacious, and there was a spot of green down below in the backyard. Besides, love—real love—beat green grass and horses any day. And love was the whole purpose for this little game of hide-and-seek across the country.

After all, he could have left Debbie with her grandparents, their horses and their swimming pool, but was that all

Debbie needed? Their coldness had ruined Sheila, and he wasn't about to let them turn his daughter into the confused, tortured human being that her mother had been.

"Nuts." The little girl glared at the offending jacks lying around her knees. "I thought I could figure out how to play this."

"Maybe we should check for an expert in the yellow pages," Ben said.

"I saw other kids playing it," she said. "It can't be so hard."

"You ready for that ice-cream cone now?" he asked, recognizing his own stubbornness in his daughter and sighing. Persistence was good to have, but it could also be a curse.

"Not until I figure this out," Debbie insisted, then frowned over toward the latticework privacy screen that separated their porch from the one belonging to the next apartment. Through the holes, Ben could see that someone had come out onto the next porch.

Debbie inched over closer to the screen to peer through. "Hello," she called out before Ben could think up a reason to stop her.

"Hi," a soft, musical voice answered. "What you doing?"

He recognized Kelly's voice. Or maybe it was his heart that did. Those tones were soft enough to smooth out the roughest waters, and he stiffened his spine against their lure. His mind played back her smile, though, and his heart wanted to weaken. Her smile, the laughter in her eyes, the wild riot of auburn curls that had turned to flame in the morning sun as she'd sat drinking iced tea with him. She spelled danger to him in every swaying movement of her slender body.

"Do you know how to play jacks?" Debbie asked the woman through the wooden screen.

"Honey, we shouldn't bother people," Ben said.

"'Do I know how to play jacks?'" Kelly repeated, ignoring Ben's words if she'd even heard them. "Hey, do birds know how to fly?"

"Yeah." Debbie's voice had an uncertain sound to it.

"Want me to come over and show you how?" Kelly asked.

No, Ben wanted to say, but couldn't find his voice.

"Oh, would you?" Debbie's uncertainty was gone, demolished by fierce excitement.

Ben eased himself out of his chair, telling himself it was all right. No, he didn't want Kelly's company, but Debbie did. She obviously needed a female coach to instruct her in the basics of jacks, and it wasn't fair for him to deny his daughter that little pleasure when he had taken so much away from her. He could be strong and ignore any stirrings that Kelly's presence might awaken.

"I'll go downstairs and open the door," he said.

"Don't bother," Kelly called.

Kelly climbed onto the porch rail on her side of the screen and swung around the post anchoring the latticework. Shapely legs seemed to take center stage as Ben watched. Even as he swallowed hard, his hands reached out to help her down, but she ignored them, jumping lightly onto the floor of the porch on their side of the screen.

"That's only for big girls to try," she told Debbie.

"And eight isn't big enough," Ben recovered enough to add.

"What if I really had to get to your side?" Debbie said. "Like if a big, bad robber was chasing me."

"Talk to your father about taking the screen down," Kelly said.

Kelly's eyes were gleaming with joy just as they had this morning, and her skin seemed to glow with the warmth of the sun. She brought both peace and a wild tension into his heart at the same time.

"Daddy," Debbie said. "Can we take it down, Daddy? I mean, in case I got to get over to this lady's side real quick."

"This lady is Miss Farrell," Ben said. "We met her and her family the day we moved in." The pleading in Debbie's blue eyes reminded him of all that was at stake here, all that was at risk, and his heart closed and locked its doors. He could look over at Kelly without the faintest tremor in his soul.

Kelly's lips split into a big smile for Debbie as she shook the girl's hand, much to Debbie's blushing delight. "Hi, Debbie," she said. "My real name is Kelly."

"Hi, Kelly."

Now what? Ben wondered. How did he gently extricate himself? But Kelly just dropped down to her knees in front of the child.

"So, do you want to play jacks or don't you?"

Debbie nodded her head vigorously as Kelly picked up the jacks in one hand and tossed them out onto the porch floor. As Ben watched, Kelly showed Debbie how to bounce the ball while picking up all the jacks, first one at a time, then two, then three. The gentle thump of the ball on the wood began to untie the knots in his stomach, just as the soft breeze cooled his worries.

The sun sank below the horizon, and the gods slowly spread the evening's coverings over them, clothing the earth in the gentle half-light of dusk. A dog barked down the block, kids played hide-and-seek in a neighboring yard and a pair of lovers gazed into each other's eyes in the alley. He and Debbie had found refuge here. Maybe not for a long time, but for now they were safe. Kelly was not a threat in any way.

"Daddy. Can we have our ice-cream cones now?" Debbie asked.

He got to his feet. "Ah, we've mastered the jacks, have we?" he asked. "Or does learning them work up an appetite?"

"Not much to master," Kelly said with a laugh. Her glance at Debbie overflowed with affection. "She just needs a little practice."

"Kelly wants an ice-cream cone, too, don't you?" Debbie told him.

"What flavor?" he asked Kelly as he opened the back door. Debbie, he knew, was a strawberry afficionado.

"Chocolate," Kelly said. "If you have it."

"That's Daddy's favorite, too," Debbie said.

Ben just went inside, letting the screen door swing closed behind him with a familiar dull thud. It sounded like the screen doors of his youth, before everything was aluminum, and his heart wanted to relax even more. He'd been secure as a kid, even with his father out of work half the time and his mother fretting that one or all of the kids were getting into trouble at school. Times had been hard, but justice had always triumphed and the bad guys had always got their due.

Ben swallowed hard as he scooped ice cream into the cones. He had to be more careful. Just because a screen door sounded like the ones back when he was a kid didn't mean that he could relax. Some people surely viewed him as the bad guy now, and were rooting for him to get caught.

He quickly went back out with the cones, heaped to overflowing. Debbie and Kelly remained sitting on the floor while he returned to his chair. There were other empty chairs, but he was just as relieved to see Kelly choosing Debbie as her companion rather than him. He ate in silence while Debbie and Kelly chatted together.

"Thank you for the ice cream," Kelly said when she'd finished.

"It was the least we could do for the jacks lesson," he replied.

"My pleasure." Her voice was laughing but sincere. She pushed herself up from the floor. "I'd better be going. Bakers have to get up early."

"How early?" Debbie asked.

"I have to start the ovens around four-thirty," Kelly replied.

"Ugh," Debbie grunted. "That's sort of the middle of the night."

"Almost." Kelly laughed and, after a little wave, reversed her previous path and dropped down on her own side of the porch. Their side suddenly seemed chilled and shadowed.

"Can we play some more tomorrow?" Debbie called out as if she felt it, too.

"I'd love to," Kelly replied.

"After dinner?"

"About the same as tonight."

Then she was gone, and the evening's silence hugged them to its soft bosom. "You'd better be hitting the sack, too, kid." He chose not to linger on the sunshine Kelly carried in her smile and finished his own cone.

"I'm not a baker," Debbie pointed out.

"You're a little kid."

"It's not fair," she grumbled, but he heard the scraping of the jacks as she scooped them off the porch floor. Then soft footsteps crept up on him and he was enveloped in strong little arms around his neck. "Good night, Daddy."

"Good night, squirt."

They kissed, then Ben was left with his thoughts. He watched them dance in the streetlights that illuminated the alley and knew that for a time, life would be good here. Debbie could make friends with Kelly, but that would only be a problem if he and his daughter forgot to keep their distance.

## Chapter Two

"Can you hold down the fort, Mom?" Kelly asked as she filled a small tray with rolls and doughnuts. "I thought I'd drop in on Ben for a minute."

"I guess," her mother said with mock hesitancy. "Though no more than a minute. I could never handle our midmorning rush alone." The smirk on Anna's face matched her smart-aleck words.

"He's new to the neighborhood, Mom," Kelly protested. "And you know the people around here can be a little standoffish at times."

"Kelly, you're just an angel of mercy," Anna said laughingly. "Now, go before his lunch rush hits and you expect him to ignore them all to talk to you."

"Mom!" Kelly protested, but then just shut the door firmly behind her and marched to the door of the sandwich shop.

At times there was just no discussing things with her mother. Kelly was not in pursuit of Ben. She was trying to be friendly, that was all. That's why she was bringing the tray of sweet rolls, as a friendly gesture from one business-person to another. If he was interested in offering her baked goods at the shop, then fine. If not, that was all right, too. She was not using it as an excuse to see him each morning.

Ben was in the front of the shop, filling napkin containers at the tables. Although he was working efficiently, with a minimum of wasted movement, it just didn't look like a job he ought to be doing.

"Hi," Kelly said, then stopped in the doorway. Would he think she was chasing him, just as her mother did? Or would he understand that she was just being friendly?

"Hello there." His smile said she had nothing to worry about, giving her the go-ahead to venture farther into the shop.

"How are you this morning?"

"Fine." He glanced at the tray in her hands. "Are you the chairperson of the Canaryville welcoming commit-tee?"

"I was hoping to get you hooked on our product," she replied. "Then, unable to control yourself, you'd spend your life's savings buying goodies from us."

A crooked smile danced on his lips. "My life's savings would get me two doughnuts."

His smile could get him two doughnuts and her life. She shook her head, willing away the unbidden thoughts. "Actually I was wondering if you'd want to have some fresh-baked goods on hand to serve. The guy who used to run this place used to buy all his pastries at the wholesaler, so they were never too fresh."

"I hadn't even thought ahead that far," Ben admitted, his smile fading. "I'm just sort of on hold right now, sticking to the basics on the menu. I haven't thought of any specializations yet."

His smile was genuine, though his eyes still held bleak-ness in their far corners. Was it from some lasting hurt, or was he suspicious of her motives? Darn her mother for making her so sensitive this morning. "Why don't I put this tray here on the counter?" Kelly suggested. "Want one now?"

"Sure. Anything chocolate." Ben went behind the counter. "I was just going to have some iced tea. Would you like some?"

"Yes, please."

Kelly brought a chocolate doughnut for Ben and a cherry sweet roll for herself and sat down at a small table near the window. It was a typical Chicago summer, heat waves shimmering off the blacktopped street outside. People moved in the slow motion of a lazy summer day. Even the cars seemed to be going at a slower pace.

Ben brought two large glasses of iced tea to the table, and they ate in silence for a few minutes, sharing the panorama of an old Chicago business street. Laughing children raced by while older adults stopped to chat with friends. A bus lumbered by, stopping to pick up passengers at the corner.

Kelly's eyes came back to Ben, watching him as he watched the people outside. The tension she sensed in him yesterday seemed gone, or at least at rest for the moment. There was a certain watchfulness about him, a wariness that said he wasn't looking for closeness. But that could mean a lot of things, Kelly told herself. It most likely meant he wanted no romantic involvement as of yet, which was fine with her. She was just getting to know him. When the time was right, she'd start introducing him around the neighborhood. Ben's eyes came back to hers suddenly, and she threw herself into conversation.

"You have a bit of an accent. Where are you from?"

"Back East."

"That covers a lot of states."

"Think I've lived in them all, too." Ben chewed carefully for a long moment as he checked out every corner of the street. "It's nice here," he said. "But I kind of miss the ocean. I didn't live too close to it as a kid, but close enough that we used to go there to spend the day. There's something about that huge expanse of water that tends to put things in perspective."

"Lake Michigan is our ocean substitute," Kelly said. "It's not as big, but you can't tell that from the shore."

Ben nodded. "Yeah, it's nice. We took a walk along the beach a few days ago."

"It really cools the city off when we get an easterly breeze."

Their eyes met, and the tingling shock waves that raced through her body were anything but cool. She was aware of Ben in ways she'd never been aware of a man before. The faint hint of his masculine scent. The thick blond hair that covered his arms. His hands, so still around his glass of iced tea, but possessing such strength. They were all physical things she must have noticed a hundred times before on other men. Yet here and now, it was all different.

Everything about Ben seemed to promise tenderness and peace, along with the fire of passion. That tingling in her soul at his every glance wasn't sympathy for his situation, but awareness of him as a man. And herself as a woman. An awareness she'd never felt with such power before.

The silence of the moment stretched on into eternity and, for one of the few times in her life, Kelly found herself straining to continue the conversation. But words seemed rooted deep within her psyche, requiring superhuman effort to pull to the surface.

"Where's Debbie?" she finally asked.

"Upstairs," Ben replied. "Drawing and stuff like that."

"You haven't drafted her to help you down here?"

"She helps a lot around the house." He was silent for a moment, then shrugged. "Besides, she's just a kid."

"She ought to meet some of the kids in the neighborhood," Kelly said. "Why don't we set something up—I can introduce her to some of my friends' kids?"

Ben had finished his doughnut and gulped the remainder of his tea, the ice cubes rattling against his front teeth. "She'll meet some kids at school."

Didn't he want Debbie to meet other kids? Was Ben being overprotective, or was she being oversensitive? He was probably right. It was better for her to meet kids at school and pick her own friends. Though, there were a lot of kids in the neighborhood. Even if she didn't become best of friends with any of them, it would be better than sitting alone and drawing in her apartment. Kelly studied Ben's face as he stared out on the street. The trace of underlying passion she had just felt in his gaze had changed. Now she sensed only worry and something that seemed almost like fear. She was crazy, she decided as a mail truck banged to a stop in front of the shop.

"One of my regulars," Ben said, pushing himself up quickly.

"Hey, Ben," the mailman said heartily. "What's happening?"

"Nothing much," Ben replied. "Coffee to go?"

"How about some iced tea?" the man said. "I'm already melting away in this heat. A hot cup of coffee would just turn me into a grease spot. Hey." The driver had spotted the tray of sweets. "Sweet rolls! Got any cream cheese?"

Ben glanced over at Kelly, and she nodded, pointing to the far corner of the tray and mouthing fifty cents. Ben rang up the total.

"You know," the driver said as he pocketed his change, "this is a good idea, you and the bakery getting together. That way if I want a snack, it's like one-stop shopping."

Ben just shrugged at Kelly after the door had shut behind the driver. "I guess it's been decided."

"Why don't I bring a tray of pastries every morning?" Kelly said. "What you don't sell, I'll take back."

"That's okay, I—"

"I've already got a source for disposing of day-old goods," she assured him. "I can bring you some sandwich rolls, too."

"Okay."

The silence came between them, charged once more with an energy not unlike the restlessness of the tides. Over and over, her heart seemed ready to pound itself on the gentle sweetness of his smile. She got abruptly to her feet. "Well, see you later. Partner."

Ben's eyes grew shuttered. "Yeah, later."

Kelly strode briskly toward her own store, trying to rein in her wandering heart. That was a good business idea, but nothing more. There was no reason to feel as though it was about to rain just because Ben hadn't seemed overjoyed to be her partner. She glanced up at the clear sky, at the hot sun that seemed more mocking than warming, and hurried inside the bakery.

"Better add a few more bismarcks," Kelly's mother said. "We don't want that handsome young man wasting away to nothing."

Kelly gave her mother a quick but mild glare and went on stacking sweet goods and rolls onto the large tray.

"And don't forget that little girl. The poor child may have a tapeworm for all we know."

"Mother," Kelly said. "I told you this was a business deal. We decided to try it yesterday. People go to the sandwich shop for a midmorning coffee break and they'll pick up a sweet roll. Or they'll ask for their sandwich on a kaiser roll. We can use the extra business, you know."

Anna nodded, but the smile of quiet amusement still clung to her lips. "We could also use a handsome boyfriend," she said.

Kelly refused to get annoyed. It didn't matter that her mother thought she couldn't be happy without a man. Kelly knew differently. There were other things in life besides love, like work and friendship and responsibility. She carefully pulled the clear plastic wrap down around the baked goods so that it was without any wrinkles. It was a well-known marketing fact that a nicely presented display attracted positive attention.

"It's been two years since Randy," her mother said, continuing her own conversation. "You should be over him by now."

Over him. Randy of the smooth tongue and the morals of a snake. Kelly clenched her jaw momentarily. That really wasn't fair to the snake world. Snakes provided beneficial services, like keeping the rodent and bug population down for the farmers. Randy provided nothing positive to anybody, not even to himself.

"Mom," Kelly said softly, "I've been over Randy ever since that slime ball walked out the door with our money."

Her mother just picked an invisible piece of lint off Kelly's T-shirt with a smile. "Say hello to that nice Mr. Peterson for me."

Kelly swallowed a sigh and picked up the tray. She beat her mother to the door, pushing it open with her back as her mother followed. Once Kelly was outside, Anna gave her a big smile and a sweeping wave as she closed the door. Kelly answered with a small wave and crooked half-smile of her own. It was as if her mother was sending her off to school for the first time. Or off on her first date.

Kelly shook her head as she carefully carried the tray around two men standing in the middle of the sidewalk, discussing the White Sox victory over the Yankees last night. Her mother just wasn't thinking straight. Not only was Ben Peterson not in the market for serious companionship, but Kelly Farrell wasn't, either! She had a million things to get done before she started dating again.

The first thing was to get the bakery back on firm financial footing, then she needed to start putting money aside so that her mother could get away during Chicago's harsh winters. After that came Mike's schooling. A bachelor's degree was preliminary for an aspiring engineer, but a masters or even a doctorate was requisite. No, she was definitely not in the market for a relationship, no matter how handsome their neighbor might be.

Ben was at the door of the sandwich shop, holding it open for her. "Something wrong?" he asked as she hurried in out of the growing heat. "You're frowning."

She put the tray down, taking the time to line it up with the edge of the counter. "Didn't you know that it takes more muscles to frown than it does to smile?" she asked, forcing her gloominess away and producing a smile. "Well, I was just exercising my facial muscles."

He put the last salt and pepper shakers on a table, then brought his empty tray back around the counter. "Just so long as you weren't regretting this partnership already."

Kelly glanced briefly at him, her heart nearly faltering on his rugged good looks. Who would regret being partnered with him? Not her, her heart cried out until common sense asserted itself.

Maybe she ought to be regretting this. If her foolish emotions weren't going to stay in line, then she should keep herself locked up in the bakery all day.

"Nope. No regrets unless they're on your side," she said. "And here's my first delivery, partner."

Ben came closer to look at the sweet rolls, and Kelly took a step back, then scolded herself for acting like a scared rabbit. The wobblies in her knees weren't due to his closeness. Or rather, they were, but it wasn't anything he was consciously causing. She had to start behaving like a reasonable, mature adult.

Ben frowned at the sweet rolls, shaking his head. "I don't know."

Kelly's heart sank. Had he changed his mind? "What's wrong?"

"I won't be able to sell anything," he said sadly.

She should have expected this. Hadn't she sensed his hesitancy yesterday? And when she went over to their porch last night after dinner to play jacks with Debbie, she had only caught a glimpse of him reading the newspaper in his kitchen. He was trying to discourage her attempts at friendship.

"So, should I take them back?" she asked.

"Maybe. They look so 'purty' I won't have the heart to let people eat them."

She saw the laugh devils dancing gaily in his eyes and was too relieved to do more than smile in return.

"No matter how 'purty,' these here rolls are for eating," she said, and reached over to loosen the plastic wrap.

But Ben was reaching over at the same moment, and their hands brushed. It was the lightest of touches, barely making contact. Yet her heart stopped.

She brushed hands like this all the time with customers and never noticed, but the gentlest touch of Ben's hand on hers started firecrackers exploding. Roman candles shot into the dark and sent a cascade of diamonds across the nighttime sky. Sparklers waved and danced in wild delight. She stared into his eyes and thought she saw the reflection of her fireworks. The air seemed still and suffocating.

"Hi, Kelly," Debbie cried. "What are you doing here?"

The suffocating cloud disappeared, and Kelly found it possible to breathe again. She turned gratefully to the little girl. "Hello, Debbie. I just brought some sweet rolls over for your dad to sell here."

The little girl walked over to the counter and looked at the laden tray. "Boy, do they look great!" She turned pleading eyes on her father. "May I have one, please?"

"They're to sell, honey," Ben replied. "Not for us to eat."

Debbie's sunshine faded slowly.

"Hey, they really ought to be tested first," Kelly said. "You know, make sure they're good enough for your dad's customers. You could sure do me a favor by trying one."

"For free?"

"On the house," Kelly said with a nod.

But that apparently only confused the issue, for Debbie turned her questioning eyes back to Ben.

"That means you have to climb on the roof to get your treat."

"Ben," Kelly protested.

"It's okay," Debbie said, woman-to-woman all over her voice. "That's just one of his little jokes." The girl emphasized the word "little," and Ben made a face behind her back.

Kelly found herself smiling, not so much at Ben's expense as at the easy rapport between the two of them. There was so much affection in everything they did that their happiness couldn't help but spread to those around them.

"What are these filled with?" Debbie asked, pointing to some rolls.

"These are chocolate filled," Kelly replied, indicating one row of bismarcks. "And these are filled with custard."

The little girl's face twisted in mock pain. "I like both."

Debbie's voice was so small and sad that Kelly didn't know whether to laugh or hug her. "Take one of each," Kelly told the girl.

"But you can only eat one now," Ben quickly commanded after the child had stolen a quick glance in his direction.

Twisting her face in deep thought, Debbie picked out one of each. Then she wrapped the custard bismarck in a napkin and took a bite out of the chocolate.

"I'll put this one in the refrigerator upstairs," Debbie said around a hearty mouthful.

"Be sure you do," Ben warned, reaching for severity in his tone but not quite making it.

Debbie just nodded as she skipped away toward the stairs leading to their apartment upstairs. At the door she turned. "Daddy and I are going to the park after supper," she said to Kelly. "Want to come along?"

Her little face was so solemn, and there was a smear of chocolate across her cheek. How could Kelly refuse? She carefully kept her eyes away from Ben, away from those eyes that could hold her captive.

"Sure," she told Debbie, and with an easy wave in Ben's direction, hurried from the shop.

It was a purely physical attraction, Kelly told herself. A normal reaction for a young woman like herself who'd been avoiding men like the plague. A nice, handsome one comes along, she lets her guard slip slightly and the next thing she knows her toes are curling inside her shoes whenever he looks her way. A purely physical attraction, she repeated. It couldn't be anything else. She barely knew anything about the man.

"Is it seven yet?"

Debbie anxiously scanned the two clocks in the kitchen. The one in the microwave turned to 6:57, and Ben knew that one on the stove would turn over in another few seconds.

"Not yet, honey," he replied. "Another few minutes."

Debbie skipped back out onto the porch, and Ben was left to sigh and stare out the window. They really should be lying low, but what could he do? He couldn't lock Debbie up in the apartment all day like some pet gerbil.

And it was obvious that the company of a woman was good for her. Ben bit his lip a moment to control the twinges that threatened to cut at his conscience. The reality was that his daughter really wanted the company of an adult woman. What else would explain Debbie's obvious attraction to Kelly?

"Hi, Kelly."

He looked up in time to see Kelly's well-turned curves, not at all hidden by her cutoff jeans and T-shirt, as she took her route around the post and dropped down onto their side of the porch. A fire began to smolder deep in his thoughts, and a silent tension tightened a knot in his soul. Debbie wasn't the only one attracted to Kelly, a little voice snickered. Ben slammed the door on that thought and went out onto the porch.

"Let's go, Daddy." Debbie was already tugging at Kelly's hand.

"Did you go to the bathroom?" he asked his daughter.

"Yes," she answered as she rolled her eyes toward Kelly, who returned his daughter's look of exasperation with a wink.

Ben locked the back door and then clumped down the stairs after them. They were already halfway down and moving fast, and he was just as relieved. He needed a moment to pull back, to regroup and check all the locks on his heart. In the small backyard, he caught up with them and Debbie grabbed his hand. The three of them went down the alley to the narrow tree-lined side street that led to the park.

"I had the custard-filled roll after dinner," Debbie told Kelly. "It was so good, I hated to eat it all."

Kelly just laughed. "I'll bring some more tomorrow."

It must be nice to be so sure of tomorrow, Ben thought. Sudden bitterness tugged at his heart, and he couldn't look at either of them on the rest of the walk to the park. Life used to be like that for him and for Debbie, where things were always as you expected them, if not as you wanted them. That nagging bitterness turned into an ache in the pit of his stomach for all the things Debbie was being cheated out of. He wanted only the best for his daughter, yet he was giving her life on the run and a suitcase full of worries.

"Daddy's it," Debbie squealed.

Ben awoke from his mopes to find they'd reached the park and that Debbie and Kelly were both sprinting away from him. "Wait a minute," he cried.

But Debbie and Kelly weren't coming back, were just hovering together about ten yards away. Debbie said something to Kelly, who leaned over the girl to whisper back in her ear. The fiery glow of Kelly's curls seemed reflected in the light in Debbie's eyes, the light of pure joy. It melted the iciness that seemed embedded in his heart. It was worth all the worry in the world to see such happiness on her face, to know that for a few hours anyway, she was a regular, ordinary, happy kid.

"All right, you two," he said in a mock growl. "Better look out, 'cause I'm faster than any man alive."

They just laughed and raced away as he lunged toward them. For the next fifteen minutes or so, they raced in madcap abandon around the trees, over the picnic tables and through the sandbox. He finally tagged Debbie, who tagged Kelly, who tagged him. When he tagged Kelly back, she tried to immediately return the favor and they all dissolved into laughing wrecks on the grass.

"Boy, Daddy sure does cheat," Debbie told Kelly.

"I'll say," Kelly agreed. "Everybody knows there's no tag-backs."

"Show me where it's written," Ben said with a grin.

Kelly was lying next to him on the grass with Debbie lying across her. The little girl was giggling, her face all aglow, but it was to Kelly that his eyes kept straying. Her face was glowing, also, but with a different sort of radiance. She looked so beautiful, so womanly, that his heart nearly cried out in pain. This was how it should be—a man, a woman and a child. All together in love and in laughter.

His hands ached to touch Kelly, to run his fingers through those fiery curls and to see if those flames had roots in her heart. He wanted to lie beside her and feel her softness and her strength. His arms wanted to hold her close and feel her heart beating next to his, knowing that—

Ben sat up abruptly. Was it the summer's heat or this place that brought just nonsense, such impossible dreams, to his mind?

"Come on, you two," he scolded, and got to his feet. "You can't be that worn out."

Debbie and Kelly got up, and they all walked across to the swings. Ben felt his heart had had enough ups and downs for one day and contented himself with pushing Debbie to and fro.

"Higher, Daddy," she ordered. "I want to touch the sky."

Don't we all? he thought.

"I used to want to touch the leaves of those trees," Kelly told them as she swung next to Debbie, but at a much tamer pace. "I could see from a distance that they hung over the swings, but they seemed to pull back when I was swinging." She smiled across at Debbie. "I kept ordering my dad to push me higher, too."

"Did you ever touch them?" Debbie asked.

Kelly shook her head. "Not yet."

Debbie looked over her shoulder at Ben. "Push Kelly, too, Daddy," she said. "You can make her touch the leaves, can't you?"

Ben glanced at Kelly's back, at her slim waist and her trim behind tucked onto the wooden seat. His hands were willing to try, even as his mind knew he was playing with fire.

"I'm not sure I want to try anymore," Kelly said, saving Ben from himself.

"Why not?" Debbie asked.

"Sometimes dreams are best left as dreams," Ben explained for Kelly. He knew all about that and had learned it all over again this past hour.

Debbie dragged her feet, slowing her swing. "Think those kids would let me play soccer with them?" she asked.

"Sure," Kelly said. "See the kid in the green shirt. That's Paco. Tell him you're my buddy, and he'll make the other kids let you in."

"Great," Debbie screamed, and jumped off in mid-swing. She landed on her hands and knees, but scrambled to her feet and raced off. Ben took her place on the swing, letting it move slowly.

"She's a neat little kid," Kelly said, watching Debbie go.

Ben just watched Kelly for a long moment, then turned to find his daughter amid the crowd of kids. Dreaming was all he'd been doing. Kelly was attractive, young and full of life. It was no surprise that he'd feel attracted to her, but Debbie was where his life and future lay. He'd made that decision months ago and, in making it, he'd chosen against certain other things. Like permanent relationships with anyone else.

"My father used to bring me out here all the time," Kelly said. "He taught me how to play baseball and soccer. Soccer was more of an ethnic sport when I was a kid, and it was pretty big in this neighborhood."

That's what dads were supposed to do—teach their kids how to play ball and roughhouse without getting hurt. That love doesn't have to be flowery and quiet. That's what he wanted to teach Debbie. He was suddenly aware that Kelly was watching him, waiting for some sort of response.

"Is your dad still alive?" he asked.

"He died when I was thirteen." Kelly had looked away and seemed to be watching Debbie playing with the other kids, but Ben was sure her distant gaze was separated more by time than distance.

"He went to all our school functions and sporting events," Kelly continued. "He'd help with coaching but most of the time he had to work late in the bakery, so he couldn't really take responsibility for our teams. But he was so much fun, always keeping everybody laughing."

"My father never seemed to laugh," Ben told her. "He was always so worried about making ends meet for all of us. But we always knew that he loved us."

"That's what counts," Kelly said.

That was true. Love was what counted. Knowing you were loved was what counted. Sheila never had that, not from her father, anyway. Ben shut the door on that thought before it brought a black cloud over him. Life was one big crapshoot. Some folks were lucky, and others weren't. His job was to see that Debbie stayed as lucky as he could make her. To be certain she grew up secure in the knowledge that she was loved.

"So, how'd the sweet rolls sell?" Kelly asked, getting up from the swing and stretching her arms over her head.

Softly rounded curves caught his eyes and tugged at his heart, but he turned to watch a kite floating in the sky above them. "Looks like we'll do a good business," he said. "I sold out before my lunch hour was over."

"Great. Want the same amount tomorrow?"

"Maybe boost it to a tray and a half."

"You got it, partner."

Partner. Was that even too much of a relationship to risk? But it was only a business arrangement, and certainly temporary.

"I think the soccer game is drawing to a close," Kelly said.

Men and women were moving about the group of kids, rounding them up and herding them off for the journey home. Debbie came running toward them.

"I almost scored a goal," she said. "But Paco grabbed me by the shirt."

"I guess you'll have to try harder next time," Ben said.

"Yeah," Debbie replied. "I'll kick him in the leg."

Laughing, hand in hand, they headed for home. The streetlights were coming on, and an easterly wind was bringing the cool off the lake inland, spreading it among the narrow streets and alleyways of their community. Ben kept a smile on his face, but his heart sighed. If he had the power, he'd just stop the world right where it was.

## Chapter Three

Delivery girl," Kelly sang out as she set the tray down on the counter the next morning.

Debbie popped out from the back room. "Hi, Kelly."

"Hi, Debbie. Where's your dad?"

"Back here," Ben called. "I need to go upstairs for a minute. Can you stay with Debbie?"

"Sure."

They both listened to his footsteps pounding on the stairs, then Debbie turned to Kelly with a little smirk on her face. "He spilled catsup on his shirt."

Kelly shrugged. "Accidents happen."

"It was a big blob of it, and he said a bad word."

"I'm sure he didn't mean to say it."

"Grandma always says you mean everything you do, even if you don't want to admit it."

Kelly raised her eyebrows in surprise. "That's a kind of tough philosophy," she said. "Are you sure she wasn't joking?"

her. And even if she wasn't part of it, its sunshine touched her and shared its glow.

"How about if you do your math this morning?" Kelly said. "Then you can have dinner at my house tonight."

"Oh, boy," Debbie exclaimed. "Can we, Dad? Can we?"

"We don't want to put anybody through extra work," Ben said.

"There's no extra work," Kelly assured him. "Mom's making spaghetti and she always makes extra for freezing. All we have to do is add a little more pasta to the water."

"I'll do all my work this morning, Daddy. And I'll clean my room right after lunch."

Kelly could see him vacillate. Was he worried that she'd get the wrong idea? Or was he fearful of imposing on them?

"Mom would really appreciate having you guys over," Kelly said. "We're not exactly social mavens, but she is getting a bit bored with just Mike and me every night."

"Okay," Ben finally said with more of a reluctant sigh than wholehearted agreement. "What time should we be over?"

"Six-thirty will be fine," Kelly said.

"I love spaghetti," Debbie assured her.

Ben's frown hadn't totally vanished, though. "We're not going anywhere if you don't finish your work, young lady."

"No problem," Debbie cried as she scurried out of the lunchroom. A few moments later, they heard her footsteps as she bounced on up to their apartment.

Ben sank onto the stool next to Kelly. "I'm not really a grouch," he said. "It's just that her schooling has been a little erratic recently, so she needs to catch up."

"I doubt that some extra math will hurt her."

Kelly took a moment to rest in the tenderness of his eyes, noticing also the worry that lay there along with his love for his daughter. It would be so easy to get lost in those eyes, in the strength that could be found there. Not for her, since she'd already fought against such weakness, but for someone else less cautious. She thought, though, that the moment Ben sensed someone becoming emotionally attached to him, he'd disappear faster than sugar on a hot muffin.

"Thanks for the dinner invitation," Ben said. "It'll be nice to get out."

Kelly just shook her head. "Don't jump to conclusions. I thought Debbie needed a treat, not you. She told me about your reaction to the catsup spill."

"My reac—"

"What you said."

Ben tried to look sheepish but failed. His eyes were bright, and his mouth curled in his efforts to stifle his laughter. "I'm afraid I'm driven to say things like that all too often. It's not just catsup that jumps all over me," he admitted. "It happens with any kind of tomatoes. Catsup, spaghetti sauce, even plain old tomato juice. I come anywhere near something with tomatoes in it, and I'm immediately splattered."

"Oh, dear," Kelly said.

"Maybe I just shouldn't come tonight," Ben said. "Debbie can come alone."

"It would probably be less traumatic for her," Kelly agreed. "But we can't let this problem lick us. First it's tomatoes, then it'll be cranberries and watermelon."

"And apples."

"Precisely." Kelly narrowed her eyes. "You know, I used to have a similar problem. When I was in school, these three boys used to follow me around every place. No matter if I tried to go home a different way or yelled at them. They were always around."

"So, what'd you do?"

"I made them let me join their baseball team."

"I see."

"If you can't beat 'em, join 'em," Kelly said. "Start wearing red all the time, and no one will know about your problems."

Ben laughed, a sweet, inviting sound that began to lure her into his web, but she stood up. "I've got to get back to work, or Mom will fire me."

"Yeah," Ben said. "My lunch crowd will be starting soon. See you tonight."

"Right." Kelly walked toward the door.

"You know, Kelly," Ben said, his voice so arresting that she came to a stop, "I find it hard to believe that it was only back in your school days that the boys followed you around. How come your evenings are free to teach jacks and solve tomato attacks?"

How come? she repeated in her heart. Was it that she trusted the wrong pair of blue eyes or that the right pair just hadn't come along yet? Ben's eyes were blue, a little voice reminded her, but she just pushed that pesty presence aside.

"Once you prove you can hit their curve ball over the fence, they kind of lose interest," she said, and left, Ben's smile following her out the door and surrounding her with warmth.

No, it was just the sun sending up waves of heat from the already baked sidewalk. Either way, Kelly had a glow on her cheeks and in her heart as she hurried back to the bakery.

"Daddy, you're not dressed yet," Debbie scolded. "You can't wear your work clothes when we go visiting."

"I'm going to change, honey," he said without looking up from the newspaper in front of him. "I'm just relaxing for a minute."

"You can relax at Kelly's house," his daughter replied. "You won't have to cook or anything."

The letters before him blurred as worries seemed to wash over him. He didn't know when they'd be able to relax, but it certainly wasn't now. Or anytime soon.

"We can't let down too much." Ben put his paper down, looking over at Debbie. "Remember, we talked about it."

She came over to lean on his arm. "I remember, Daddy. Honest, I do."

Weariness tried to capture his soul, and for just a moment, he gave in to it, leaning lightly against his daughter. Was all this really for her sake, or was he just doing it for selfish reasons of his own?

"We have to be careful what we say," he warned her.

Debbie nodded. "I know. Don't talk too much about Mother, or where we come from or about Grandma and Grandpa."

He pulled her into arms. "I'm sorry about all this, baby," he murmured into her hair.

She lifted up her head, put her arms around his neck and grinned. "No problemo, Daddio."

In spite of his mood, a half smile forced its way onto his face. "'No problemo, Daddio'? Where did you learn to talk like that?"

"From Paco."

"You mean the kid that kicked and tripped you during your soccer game last night?"

"Yeah. He's a cool dude."

A cool dude. Ben could only smile and shake his head.

"Anyway," Debbie said, "you're supposed to be getting dressed."

He sighed and folded his newspaper. "Okay, but remember we have to be careful."

"Don't worry, Daddy. Grandma and Grandpa would never think of looking for us here. And if they do, we'll just go someplace else."

Ben stopped and stared at his daughter, at her calm acceptance of life on the run. God, how he hated to do this to her.

"Daddy," Debbie said patiently. "This is sort of exciting. And besides, we get to meet a whole bunch of nice people."

And get close to none.

"Kelly makes the best chocolate doughnuts in the whole world."

"Well, that certainly makes the trip worthwhile," he said with a laugh.

"I bet Kelly's mom makes real good spaghetti, too."

"I don't doubt it," Ben replied.

"Well, then get dressed up," Debbie said, pushing him toward his bedroom. "Or there won't be any left. Can I pick out your clothes?"

"All right. You pick out my clothes while I shower real quick."

Ben closed the bathroom door behind him and stared at himself in the mirror. There were dangers in going out, but Debbie was pretty careful not to let anything slip. He closed his eyes for a moment, shaing his head. Eight years old and the kid was already an expert double agent.

Taking a deep breath, Ben pulled his shirt up and over his head. Disclosure wasn't the only danger that would stalk them tonight, though. He threw his shirt onto the floor. Kelly and her smiling Irish eyes presented a danger all their own.

He dropped the rest of his clothes on the floor. Her eyes, her smile—they all radiated a constant message. Calm dependability. Someone to travel the long road with. Someone that you didn't have to look around for because you knew they'd be there, no matter what life handed you.

The shower was just the right temperature and felt good, warm streams hosing away the weariness from body and soul. Closing his eyes, Ben put his face right into the water.

Kelly was so different. Sheila had been like a caged wild bird. Garish clothing styles made up her bright plumage, and authority of any kind was the cage that she beat herself against.

He moved back from the spray and began soaping himself.

He'd first met Sheila back in his high school days, when he'd been into rebellion himself, although not into avantgarde clothing styles. River rats like himself had been into blue jeans and jackets painted with gang emblems. Their little town had the blue-collar folks down by the river and the "swells" up on the hill above the main part of town. Kids down by the river had known all about rebellion—they just hadn't had the money for weird clothes.

He and Sheila had never really dated in high school. Sheila just hung around with the greasers, trying to be tough like them. But, of course, she wasn't. The police certainly knew that. If their group was caught in a sweep, speed trap or any other dredging activity by the law, people like Sheila were taken home in a squad car. Ben and the others were taken to the station, where their parents had to come pick them up.

Somehow his parents had gotten through to him, though, and he'd buckled down in his later years of high school. His class standing improved enough that he was accepted at M.I.T., where he studied engineering.

Much to his surprise, Sheila had also wound up at M.I.T. She was still the wild bird, given to outrageous dress and even more outrageous behavior. And Ben still found himself attracted to her. At first she was just fun, a party girl. Then slowly, as they spent more time together, Ben began to see the real human being behind the rebel facade. What he saw was a tortured and confused little girl.

He'd grown up in a blue-collar home where the basics had been provided for, but not much else. Sheila had had clothes, cars, trips to Europe and summer camps lavished on her. His parents gave him love; hers gave her stuff. It wasn't until he matured and went to college that he saw he was the lucky one.

During their college days, they experimented with love. Then Sheila had come to live with him. It was a roller-coaster relationship whose primary purpose, Ben later learned, was to torment her parents.

Sheila hated her parents and would do anything to bring them anguish, and for this and other reasons, Ben didn't like being used. He wanted to break off the relationship, but was young and inexperienced. And, most of all, poor Sheila seemed to desperately need someone. He would wake up at night to find her crying in the bathroom.

Then Sheila became pregnant and initially she was a different person—happy and loving. But the baby came, and her parents rarely did, and she grew even more vicious than before.

Ben wanted to marry her, but Sheila turned him down, time and time again. And once Debbie was born, he realized that all he and Sheila had shared was passion, not love—true, unselfish, giving love. Motherhood didn't change Sheila a bit—she was still the wild bird, flying free. He was the one who'd care for Debbie, take her on an outing to the park, walk her if she were fussy at night. His little daughter in one hand and his class notes in the other.

Debbie's birth had put Ben solidly between a rock and a hard place. He'd wanted to break up with Sheila before she'd become pregnant, but hadn't known how to handle it. After Debbie was born, he didn't know what to do. He couldn't leave Debbie in Sheila's care, since she was too unstable. Yet they weren't married, and he didn't think he had a legal leg to stand on in getting custody of Debbie. So he stayed, giving all his love to a beautiful, growing human being. Her parents sent money, but rarely came to see them.

Then there was the accident. Sheila had been drinking and drove her car off the road into an overpass abutment, dying instantly. A few days later, Ben found out that Sheila had left a will, made shortly after Debbie's birth, giving custody of the child to her parents.

Ben couldn't let that happen. Sheila had told him about the coldness of her parents, how they seemed incapable of loving anybody. And how they hated him, blaming him for Sheila's rebelliousness. Once they got their hands on Debbie, he'd never be let near her again. After long hours spent with a buddy who was also a lawyer, Ben knew he had no alternatives. Right or wrong, the system was on the side of Sheila's parents. They had the money, the clout and that damn will. A legal battle would probably win him visitation rights, but could take years if the Websters so chose. The law was anything but swift. Ben had taken about two seconds to think over the possibilities, then he and Debbie had hit the road.

Ben stepped out of the shower and rubbed himself slowly. It was just about a year now since they'd fled Massachusetts. Their life in Delaware had ended after three months when a call to his mother had apparently been traced and they'd come home from the movies to see two strange men on their doorstep. He was more careful during the seven months they spent in Atlanta, but they'd had to move when Debbie's picture had appeared in a newspaper article about the citywide spelling bee. They backtracked to Washington, D.C. for a few months, then came out here to Chicago. So far, so good.

He and Debbie were still together and were going to stay that way, regardless of how far or how often they had to run. If they found friends along the way, that was great, but friends didn't count in the long run. One sniff that trouble was on the way, and they'd be gone. No matter how close the friends, they'd be left behind. That was just how it had to be.


"Anyone want dessert now, or should we wait?" Kelly asked.

"Later," the adults all chimed, but Debbie hesitated, the agony of waiting weighing heavily on her face.

"If you're not full yet, you can have a brownie now," Kelly said.

The elfin little face lit up like a Christmas tree. "Can I, Dad?"

Ben nodded slowly. It was good of Kelly to read Debbie's disappointment. She seemed so attuned to the little girl, a fact he viewed with mixed feelings. While that closeness would be good for Debbie, it would also make the leaving harder for her.

"Why don't you guys clear out of here so I can clean up?" Kelly said.

"I can help," Debbie said.

"No, that's okay, honey," Ben said. "I **will**."

Mike looked at his watch. "What do you say we go watch that Garfield the Cat special that's coming on in a few minutes?"

"All right!" Debbie cried, and raced after Mike into the living room.

"I guess I'd better go keep an eye on the children," Mrs. Farrell said. "Call if you need more help."

"Okay, Mom."

The room was silent and still, with everyone else gone. Kelly seemed closer than he expected, and her eyes seemed filled with mystery and longing. He could see the pulse beating at the base of her neck and swallowed hard as he got to his feet.

"This is your turf," he said softly. "Tell me what you want me to do."

"Why don't you clear the table?" she said. "I'll put the dishes into the dishwasher and wash the pots."

"Okay. And I'll dry."

Ben cleared the table, stacking the dishes on the counter next to Kelly while she concentrated on rinsing them. She worked quickly with a minimum of fuss. Sheila had been such a fluttery little bird, whereas Kelly seemed about as far from a bird as a person could get. She stuck with something until it was done without flying from place to place. Chattering didn't seem in her nature, and neither did flightiness.

"Have you always been a baker?"

Kelly looked up from the dishes. "I was a little girl first," she said, laughing.

The sound of her laughter diffused the stillness that had been hanging over the kitchen. "You weren't born in an apron, then."

"Hardly. Actually I went to college for a while in California and then tried acting."

She sounded as if she was scolding herself. "No harm in that," he said. "A person needs to try different things before they find what satisfies them."

"As long as there is no harm in it," she said, twisting his words slightly. She met his eyes briefly and sighed. "I met this guy out there, a would-be actor, also. He hadn't been in anything I'd ever seen but, boy, he was good enough to win an Oscar."

Ben said nothing, and it was as if his silence opened the floodgates. Kelly began filling the sink to wash the pots.

"He had a sick mother," she said.

"That's a new line," Ben said. "Were you supposed to comfort him?"

Kelly shook her head, a wry grin surfacing as she swirled the spaghetti sauce pot under the running water. "You're on the wrong track," she said. "But the same one I had been on. Everybody out there seemed to be on the make, so when he didn't come on to me, I trusted him without question." She glanced up at Ben briefly. "I know, dumb."

"Not dumb," Ben argued. "Young."

Kelly shrugged away the difference. "Anyway, he said he'd come to Hollywood to try to make some quick money to help pay his mother's medical expenses. He was willing to do anything, even porno flicks because he was so desperate. Then he got a big offer, or so he said, for a film with big-name movie stars. It was just a minor role, but would pay great, once they started filming. The only trouble was, he didn't think he'd get paid in time."

Kelly turned off the water and began to scrub the pot from the pasta. "It seemed so simple. I knew that Mom had money put aside for my college education that I wasn't using. Why not lend it to Randy? He'd pay her back when the film was made. So he came to Canaryville for a visit and charmed everybody, and Mom gave him not only my college fund, but Mike's, too, and the little bit in her retirement fund."

"And he walked out into the sunset," Ben finished for her.

"Never saw him again," Kelly agreed. "The film was a lie, of course, as well as everything else he told me about himself. The man he claimed was his agent had never heard of him."

Kelly rinsed the pot slowly. "The hardest thing I'd ever had to do was come back here after I figured out we'd been tricked and tell Mom."

He guessed everybody had demons. "You were lucky all you lost was money."

She put the pot into the drainer. "I guess, but it doesn't make it any easier to sleep at night knowing that I jeopardized Mike's education and Mom's retirement. Of course, it does give me incentive to get up at four in the morning."

"It doesn't sound like you were the only one who made the decision," Ben noted.

"But I brought him here. I should have checked him out better."

"Called the Better Business Bureau or run a credit check?" Ben asked, drying the pot as he spoke. "You were young and gave out of the goodness of your heart. Don't paint yourself a villain just because he was."

She just grunted a reply and concentrated on cleaning the spaghetti sauce pot. "I'm not certain that I only lost money to him," she said. "I've been a bit short in the trust department since then. Even once I get Mike through school and Mom in a condo down in Florida, I'm not sure I'll be ready to tackle love again."

Ben found that funny. "If you consider yourself suspicious now, you must have been a real pushover before," he said.

"Now, wait a—"

"Look at how you've adopted me and Debbie. How do you know I'm not some con artist out to siphon off the last few pennies?"

"Come on," she protested. "That's not fair."

"No, I could be. You know nothing about me." In some ways, she was like Debbie—needing reassurance and gentle teasing to put things back into perspective. He put the pot down and leaned against the counter. "So, how do you know that I'm not going to use you for my own nefarious schemes?"

"Most con artists don't use kids."

"Why not? Who evokes trust faster than a poor little kid?"

"You seem honest," she said lamely.

"So did Randy at first, I'll bet."

"You haven't asked me for any money," she pointed out.

The acceptance she'd given them was worth far more than any check she could write. "Maybe I was waiting until after the dishes were done. You know, warm you up by helping out."

Kelly couldn't help but smile. "Well, maybe I asked you here just to get some help with the dishes. Maybe I'm using you."

"You mean that's all this has been?" He was glad to see the glimmer of laughter in her eyes. Maybe he could pay her back in a small way for the smiles she'd brought Debbie. "The doughnuts, the jacks lessons, even the dinner were just part of a grand scheme of yours?"

"You better believe it, buddy," Kelly said. "And I'm going to throw you out unless you get caught up on your drying." She nodded at the drainer, overflowing with pots, lids and utensils.

"Well, as part of my grand scheme, I'm going to dry these just to get on your good side," he said.

Kelly chuckled quietly and put the last pot into the drainer, letting the water out of the sink. Television voices drifted in to fill the silence in the kitchen, and everything seemed just right. As though they were an old married couple doing the dishes together, talking over the day. Because of this surprising peace that she'd given him, this little oasis in the middle of his flight, he was even more in her debt.

"I'm not sure why I told you all that," she said. "Most everybody around knows that I got burned by Randy, but just Mom and Mike know that it wasn't just an emotional burning."

He dried the ladle they had used for the spaghetti sauce. "I'm not going to tell anyone."

She rinsed out the sink with the spray hose, watching the soap suds swirl around before disappearing. "I didn't think you would."

He couldn't help but tease her. "See? You're trusting again."

She glanced up at him, with obvious disapproval. The spray hose in her hand turned slightly, and he jumped back.

"I hate it when people say I told you so."

"I hate it when people can't admit someone else is right."

She squeezed the trigger on the hose for just a short burst that mainly fell onto the kitchen floor, though a few darker, round patches appeared on his shirt.

"Hey, you're vicious," he said.

"You'd better believe it." She aimed the hose at him again, though kept it off. "Now, take it back. Say I'm not a trusting person."

He moved carefully to the side, his eyes on the spray hose. "Never," he vowed. "I'll stand a martyr to the truth."

"Oh, will you?"

But even as she turned to follow his movement, he darted in closer and grabbed the spray hose. She wouldn't let go, though, and for a moment they both struggled for possession, his hand over hers. She struggled to aim it directly at him, attempting to squirt him again, a real squirt this time, but he kept it pointed toward her.

"It's not nice to squirt your hostess," she warned.

"And it is to squirt your guest?" He still held on tightly.

"Just let go, and I won't squirt you again," she promised.

"I'm supposed to trust you?" he scoffed. "You who claim not to believe in trust?"

That apparently did it. She made a sudden jerk of the spray nozzle so that it faced him, then pressed the trigger. Prepared for such a maneuver, he reversed it back toward her just as the water escaped the hose. He got some on his arm, but she got sprayed all down her chest. Letting go of the hose, they both dissolved in laughter.

"That wasn't fair," she cried as she hung over the sink, laughing.

"Fair? Now you're wanting things to be fair?" He took a towel and wiped off his arm, but stopped short of wiping off her chest. Maybe that was carrying his gratitude a bit too far. "Uh, maybe you'd better take care of that."

She stared down at her soaked shirt, clinging to her chest with rather obscene clarity. With a giggle she pulled the shirt out from her chest and let it go. It fell back against her like a second skin. God, she was beautiful.

"Lot of good that towel will do." She tucked the towel into the neck of her shirt so that it hung like a long bib down the front of her. "Unless I wear it."

"I didn't mean for you to get that wet," he said.

"Sure, sure," she teased. "And to think I trusted you were a gentleman."

"See, I knew you trusted."

She made a sudden grab for the hose again, but his hand got there first. He had just been touching hers, his hand had been on hers not more than a minute or two earlier, but this time it was different. The world seemed to stop, the sounds from the living room dying away as only the pounding of his heart could be heard.

Her touch was so warm, so safe. He wanted to pull her into his arms and hold her there forever. His eyes bored into hers, as if they would reveal her thoughts and her desires, and even as he watched, a flame seemed to flicker to life as she returned the penetrating stare. His breath caught, and his hand tightened on hers. Then a burst of laughter came in from the living room, Debbie's voice distinguishable among the others, and he pulled back into himself.

Kelly took a deep breath. "Truce?" she asked lightly.

"Truce." He turned back to the dishes, drying invisible spots on things he'd already dried.

## Chapter Four

The walk over to the sandwich shop the next morning seemed the longest Kelly had ever traveled. She had been so silly last night, letting a simple job like doing the dishes turn into a major embarrassment. Somehow she was going to have to set things straight with Ben. When she reached the door of the shop, she took a deep breath and went in. No one was there.

"Hello," she called out.

There was a long moment of silence as she lugged the tray of goodies up to the counter, then Ben looked out of the back room.

"Hi," he said with a frown. "Want to put the stuff down on the counter where it usually goes?" He disappeared into the back room.

Oh Lordy, Kelly thought, she'd ruined a perfectly good friendship by going all weak-kneed last night. Ben probably thought she was after him and, not ready for that type of relationship, had decided to put some distance between them. Hesitating for only a moment, Kelly walked around the counter and into the back room. Ben was sitting on the edge of a table, his back to her.

"I have a second tray for you today," she said.

"I'll try to get by for it in a few minutes." His voice was sharp and abrupt, and he hadn't even bothered to turn around.

Kelly stepped farther into the room and saw Debbie in front of Ben. The little girl was close to tears, and Ben looked about ready to explode.

He looked up, glaring at her intrusion, and then snapped, "She wants her hair braided."

"I don't like it loose when I run around in the summer." Debbie's lips were trembling. "It makes my neck all sweaty and yucky."

The offending hair hung down the back of the girl's neck, twisted into a braid but hanging limp and loose like old yarn.

"It comes out all loose," Ben said, pointing accusingly at the offending strands. "But when I try to tighten it, she says I'm pulling her hair."

"Well, you were." Debbie's voice was as close to petulant as Kelly had ever heard it.

"I enrolled her in a day camp at the park," Ben said. "And we've been fighting this hair thing all morning."

He glanced at his watch while Debbie stared at the tips of her shoes.

"Now she's supposed to be leaving in a few minutes, and I barely have things set up for the lunch crowd."

"Would you like me to braid it?" Kelly asked.

Debbie's eyes lit up like two stars. "Would you?"

"Be my guest," Ben growled, and stomped out into the dining room.

Kelly waited until Ben left, then quickly undid his braid, combing Debbie's hair out. Then, starting at the top of Debbie's head, she wove the strands together to make a

French braid. A rubber band at the bottom secured the loose ends.

"There. How's that, kid?" Kelly asked.

"Super duperino," Debbie exclaimed, looking at her reflection on the refrigerator door. She turned her head one way, then the other. A wide smile never left her face.

"The trouble with you, honey, is you have too phlegmatic a personality."

"Huh?" Debbie responded.

Kelly laughed and kissed her on the cheek. "That means you're a real neato kid."

"You're real nice, too." Debbie reached up and hugged Kelly hard around the neck, then raced into the lunchroom. "Daddy, look."

Ben was busy stocking condiment boxes over the stove, but he managed a sheepish smile. "You look beautiful, princess." He glanced up at the clock on the wall, and some of his aggravation seemed to return, settling in his shoulders and weighing them down.

"Come on, honey," he said. "I'd better get you to the park so I can get back here before my customers start arriving."

"Why don't I walk her to the park?" Kelly said. She could take Debbie, then come back for a quick chat with Ben. Nothing major, but hopefully she'd be able to tell if his ill humor was due to his inability to braid hair or to those tense final moments they had shared last night. But before she and Debbie even got to the door, Mrs. Farrell came in, carrying the other tray of sweet rolls.

"Kelly, Mr. Abrams from that machine shop over by the tracks just called," Anna said as Ben hurried to take the tray from her. "They need a special anniversary cake by three o'clock, and I said you could do it. But they want a large one, so you'll have to bake it in sections. I figured you've got just about enough time."

There went her talk with Ben. "Okay," Kelly said with a sigh. "No problem. If you can walk Debbie to the park for her day camp."

"I don't want to impose," Ben protested.

"Oh, I could use a walk," Anna said. "I need the exercise, and Mike's at the bakery if Kelly needs any help."

"Let's go, then," Debbie said, reaching up to take Mrs. Farrell's hand.

"Now, don't go running ahead," Mrs. Farrell warned. "I'm too old for that kind of stuff."

"I won't," Debbie assured her. "And I'll hold your hand when we cross the street."

The door closed behind them. Kelly could see her mother's lips moving, but the rest of the conversation was lost. She and Ben stared out into the street for a long moment.

Maybe she should stay now for a quick chat, but the shop seemed so still and Ben seemed so close. Her nerve deserted her.

"Well," she said. "I have to get going. I've got that special cake to put together, and you have to get ready for lunch." She moved briskly toward the door.

"Kelly." Ben's hand was on her arm, stopping both her movement and her heart. "I appreciate your helping us this morning. Sorry I was so grumpy. Things have been kind of hard lately."

"Hey, no problem." She moved a bit, just enough so that his hold on her arm loosened—she could breathe again. "My friends and I used to braid our hair all the time."

He looked at the floor and sighed. "Yeah, I missed that part in Parenting 101. Must have been absent that day."

Her self-consciousness washed away with the flood of weariness in his voice. Here she was worrying about his misinterpreting her actions last night, and he was trying to do his best as a single parent—and feeling like he was failing. Romance was the last thing on his mind, and she felt silly and selfish for fretting over it so.

"It really was no problem," she assured him. "You can't be expected to know and do everything. Mothers don't, so fathers shouldn't have to."

"I guess." His sigh was audible, but not nearly so tired sounding. "Debbie and I are lucky to have stumbled onto you."

Kelly shrugged. "Neighbors help each other. At least in this neighborhood they do."

"Well, thanks." Suddenly he stepped closer and pressed his lips ever so lightly on hers. "I really appreciate it."

The kiss was as soft as a butterfly's footsteps, his voice as gentle as a country stream meandering through a meadow, but the roaring echoes in her heart were anything but peaceful. She wanted to throw herself into the haven of his arms and tell him to stop worrying so. But that might not be the best way to promote a strictly-friends relationship between them.

"Well, I gotta get going," she said.

"Yeah," he said. "I'd better get to my chores."

She moved quick as a bunny to the door, letting it close behind before she breathed a deep sigh of relief. Ben needed someone to talk to, someone to help out on occasions, but not someone who was looking for happily ever after. She certainly fit the bill, but could she keep her heart in line?

"Good afternoon, Mrs. Shay."

"My goodness, Kelly," her neighbor said, "you look close to a collapse."

Kelly leaned forward, her elbows on the counter. "This has been one heck of an afternoon. Acme Machine Tool down by the tracks called in a special order that I had to bake in six sections. And then Mrs. Konek wanted a special birthday cake for her grandchild, all chocolate—icing and cake. And I had four sheet cakes to do for the Franklin Home and School Association, decorated with the school mascot."

Mrs. Shay chuckled sympathetically. "Sounds like you've barely enough time to turn around, much less think."

Kelly just nodded in reply. She didn't want to tell Mrs. Shay or anybody, but time to think was the last thing in the world that she wanted. Because if she had the time, she wouldn't think of anything substantial.

The corners of her mouth flickered. Actually at six feet plus and almost two hundred pounds, Ben was fairly substantial. And that was even before one considered that rough-cut face and those cool, calm eyes. Oh, one mustn't forget those eyes.

Kelly pushed herself away from the counter. There was really no need for her to think. All it would give her was trouble. She closed her eyes for a moment and took a deep breath. Any more of this, and she'd be ready to write soap opera scripts.

"What can I do for you today, Mrs. Shay?"

"I'm not sure yet. My Jimmy likes something sweet in the evening, and I'm just looking."

"Okay," Kelly replied. "I'll be in back. Call me if you need me."

"Oh, Kelly." Kelly paused in midstep. "I saw you and that nice young man from next door at the park the other night."

"Yes," Kelly said slowly. "We took his daughter there. They're new to the neighborhood, so I showed them where to go. You know, where the best swings and monkey bars are."

"She's such a pretty little girl. The three of you together looked just right."

"Just right?"

"Oh, you know what I mean," Mrs. Shay said with a hearty laugh. "A man, his woman and child. A regular family."

His woman. Kelly didn't like the gleam in her neighbor's eyes at all. "How about a cherry pie, Mrs. Shay? Doesn't Mr. Shay just love cherries?"

"That he does. Why don't you pack one up for me?"

Kelly, moving with lightning speed, had the pie boxed, took Mrs. Shay's money and returned her change in nothing flat. It wasn't as if she wanted to get rid of the dear old woman, but it was only right that she get home to care for her husband.

"Thank you, Mrs. Shay." Kelly was pleased at how brisk and businesslike her voice sounded. "Nice to see you. Do come in again, please."

Kelly let her breath out in a mad rush as the door closed. Strange how some people could jump to conclusions. But then the poor woman had only her husband to care for, and an arthritic hip kept her from getting out much, so she had time on her hands. More than enough time to let an active imagination grow a piece of nothing into full-blooming nonsense.

The mailman came in before Kelly got to the back room. "Hi, Rob. Hot enough for you?"

"More than enough." He wiped his brow with an extra-large handkerchief, then reached into the broken cookie basket for a couple of samples. "I could almost fry me a burger out there."

"If it's this hot in July, what's August going to be like?" Kelly said.

"Say," the mailman said, speaking around a mouthful of chocolate chip. "I hear you got yourself a fella."

"A fella?"

"Yeah, that young widower from next door."

Kelly stood there, her mouth hanging open, but no words came out. She couldn't believe her ears. Where did people get such wild ideas? She didn't have a "fella." She fixed other people up, but she wasn't in the market for a "fella" of her own at the moment.

"My sister saw the three of you in the park the other night," he said. "You know, you, the widower and his daughter."

"I was just showing him the neighborhood," Kelly explained.

"Oh?"

"Yeah." She felt her head nodding and bobbing like one of those dogs with spring necks that people put on the back ledge in their cars. "They're new to the neighborhood. And, you know, kids like to play around and that kind of thing."

"Oh." The mailman nodded solemnly as he finished the rest of his cookie pieces. "See ya tomorrow," he said as he went out onto the street.

Kelly just waved at him, as her vocal cords seemed unable to function. Good Lord. Did the whole neighborhood think she and Ben were an item? She'd better get busy and find someone for him before the whole city had them married off.

That decided, she spent an hour or two rearranging the remaining cookies and doughnuts on their trays. Unfortunately that wasn't quite enough to keep Mrs. Shay's and Rob's conversations from replaying in her head. By the time Mike came home late that afternoon, Kelly had a good start on grinding her molars.

"Hi, sis." He gave her a questioning look. "Have a hard day?"

"Somewhat." She slipped the last tray back into the case and slid the glass door shut.

"Lots of special orders?"

"A bunch."

He nodded. "Yeah, those things can tire you out."

"I can handle special orders quite well, thank you," she said a little more sharply than she intended. But what did he think? That she couldn't hold up her end of things anymore?

"Right." He stepped cautiously around her and put his books on the shelf just inside the storeroom. "You've always been a pillar of strength."

His voice sounded suspiciously as though he was mocking her. "Keep that up, kid," Kelly said, "and you'll be eating pablum until they make you a new set of teeth."

"Hey," he protested, his eyes honestly puzzled. "What gives? All I'm doing is praising you."

Her irritation fought with guilt and lost. "I'm sorry." She gave her brother a quick hug and leaned against him. "The whole afternoon, everybody and their cousin has been coming in and telling me that Ben Peterson is my new boyfriend."

"Yeah," Mike said, nodding. "You did go to the park with him a few days ago."

"What's with you?" Kelly cried, annoyance making a comeback. "We took his daughter to play on the swings."

"Jeez, Kelly. Don't bite my head off."

"Sorry," she grumbled.

"A lot of people saw you there. And you know how this neighborhood is. It's like some small town. Everybody watches everybody and talks to everyone else about it."

She slumped back down on the counter. "Yeah, I know. I guess I'm just tired."

"You want to go lay down?"

Kelly shook her head. What for? She'd only lie awake brooding. "Got any homework?" she asked.

"A little. But I could do it while I'm watching the store."

"Nah, get out of here. I have some stuff to clean up."

"Okay." He took a chocolate-covered long john and made his way upstairs.

It wasn't that Ben wasn't attractive, she told herself. Lord knows, his smile could weaken the knees of any woman within a hundred miles. And on top of that, he was considerate, intelligent and had a good sense of humor. She admitted he'd be a real catch for some lucky lady, but it wouldn't be her.

There were times, mostly in the early hours of the morning before that persistent alarm would ring, when she wondered if she'd ever have a family of her own to care for and love. It really hurt then, that emptiness in her heart, but when morning came, so did her responsibilities and so did the reminders of the past. The money was part of it, Kelly knew, but there also was a fear down deep in her heart, a fear of trusting again that none of Ben's teasing could erase.

A Hispanic lady came into the bakery, and Kelly pushed herself away from the counter.

"Hi, Mrs. Reyes. What can I do for you?"

"Two loaves of light brown bread, please, and a banana-cream pie."

"Coming up."

"I saw you in the park a few days ago," Mrs. Reyes said.

Kelly felt her back stiffen but she continued assembling the carton for the pie.

"My Paco says that little girl is gonna be some soccer player."

"Yes." Kelly composed her face into a pleasant smile by the time she turned around. "Her father runs the sandwich shop next door."

"I heard that."

"He's a widower, poor man. His wife just died."

"Oh, that's too bad."

Kelly wrapped the loaves of bread. "Yes, I'm going to introduce him around." She pushed the goods toward Mrs. Reyes. "You know, once he gets over things."

The woman nodded sagely as she pulled money from her purse. "Yes, men usually have a harder time getting over such things than women. They aren't as tough as we are."

"Probably not," Kelly said with a smile as she counted out the change.

Mrs. Reyes bid farewell and left. Kelly leaned forward, a satisfied smile on her face. All those silly rumors would stop now that she had started the truth circulating in the neighborhood. She wondered why she couldn't feel her smile down in her heart.

"Are you closing up?"

Ben looked up at the two elderly ladies dressed up in their Sunday best. "In a little while. Can I get you anything in the meantime?"

"We were just visiting a friend over to Mercy Hospital," the taller one said.

"And it's so hot out," her shorter companion added. "We were wondering if we could have something cool."

"Sure." He put down the cloth that he was wiping the counter with. "What'll you have?"

"Lemonade," they chorused.

"Counter or table?" he asked as he filled two tall glasses with shaved ice.

"Right here is fine." The taller one indicated a table near them.

Ben poured the lemonade over the ice and brought the glasses to them. "A dollar-seventy," he said.

The shorter one counted out even change for him. "You're new here, aren't you?" she asked.

Ben's stomach tightened, but he forced himself to nod slowly. "Yes, I came here a few weeks ago."

"Where are you from?"

"Ohio," Ben replied quickly. He and Debbie passed through Ohio, so technically he wasn't lying. Besides, it wasn't anyone's business where he came from.

"How does your little girl like it here?"

Damn. They'd seen Debbie. But then why wouldn't they see her? After all, he didn't keep her locked up in the basement.

"Fine," he said. "She likes it just fine."

"That's good," the shorter one said.

The taller nodded. "Will her mother be joining you soon?"

Ben paused. If they were agents working for Debbie's grandparents, they'd know that Sheila was dead. On the other hand, they could be trying to trick him.

"Her mother died," he said. "Last year."

"Ah, poor thing."

"True," the other agreed. "But there are a lot of children in the neighborhood."

"Oh, yes. There are many fine families."

"But there are single people, too."

"Oh, dear me, yes. A lot of single people."

"And a few young widows."

"A few."

His sense of relief almost caused Ben to laugh outright. They were just neighborhood ladies checking on his availability. It was funny that in this day and age a husband was still considered to be a prized possession.

"And don't forget the divorced ones. There are many fine divorced ladies."

"Oh, yes, many."

"One mistake shouldn't doom a person for life."

"It certainly shouldn't."

Ben backed away from the happily smiling pair. "I still have some cleaning up to do," he said. "Let me know if you want anything else. Stay as long as you like."

They smiled at him like a pair of cats watching a canary. He hurried away and left them to their whispered conversation.

Whew, he sighed to himself once he was out of their sight. Maybe he should contract some incurable disease before they began interviewing prospective brides. They'd probably select one for him and then carry out the marriage at gunpoint if his enthusiasm lagged. He shook his head and smiled as he loaded dishes into the dishwasher.

Actually he'd handled things quite well once he got over his initial scare. And that was probably even silly. It was pure chance that he'd stumbled onto this job and the apartment that came with it. And hopefully it was one of the last places on earth that Sheila's parents would think to look. They probably thought he'd run for the West Coast. Everybody else did. Instead he was squirreled away in this little Irish enclave in the center of Chicago.

Very few new people came to a neighborhood like this, but once they were accepted, Ben knew that they'd be safe. And judging from the matchmaking activity directed toward him, it was probably a good bet that they'd been accepted. In a neighborhood like this, if they didn't accept you, they threw you out.

The neighborhood people themselves were rather close-mouthed and not inclined to answer questions, especially from private investigators. Odds were high that if someone got hot on his trail, he would be warned in time to run.

"Goodbye, young man."

His inquisitive visitors were leaving, and Ben stepped out to bid them farewell. He locked the door after them and cleaned up the table. By the time he was taking his garbage out of the back, he was chuckling to himself. Kelly would get a kick out of the story, he thought. Then he frowned.

Kelly. He'd been avoiding the thought of her all day. Somehow he'd thought he was immune to her charm after that first night when she swung over the railing to teach Debbie jacks. Tussling with Kelly over that water sprayer sure taught him differently, though. And last night's attraction was far more dangerous than that first night's.

Last night it hadn't been just her fiery curls and the sparkle in her green eyes that had lured him closer. It had been that sense of peace and belonging that she had given him. A gift that was all too precious and rare. It had caught him unawares and let him dream that if he could just hold on to Kelly, he could also hold on to the peace. Luckily the dream had evaporated in the light of day. Kelly came out into the alley just as he was closing his dumpster.

"Need any help?" he asked.

"Nope."

Ben watched in admiration as she hoisted her own garbage bags into the commercial dumpster. There was something about a strong woman's curves that was like nothing else on earth. They were such a unique blend of power and softness. Just as Kelly was a blend of strength and gentleness.

She turned and, judging from the slight frown on her face as she slowly closed the dumpster, noticed him looking at her.

"Got a minute for a cool drink?" he asked.

"Sure."

He held the back door open for her, and they walked into the lunchroom. The room was silent and still. They were together, but the hungers that had haunted him last night were gone, locked away deep in his soul. He breathed a sigh of relief and headed around the back of the counter to get some iced tea.

"There were two old ladies in here just a few minutes ago," he told her as she sat down at the counter. "And you should have heard the third degree they were giving me."

"They probably have some unmarried granddaughters," Kelly said.

"They seemed to be checking me out for the whole neighborhood."

Kelly smiled. "That's all right. I had my share in today. Not exactly checking me out, but congratulating me on snagging you for myself."

Ben started. His situation made emotional attachments impossible, but of course Kelly wouldn't know that. Did she share the neighborhood's view that she had him 'snagged'? No, not if the laughter in her eyes was any indication. Ben sagged in relief.

"I didn't realize I was such a prize," he said.

"Who said you are?" Kelly responded as she sipped her iced tea. "Maybe it's just that they're all anxious to get me off the market."

He leaned on the counter, coming closer to those inviting green eyes. "And are you anxious to get off yourself?" he asked, more interested in her answer than reason dictated.

She made a face. "As far as I'm concerned, I'm not on the market, so there's no need to get me off. When and if I settle down, it'll be well into the future."

Ben stared into his glass for a moment. The wedge of lemon bobbed to the surface, a thin yellow smile of sunshine. "I'm not on the market, either," he said. "Part of it is Sheila's death and getting adjusted to a new sort of life. But it's also that I need to settle down with Debbie, too, and make a home for her."

"Debbie has to come first right now."

"Exactly." For some reason he was relieved she understood, but also had been certain she would. "Though I'm not sure that's something I can explain to the marriage-minded ladies who come in here checking me out."

Her eyes were pools of safety, calm and serene, inviting him to hide in their depths. "You won't need to," she said. "Once the word gets out that I've got you snagged, they'll all leave you alone. Nobody would dare trespass on my territory."

"You're that feared?"

"Hey, I'm that loved," she corrected. "And down here, loyalty is everything. Look how we've stuck with the White Sox in spite of their years of losing."

"Are you a baseball fan?"

"Do birds fly?"

Ben drank down the last of his iced tea, reluctant to let their little interlude end. "I used to be a Yankees fan," he admitted. "But they just aren't the same as they used to be."

"Good thing you said 'used to be,'" she said. "If you still were for the Yankees, I would have had to 'unsnag' you, and even the little old ladies around wouldn't want you for their granddaughters."

His feeling of ease and belonging increased with her teasing. Life was tossing him sweet moments of pleasure in the midst of his worries. "What if I was a Cubs fan?" he asked.

"Not quite as bad as the Yankees, but it would brand you as a yuppie."

"That bad?"

"Well, it's not good. You don't see too many luxury cars in this neighborhood, do you? That kind of person just doesn't belong, so no one makes any effort to keep them."

Did he belong here? He'd thought at first that this place would be a safe hiding spot for a few months or even a year. He hadn't expected to feel so at home here or so certain he would miss it when they had to leave.

"But don't worry," Kelly was going on. "We plan on keeping you around."

That he and Debbie were wanted here suddenly seemed an unexpected burden. He put his glass in the dishwasher. "That clock keeps reminding me that I have to get Debbie from the day camp," he said. "You can stay and finish your iced tea if you want, though."

"No, I'm through," she said, gulping down the last few drops. "I've to finish cleaning up the bakery, too." She got to her feet and walked with him to the door. "Thanks for the break, partner."

"Anytime," Ben rejoined as they parted ways. But his feet seemed heavy as he walked toward the park. Maybe Kelly wasn't exactly snagging him, but something here was.

## Chapter Five

"Think this will be enough?" Kelly asked as she placed the tray of sweet rolls on the counter. It was just past six-thirty in the morning, far earlier than she normally brought Ben's bakery goods over, but he'd decided to try opening for breakfast.

Ben shrugged as he poured water into the coffee maker. "I don't know. I'll have to wait and see what the demand is. I'm just going on the word of a few guys who said they'd like to stop by early."

Kelly sank onto a stool by the counter. "You've really done wonders with this place," she told him. "You should get Mr. Chapman to pay you a bonus, or you should buy the place from him. You're the fourth one to run this diner in the last five years, and every other one definitely helped reduce the number of customers."

"I don't think I'm in a position to buy," he said, and wiped his hands on his apron. "Got time for some breakfast?"

"Going to practice on me? Sure, I'm game."

"Bacon and eggs okay?"

"If you're going to join me."

She watched in silence for a few minutes as Ben started the bacon grilling. He moved with quick, sure movements. But something was wrong with this picture—Ben, endowed with a splendidly athletic build, slaving over a hot stove. "You sure know your way around a kitchen," she said. "But you're not a professional cook, are you?"

"Not until a few weeks ago," he said. "What gave me away?"

"The way you crack eggs. As if you're afraid you're going to get shell in everything."

"I do, a good number of times," he said. "Want some orange juice?" When she nodded, he poured them both a glass.

She took a sip of hers before she pursued her earlier subject. "So, if you aren't a professional cook, what do you consider your profession?"

He slipped bread into the toaster and put their bacon on plates. "Oh, a little of this and a little of that. I learned to cook from my mother. She thought that everybody should know how to take care of themselves."

"Wise woman."

"Yeah, I miss her." He slid the eggs onto plates just as the toast popped up.

"She dead?" Kelly asked.

Ben shook his head. "No, but I don't get back to see her nearly as often as I'd like."

No answer seemed suitable, not with that quiet finality in his voice, so Kelly started eating. She couldn't imagine being very far away from her family. Her whole life revolved around them, and even if she should marry some day and have children of her own, she'd still count Mike and her mother as two of the people closest to her.

"Where's Debbie?" Kelly asked after a moment.

"Still asleep. She's not an early-morning flower."

"Too bad. She's missing a good breakfast."

"Thanks."

"Plus the best time of the day," she added.

Ben's eyebrows rose. "Now is the best time of the day?"

"In some ways," she said. "Maybe it's just being a baker and always having to be up before the sun, but I really like the early morning. It's so peaceful and quiet. You get to see the day starting to shake itself awake."

"I never thought of it that way."

They sat in silence, staring out the door. The July sun was just up over the lake, and the air was still cool. Ben hadn't turned the air conditioner on yet, and the front door was open, letting the damp smell of the recently washed street float in along with the sounds of a city street awakening. The mood hanging in the air was soft and comfortable. Kelly finished her eggs, then got herself some hot tea and Ben a cup of coffee before she was willing to break the spell.

"I bet the banks would be willing to discuss some arrangement for you to buy this place," she said.

"Maybe."

"No 'maybe' about it," she argued. "You're building a good reputation in the neighborhood. They'd see it as a wise investment."

He finished his toast before he spoke. "I'm not certain this is what I want to spend the rest of my life doing."

"It doesn't have to be the rest of your life for it to be a good investment."

"I guess." But the tone in his voice suggested that the subject was closed.

Kelly said nothing for a time, but just sat there in silence as she played idly with the crust of her toast. She didn't feel so much rebuffed as left out. Ben hadn't been angry at her suggestion, but neither did she believe he was going to consider it for even a minute. Was it really that cooking meals for a living wasn't his cup of tea, or was he not certain this was where he wanted to stay? But if he didn't like cooking, why had he taken the job? But most of all, why did the answers matter to her?

Kelly looked down and swirled her tea. A few tea leaf particles had escaped their gauzy prison and were floating near the bottom of the cup. Were they trying to give her a message? There used to be a gypsy woman over near County Hospital who could read tea leaves. Mike would know if the woman was still there.

"Want any more tea?" Ben asked.

Kelly shook her head. "Nope, I've got to get back soon. Today is apple pie day, and I've got a lot of apples to peel. Want me to save you and Debbie some turnovers?"

Ben made a slight face. "I'm not really an apple person," he said. "Strawberries are my favorite fruit. Big juicy strawberries. I like anything made with them. Jellies, jams, jello."

"Me, too," Kelly said. "Strawberry pie is one of my favorites."

"Oh, yeah?" Ben said. "So, when does strawberry day roll around?"

"Not for another year," she told him. "The season is past for Michigan strawberries, and the other ones just aren't as good. I'll make you one next June."

She thought she saw a cloud pass over his eyes, but then he turned away, beginning to clear up the breakfast dishes. "Looks like it's going to be another scorcher," Ben said with a forced-sounding laugh. "I'm surprised anyone lives in this city. I've heard the winters are killers, but the summers can sure do you in."

"But fall and spring are great."

"Must be why we came. As far as I'm concerned, there's nothing that can beat fall. The leaves turning color, Indian summer, pumpkin pie, football and the sharp snap that you get in the air. There's nothing like it."

She knew just what he meant. And knew, too, that he must have come from north of the Mason-Dixon line to feel that way. South of it, they didn't have true fall, not like what he'd described.

"So, is football your favorite sport?" Kelly asked.

"Not really." He pondered a moment. "I like football, but I'd have to say that baseball is my favorite."

Kelly laughed out loud. "It's my favorite, too," she said. "It has such a comfortable pace to it and is so precise."

Ben grunted. "Maybe I ought to have you talk to Debbie."

"Doesn't she care for baseball?"

"Care for it?" Ben shook his head. "She thinks it's a stupid game where two guys play catch with a ball that once in a while a guy in the middle hits with a stick. The only excitement she sees in it is when the outfielders run into each other or the wall."

Kelly laughed again. Being here with Ben had such a comfortable feel to it. At times like this, it felt as though they were old friends. At other times, it had a hotter than friendship feel. "What sports does she like?"

"Football and pro wrestling," he said, making a face. "She's a violent little thing, always wanting to wrestle me."

Kelly shrugged. "Little girls like to roughhouse with their daddies as well as little boys."

"Yeah, but little boys probably don't pound their daddies into a pulp."

But there was no disguising the love and pride that glowed in Ben's eyes, those gentle eyes in his rock-hard face. Her mother would probably say that was the combination of a tolerant man. A man that could easily cradle a little girl in his arms but wouldn't be at all bothered if she jumped on his back wanting to roughhouse or play horsey. A real father. Or maybe a real man.

A man really showed his strength through his gentleness. She'd always thought that fatherhood was the real proof of a man's character. Trouble was, you didn't usually see that before the wedding. The woman who eventually got Ben would be very lucky. Kelly hoped that that woman would appreciate what she was getting. Of course, Kelly could search to make sure he met just the right woman when the time was right. Until then, she'd be happy to befriend him. And just how happy was that? a little voice asked.

"Hi, Ben. Kelly." It was the soda vendor about to make his deliveries to the various vending machines in the area. "Hear you're serving breakfast here now."

Kelly got to her feet, welcoming the distraction so she could lock up her errant thoughts. "Well, I guess I'd better get to work," she said.

"Me, too," Ben said and put their cups by the dishwasher on his way over to take Lou's order.

"I'll check you later to see if you need any more pastries," Kelly said, and let herself out.

She barely saw Ben's nod as she hurried back over to the bakery. It was warm already, the sun scattering the coolness of the early morning. Looked like Ben was right—it would be another scorcher. Maybe a break in the heat was what she needed to regain some common sense.

"Hi, Walt," Kelly greeted her customer. "Come for that anniversary cake for your parents?"

"Yeah."

Kelly went in back, took the whipped cream cake out of the refrigerator and boxed it.

"Keep the cake cool until you're ready to eat it," Kelly said. "And cheer up. It's gonna taste great."

"Hey, it ain't that." He shrugged as he handed her the money. "And it ain't like I begrudge my parents a fiftieth anniversary. But I don't know why my sister says we have to celebrate it the same night I got tickets to the White Sox game."

"Tonight's game?" Kelly asked as she counted out the change.

Walt nodded glumly. "Three box seats. For me and my two boys. We were going to make a night of it."

"Should be a good game, too," Kelly said. "The A's are as tough as opponents come."

Walt sighed. "This party was supposed to be next week, but my parents got an invite to visit some friends at their cottage in Michigan. And it couldn't be this weekend, because we have a cousin's wedding. My sister just decided on the date yesterday."

"Well, I hope your absence from the game doesn't jinx the Sox."

"Me, too." He stopped, his glum look brightening slightly. "Hey, why don't you take the tickets off my hands? I was gonna give them to my neighbor, but he'd just root for the A's to be ornery."

"Gosh, I don't know," Kelly said. "Tonight's Mom's canasta night, and I don't know if Mike's got plans or not."

But what about Ben and Debbie? Kelly asked herself. Ben said he liked baseball and, even if Debbie didn't, going to an actual game was a lot of fun. Popcorn and hot dogs ensured that. It would be great to share their company for an evening, to give Ben an evening out for laughing and relaxing.

"On second thought, I will take them," Kelly said. "How much do I owe you?"

Walt fished the tickets out of his wallet and gave them to her. "Don't worry about it."

"Don't give me that."

They argued for a few minutes. Walt said he'd got the tickets at a discount at work and finally agreed to a dozen doughnuts.

Glowing with anticipation, Kelly stuck the tickets in her jeans pocket, but as the afternoon progressed, she grew more and more antsy. She wanted to run next door to tell

Ben about the tickets, but there never seemed to be a free moment. She had to content herself with humming the old familiar baseball anthem as she packed up cookies, doughnuts and bread.

Finally she was able to lock up the bakery and hurried through the alley to the sandwich shop. She knocked on the door and let herself in as Ben came into the back room from the dining room.

"Guess what?" she exclaimed. "I got tickets to a White Sox game tonight."

"That's nice."

"I got three tickets." His face remained unchanged, and Kelly realized she hadn't been too clear about things. "The three of us can go."

A shadow flickered across Ben's face, and it seemed for a moment that he tried to fight it away, but it took root in his eyes.

"You know," Kelly went on, despite the fact that her stomach was sinking as if she'd had gravel for lunch, "like you, me and Debbie."

Ben's face seemed to be carved in stone. His eyes were icy and remote. "Thank you," he said, though his tone belied his words, "but we can't."

Her perfect evening fell into sudden ruins. "Why not?" she asked. "What else do you have going for tonight?"

A dark cloud covered Ben's face. Part of it was anger, part was something else. Regret? Bitterness? He turned away. "I didn't realize I had to get your approval for my social calendar."

Kelly felt as if she'd fallen from the swings at their highest point. She swallowed hard, trying to drive the hurt away. He was right—what he was doing for the evening was none of her business. She'd been taking too much for granted. Just because they had some pleasant times together and were partners in a business venture, it didn't mean either of them had any hold over the other. She had assumed too much.

"I'm sorry," she said quietly. "I just thought it would be fun. And you don't seem to go out that much."

"Maybe because I don't want to." His voice was tight, emotion reined in by iron control.

Kelly felt a slight stinging around her eyes and all she could do was back away, open the door and step back out into the yard. Dignity wasn't much, but it was all she had at the moment.

"I'm sorry," she repeated with a shrug.

"I'm sorry, too," Ben said. This time his voice echoed with regret instead of anger, but still he shut the door firmly behind her and turned away.

Somehow Kelly's feet took her around to the back of their building and dragged her upstairs. Mike and her mother were in the kitchen, getting ready to make dinner.

"Hi." Her greeting came out more as a mumble, and her family stared at her. She shook her head, a deep breath burying all her disappointments. "Guess what? I got three tickets to the White Sox game tonight."

"Is that all?" Mike said with a grin. "The way you looked, I thought maybe you had got tickets to a Cubs game."

Her mother just frowned, her eyes obviously reading more into Kelly's gaze than Kelly wanted. "You said three tickets?" Anna asked.

Kelly just nodded and turned away to sort through the mail.

"Ben couldn't go?" her mother asked.

"He didn't want to," Kelly said in an attempt at off-handedness.

The silence began closing in on her, and Kelly opened a letter addressed Occupant and began to read about a new driveway paving firm with interest. She could feel her family's sympathy hovering in the air, but didn't need it. It wasn't as though she and Ben had a thing going, no matter what the neighbors thought. She hadn't snagged him. But she wasn't really hungry tonight. Tentacles of a headache were beginning to reach around and take hold. Maybe she would just go to her room and lie down.

Her mother coughed slightly. "I don't know about anybody else," she said. "But I sure wouldn't mind going to the game. I'm getting tired of canasta every Monday night. How about you, Mike? You in the mood for a baseball game?"

Her brother looked up from the chicken he was getting ready to cook in the microwave and shook his head. "Not me, Mom," he said. "I'd rather do something useful and worthwhile, like staying home and making dinner."

"You haven't done that in a while," Anna said, a semi-grim look on her face.

"I know," Mike said. "I know. And it's really been bothering me."

"Then we shouldn't let him cook, should we, Kelly?"

"Mom, I—"

"We should make him suffer," Mrs. Farrell said. "Deny him the pleasure of making dinner for us."

"Mom." But both of them had a look of mock seriousness on their faces, and Kelly couldn't keep herself from laughing. "All right," she said, putting her arms up in surrender. "All right, I give up. We'll go to the game. Just let me go change."

Kelly went down the hall into her bedroom, and her mother followed her. "I know we weren't your first choice, honey," she said. "But I think we're a better alternative to staying home and moping."

"What do you mean, you weren't my first choice?" Kelly asked briskly, throwing the remnants of her gloominess under her bed along with her shoes. "I just asked Ben because of your canasta. I'd rather go with you and Mike any old day of the year."

"Sure, you would, honey." Anna patted Kelly's cheek gently. "You change your clothes and relax. We'll have such a good time tonight that you won't have time to think."

It seemed to be Kelly's one goal in life lately—to be too busy to think.

"Don't you feel good, Daddy?"

Ben looked up into a pair of concerned eyes, framed by a small pretty face all wrinkled with concern. "I'm fine, baby."

"You've been awful quiet tonight. Are Grandma and Grandpa getting close again?"

Guilt and sorrow swallowed him up, and he hugged Debbie tightly to him. Just because he was feeling awful about the way he treated Kelly didn't mean that Debbie should feel his gloom. "No," he said, "Grandma and Grandpa are far away. Don't you start worrying about them. I'm only quiet because I'm tired."

"Me, too." Debbie squirmed out of his embrace, then climbed up into his lap, yawning widely as she leaned her head on his chest.

"Have a good time at your day camp?" he asked as he put his arm around her waist.

Debbie yawned again, nodding her head. "I sure did. We do all kinds of stuff. We run around, swim, and we make stuff and we just do a whole bunch."

As always, even in his darkest moments, the sweetness of her face just melted his heart, and he felt an overpowering flow of love. At these times, his throat would get so tight he couldn't talk, so he just hugged her hard. She yawned again.

"You'd better hit the sack, sleepyhead."

"I guess," she replied as she snuggled closer.

"I mean you have a whole bunch more stuff to do tomorrow."

Debbie nodded her head.

"You want a ride to bed?" Although she ducked her head, Ben knew that she was wearing a big grin. "You're really a big con artist," he said. "You know that."

"No, I'm not. I don't draw good at all."

Chuckling, Ben stood up with his daughter still in his arms and carried her into her room. He dropped her on her bed, but strong, skinny little arms grabbed him around his neck. She gave him a big kiss and then dropped back on the bed.

"Brush your teeth and get into your pj's," he said.

Debbie slowly pushed herself up into a sitting position. "Okay."

"Want a story?"

She shook her head as she yawned again, so Ben just walked softly out of the room. Debbie usually liked a story to relax her at bedtime, but several hours in the fresh air and sunshine, crammed with swimming and other activities, seemed to have taken a good bit of her energy.

He took a can of beer from the refrigerator and sat down before the television, turning on an early edition of the evening news. Ben stared at the set but saw and heard nothing.

Damn. He'd handled that thing with Kelly so poorly. He knew that he'd hurt her feelings. He'd been an absolute jerk about the whole thing.

But what was he to do? Tell Kelly the truth? That he was afraid to go to the ballpark because sometimes camera crews panned the faces in a crowd, especially when there were cute little kids involved? That he didn't want to pick up and run again because somebody might see their picture on national television and send some private investigators out to Chicago?

Of course, he couldn't have told her, but he certainly could have handled it better. He could have pleaded that he was sick, that Debbie was sick, any number of things.

Damn it. She'd just caught him by surprise, marching in with an offer like that. He'd just frozen and hadn't known what to say, so he'd lashed out. And that had been so unfair after all the kindness she had shown them. She knew nothing about them, yet had opened her heart and her home to them. And how had he repaid her? By slamming the door in her face.

The news ended, and the station brought on some teaser scenes for an old private eye adventure series. Ben turned the television off and stared off into the emptiness of his room.

He wished that he could tell people about himself and Debbie. He was so tired of their living alone, locked in their own little world, unable to be open and trusting with anybody. It would be nice to talk to someone like Kelly. She would understand and care. She would help them over the rough spots and bring a time of sunshine into their shadows.

It wasn't just that he was sorry he'd been rude to her—he was sorry that he hadn't been able to spend the evening with her. White Sox or Red Sox—that didn't matter. But an evening with Kelly would have left him with warm memories that would brighten even the darkest and loneliest of times in the future. It would have given him hope that summertime could find them no matter how often they moved and no matter how bitter the world seemed.

Getting up, Ben dropped his empty can in the garbage under the kitchen sink, then went out on the porch, sitting down in one of the chairs. Debbie was so wonderful, and she filled a big part of his life, but—

Sighing, he rubbed his face with his hands. Hell, she was just a little kid, and his daughter. Like any man, he was lonely for the companionship of a woman. Not just any woman. Kelly.

Throwing himself up out of the chair, Ben went to the edge of the porch and sat on the railing. Even if he let himself grow to care for her, what the hell did he have to offer?

A bitter smile twisted his lips. He could just envision his proposal. Oh, sweetheart. I love you dearly. I want you to share my life with me. Come, be a fugitive with me for the next ten years or so. And if we're caught, you, too, can be charged with kidnapping. You, too, can go to prison for the rest of your natural life, but until that time, your life will be limited to running and hiding with me, living and pretending, working in lousy, low-paying jobs and calling your family only at specified times and through prearranged channels.

Closing his eyes, Ben slumped back against the post. No, he had nothing to give Kelly or any woman. Nothing but trouble. He'd chosen his path, and there was nothing to do but travel it alone. Alone with Debbie. He had no right to dump his burdens on anyone else.

As for women in Debbie's life, she'd have to get her counseling from schoolteachers, girl scout leaders and what have you. He wasn't the first or only single parent in the world. Life was hard, but that was just the way it was. He was a mature adult and he'd just have to suck up his gut and hang in there. His daughter deserved no less.

Voices in the alleyway called for his attention, and he looked down into the brightly lit area. From his perch he couldn't see faces but he knew one of the persons was Kelly. He could tell from that pert, bouncing walk she had. He hurried downstairs and waited for them at his gate.

Kelly saw him first and stopped. Her mother looked from Kelly to Ben and back.

Ben cleared his throat. "Hi, Kelly." Then he nodded to her companions. "Mike. Mrs. Farrell."

They all returned his greetings.

"Could I talk with you a minute, Kelly?"

"Sure," she replied.

"Would you care for something cold to drink?" Mrs. Farrell asked.

"No, thank you, ma'am," Ben replied. "I need to stay close by, anyway, because Debbie's asleep."

"Is she going to the park tomorrow?" Mrs. Farrell asked. "If she is, I'll be by to walk her. The doctor told me I need to walk more, and it's more fun with that little one."

"She'd like that," Ben assured her, another nail thrust into his heart. They were all so kind, so giving. And how had he responded? He held his thoughts in check until he heard the sound of their footsteps on the wooden steps of their porch.

Ben cleared his throat again. "I'm sorry about this afternoon," he said, getting right to the point.

In the glow of the streetlight, he could see Kelly shrug. "That's okay." She shrugged again. "I guess I took you by surprise."

He clenched his teeth a moment. "You just caught me at a bad moment. I was a little blue and I don't always handle myself maturely. It wasn't your fault at all."

She looked off into the distance, as if her hurt lay far beyond the horizon. "I'm still sorry I bothered you."

"Damn it. It wasn't your fault. I'm sorry."

Her eyes opened wide for a moment, but then a grin wiped every other emotion out. "You want to Indian-wrestle?" she asked. "Winner gets to take all the blame."

Ben couldn't do anything but laugh. He opened his arms, and Kelly slipped right in, comfortably and snugly. Their lips met and, for a moment, Ben was in heaven. She felt so soft, so womanly. All the loneliness and days of worry merged into a single, hungry embrace. He pulled her closer into his arms. Her breasts were crushed against his chest, and her gentle scent surrounded him, taking him prisoner and promising no release.

The warm wetness of her mouth brought him the rebirth of spring. He no longer felt tired or weary of his flight, but alive and young. Words wanted to spill off his tongue. The truth about Sheila—that they weren't married. That she'd never acknowledged Debbie was his child. That he wasn't so stricken with grief as to shy away from love, but so hurt by love in the past that he'd chosen a life that wouldn't allow it.

But then she pulled gently from his arms, and shadows claimed her eyes. He couldn't see what she was thinking or feeling, and the cool night air brought sanity back to him. There were no confidences to be shared now or ever. He, too, took a step back, away from her.

"Good night," he whispered.

"Good night." She took a step up her stairs. "See you in the morning."

"Right." His words came out hoarse and husky.

He watched her disappear into her yard and then took a deep breath, letting it out slowly.

## Chapter Six

"That looks like one big church down there," Debbie said, pointing out the bus window toward the south. She was kneeling on the seat ahead of Kelly and Ben, alternately staring out the window and turning back to face them.

"That's the University of Chicago," Kelly said. "Those are classroom buildings."

"They must have a lot of money to build big stone buildings like that," Debbie said.

"A Rockefeller gave them money to start up about a hundred years ago," Ben said, surprising Kelly.

"My, you're a very knowledgeable tourist," she said.

A shadow passed over Ben's face. "I read about it in some book or magazine," he said offhandedly, and turned to stare out the window at the university buildings they were passing.

Kelly couldn't help feeling shut out, but told herself she was being stupid. A person gained a lot of tidbits of knowledge along his way through life. No one needed to justify or explain where that knowledge came from. It was just that so much of Ben's life seemed closed off from her. At times she felt so close to him, then at times she felt she didn't know the man at all.

She forced herself to lean back and relax. It was a beautiful sunny Sunday afternoon, the perfect early-August day. Ben and Debbie had invited her to go with them to the beach, the closest of which was the point out beyond Chicago's Museum of Science and Industry. It was a day to be happy, to celebrate their friendship, not a day to brood.

"Oh, look," Kelly exclaimed loudly. "There's the Museum of Science and Industry."

Both Ben and Debbie turned to stare at the large Greek-inspired building to their right, but neither said anything.

"It's really a neat place," Kelly said. "It's got a coal mine and a submarine. In the spring they have baby chicks and, around Christmas, they've got about fifty Christmas trees, decorated by all the different ethnic groups that populate the Chicago area."

"I thought Christmas trees were Christmas trees," Debbie said.

"Nope, different groups decorate theirs differently. Some use ribbons and some hang fruit. For instance, one country has delicate wooden ornaments and others use crystal and glass ornaments. The Christmas trees we have in our homes are really a mixture of a lot of ethnic customs."

"Boy, it sounds neat." Debbie turned to her father. "Can we go see it, Daddy?"

Ben smiled at his daughter, but his shoulders seemed to sag. "We'll see, sugar."

Some of Debbie's glow faded, and she turned back to the window. "Oh, yeah."

"I could take you," Kelly offered, not certain what the big deal was.

"That's not necessary," Ben said.

Debbie turned enough to face Kelly. "Daddy just doesn't like to plan things real far ahead. You know, I might have a cold or something."

Or the world might come to an end, Kelly thought. "The display's there for a month at least," she said, trying not to feel annoyed. Debbie wasn't her child, Kelly reminded herself. She was Ben's, and he had the right to raise her the way he saw fit. But what was the harm in promising to take her to see a display of Christmas trees? Kelly suddenly caught sight of the bus stop ahead.

"Oops," she cried, jumping to her feet. "This is our stop." She put a smile on her face and led them out of the bus.

After crossing the street, they climbed the stairs to the Fifty-Seventh Street pedestrian bridge that took them across Lake Shore Drive. Debbie walked slowly, gazing down the whole while at the cars roaring down the expressway underneath their feet, before she was distracted by the lake.

"Look, Daddy," she exclaimed. "It's as big as the ocean."

"Not quite," Ben said, laughing.

Debbie started running across the footbridge. "Don't be such slowpokes," she called back.

"Wait for us at the bottom of the stairs," Ben said.

Then he stopped and turned toward Kelly. "Speaking of slowpokes," he said, "come on."

His hand was extended and she took it, then the two of them ran after Debbie. Kelly's earlier clouds were blown away by the gentle breeze coming off the lake and the laughter floating in the air. At the bottom of the stairs, they turned north and walked among the people already settled there to find a spot for their blanket. Ben barely had it spread out before Debbie had taken off the T-shirt and shorts that covered her bathing suit and was racing for the water.

"Stay close to the shore," Ben called after her.

She only went in up to her knees, then began to dig in the sand where the waves lapped up over it. Ben seemed to relax and settled down on the blanket himself.

"Somehow the sand is just as much fun as the water," Kelly pointed out.

Ben just nodded and began to unlace his shoes. Kelly'd already kicked off her sandals, but just sat for a moment, reluctant to take off the long T-shirt that covered her bathing suit. This was silly, she told herself and, after a deep breath, pulled the shirt over her head. Her two-piece suit was very becoming, but certainly not the most revealing around.

"Very nice," Ben said, and she glanced up to find his eyes—warm and smiling—on her.

She blushed, a deep fiery red, she feared, but was determined to play it cool. "You're not too bad yourself," she said.

He'd taken off his T-shirt to reveal a chest of solid muscle. Fine blond hairs that invited touching covered his chest and arms. Whatever Ben had done before he came here, he had managed to stay in shape. A great shape. The fire of her blush spread over her whole body, trying to engulf her, and she turned to look for her sunscreen in her bag.

"You burn easily?" Ben asked.

Could she claim her blush was sunburn, a sudden and strong case? "Yeah, most redheads do." She spread the cream over her arms and legs.

"Want me to do your back?" Ben offered.

To refuse would seem strange. "Sure." She handed him the bottle and turned her back. His touch was gentle and ever so soothing. Enough to turn her insides to jelly if she'd let him. He's just a friend, she reminded herself. Just a friend. Of course, the difference between friend and lover could be defined in terms of commitment.

"Mind if I use some?" Ben asked.

"Help yourself," she said. "I'll do your back if you want." Her voice was almost steady.

He handed her the bottle, and she carefully spread the cream over his shoulders. The muscle beneath the skin seemed rock hard. His arms must be strong enough to carry half the world, and she wondered what it would be like to lie in them, safe and secure. Her hand moved farther down his back. Randy had been thin, almost bony, and that gave him a vulnerable appearance, but Ben was solid. He gave the impression of someone who would do the protecting, not someone others would have to take care of. It was a nice, comfortable difference.

"All done?" Ben asked.

"Yep."

She closed the cover of the bottle and moved over to claim her own space on the blanket where common sense could take hold once again. Debbie was still playing in the sand, now with two other little girls of about the same age.

"She sure makes friends easily," Kelly noted.

"Yeah." Ben watched the girls playing for a few moments, then turned back to Kelly. "She's a pretty good judge of character, too. Look how she picked you for a friend."

Kelly smiled and stretched out on her stomach, propping herself up on her elbows and facing the lake. "I wasn't sure who picked who. Sometimes I feel as though I sort of forced myself on you two."

Ben joined her on the blanket, lying on his stomach at her side. "Are we back to that whole baseball game fiasco? Why can't you believe it was temporary insanity on my part? I shouldn't have reacted the way I did."

Kelly looked down, drawing lines in the sand with her finger. "It's not that, not really," she said. "I just don't want to be intruding."

"You aren't." She felt him move, and she turned to see him lying on his side, facing her. "Is this about your offer to take Debbie to see the Christmas trees?"

She just shrugged. "Not entirely."

"I have nothing against her going. Not with me, or you, or the two of us. I just have gotten real careful about promising her things. She's had a lot of change in her life this past year, and I think she feels safest when I'm honest with her."

"I can see that." Kelly lay flat on the sand, resting her chin on her crossed arms and staring out at the water. The hot sun beating down on her back seemed to melt her hesitations, giving her hidden thoughts a chance to sprout. "I guess this is all because I want to be sure we're both passengers on the same train. After the past few weeks, when half the neighborhood has been congratulating me on snaring you, I didn't want you to think that I was starting to believe them."

"That wasn't why I turned down the chance to go to the baseball game."

She rolled onto her side. "Will you get off that?" she said with a laugh, then sobered. "Look, I think Debbie is a really neat little kid and I think she needs me. I'm not saying she looks upon me as a mother substitute and I'm sure not trying to be one, but she seems to like having a woman to talk to. I'm just glad it's me. I'll be here for her as long as she needs someone, but I'm not trying to push my way in any closer. I want you to know that."

"I do." Ben sat up and wrapped his arms loosely around her knees. "Debbie's not the only one who needs you," he said slowly, his eyes on some far and distant point. "I do, too. There are times I really need someone to talk to. Someone who can braid hair," he added, and brought his eyes back to her as he squeezed her hand.

She felt closer to him then than she had felt to anyone, other than her family, in a long time. Their pasts didn't seem to matter, and the future was too far away to worry about. That only left today, right now, and it was proving to be sweet and special.

"I've just needed a real friend, and that's what you've been," Ben went on. "I never get the feeling that you're misinterpreting what I say."

"Or hearing wedding bells in the wind," she added.

His smile was rather sad. "That's one sound my ears can't hear."

"Good." She sat up. "Because I'm allergic to talk of forever. What do you say we help Debbie build a sand castle?"

Kelly and Ben walked slowly down Fifty-Seventh Street, hand in hand as Debbie bounced along ahead of them. Narrow side streets branched off north and south of them. Some lined with contemporary town houses, while other streets had retained their old charm with vintage homes put up not long after the turn of the century.

"This is a very nice urban neighborhood," Ben said.

"Yep."

Kelly felt so comfortable and relaxed, and their fingers were intertwined. She forced her mind back to the houses and the nice urban neighborhood.

"The university's worked hard to keep it this way," Kelly said. "Back in the fifties and sixties, this area came close to becoming a slum. I think the local folks were on the brink of moving."

"That would have been hard," Ben said. "These buildings have a lot of tradition behind them."

"Hey, look," Debbie shouted back to them. "There's a park." She started running. "Last one there is a rotten egg."

"Where does she get all that energy?" Kelly asked, laughing.

"I think she stole it from me," Ben groused.

"She did not. You're just getting old."

Ben looked at her long and hard. There seemed to be a dark, passionate power shining in his eyes. For a long moment, time stood still as they stared at each other. Their talk earlier had dispelled happily-ever-after from their script, but strangely it seemed to free up the attractions stirring between them. At least for her.

These fires that lay smoldering beneath her surface seemed ready to consume her at any moment, at any provocation from Ben. A glance, the touch of his hand, his laughter that seemed to settle in her heart. She wasn't afraid of the desires, and the tightness in her stomach brought delicious tensions to her trembling soul, but she wasn't ready to face them squarely yet, either. She had more of a need to laugh and sing. Or run.

Kelly eyed Debbie ahead of them in the park, then turned to Ben at her side. "Last one there is the rottenest egg of all," she teased, and sprinted away.

When she reached Debbie, Kelly turned around and was disappointed to see Ben walking after them. "What's the matter?" Kelly called. "You all worn out?"

"Haven't you heard?" he said as he came up to them. "I'm getting old."

He held her for a moment with eyes that looked anything but old before Kelly pulled herself away. Time enough later to ponder the messages in his gaze.

"Want to go on the teeter-totter?" Kelly asked Debbie. "Okay."

The girl ran over, and Kelly followed, but they quickly found that it worked best with Kelly and Debbie on one end and Ben on the other. Up and down they went, just as life had its ups and downs, Kelly thought. But now she was definitely on one of the ups.

From there they went to the swings, Debbie laughing and screaming for her father to push her higher. When three other children came into the park, Debbie raced over to join them on the monkey bars and related climbing equipment.

"Those little kids came just in the nick of time," Ben said with a laugh. "They rescued me from demonstrating the ravages of old age."

Kelly laughed. "Poor baby."

He put his arm around her. "I do have marvelous powers of recuperation, though."

"That's good to know," Kelly replied. "I may decide to test them out."

His arm was comfortable around her shoulders. Obviously strong, but so gentle. Strong and gentle. Those two words described Ben completely. The woman he had loved had been very lucky. A touch of melancholia settled on Kelly's shoulders along with Ben's arm, and, sighing, she moved a fraction of an inch away from him.

"Getting hungry?" he asked.

Kelly willed her mind to concentrate on the mundane. "Yeah, I think so."

"I'm sure there are some restaurants along here," Ben said.

"There are. This is the business strip for the student neighborhood. There'll be a number of hamburger joints and pizza parlors along the way."

Ben stood up and held his hand out to help her. Even when she was standing, he kept a hold of her hand, and she let him. Who was it hurting to explore all the avenues of friendship? As long as they both understood the rules, no one would be harmed.

"Let's go, Debbie," Ben called. "We need to eat and get home."

They went back to Fifty-Seventh Street, walking slowly along its tree-lined walks. After a block, Debbie let go of Kelly's hand and pointed. "How about there?"

"The Blue Goose," Ben read aloud. "Sounds like some kind of sixties coffee shop."

"It's a pizza joint," Kelly said. "I remember Mike telling me about it. He says they have fabulous deep-dish pizza."

"They have a neat sign," Debbie pointed out. "I vote yes."

Apparently that was all the votes needed, and they went inside. The interior was shabby and worn, and something crunched beneath their feet as they walked in. Video games winked in the shadows.

"Pleasant-looking little dump," Ben said.

"That's usually where you get the best pizza," Kelly said.

"Oh, yeah? Then why are we the only ones here?" Ben asked.

Kelly shrugged. "Students aren't back yet. I imagine summers are slow for them."

"Can I play the games?" Debbie asked.

Ben gave her a few quarters, and he and Kelly sat down. After ordering a cheese, sausage and green-pepper pizza, they sat back, letting the events of the day rest in the blanket of silence between them.

A waitress brought them their wine, and Kelly sipped at it. "Debbie seems to be adjusting very well to the loss of her mother," she said.

Ben stared into his wine. "She's a tough little kid," he said.

"You are what you have to be." Kelly drank some more, then sat back. Maybe it was the dim lighting that seemed to invite bravery, or else it was the wine weakening her defenses in short order. "What was she like, Debbie's mother?"

Ben just sighed, still staring into his glass, and for the longest time, Kelly thought he wasn't going to answer her. "Intense," he finally said. "Hyper, almost."

"That where Debbie got her energy from?"

Ben shrugged. "She's not as intense as Sheila ever was. I guess my genes are tamer."

"Whatever," Kelly said. "It seems to have been a good mixture in Debbie."

"We got lucky, I guess."

There was a sadness about him, a stillness, but he hadn't seemed to have shut his doors. Did their newly professed friendship include the right to question? She pressed on. "Debbie said her mother was sick a lot," Kelly said. "Did she die of cancer?"

Ben looked at Kelly, then at Debbie before taking a long, slow sip of his wine. Why was she asking these things? Kelly asked herself. Ben was her friend—she cared about him. She didn't want to bring him further pain.

"Never mind," she said. "It's none of my business. I wasn't really being nosy. At least I don't think I was. It's just that Debbie rarely mentions her, and sometimes talking about someone is the best way to get over grief."

"Sheila was killed in an automobile accident," Ben said simply. "She drove her car into a concrete abutment."

"She drove—" Kelly swallowed. "You make it sound—"

"Like she did it on purpose?" Ben finished for her. "I think she did. She was extremely depressed at the time of her death and refused to get help."

Kelly's heart wanted to break at the suppressed pain in his voice. "Oh, Ben." She reached out for his hand and just held it. He tightened his grasp on her.

"The police said it was an accident, and I didn't argue, but it would not have been totally out of character for her."

"You mean she tried other times?"

"She led a life that seemed bent on self-destruction. Reckless, wild behavior was the norm for her."

Kelly leaned closer to him, her hand providing strength and deliverance. "How awful for all of you," she said softly. "But someone you love, to watch them hurting must have been hell for you."

Ben's eyes went to Debbie even as his shoulders seemed to be visibly wearying. "Sheila was vibrant and beautiful," he said. "And out of reach because I came from the wrong side of the tracks. Me, I was forbidden territory—that was my main allure to her. At first I was pleasantly shocked by her attentions, then enthralled with her. By the time the rose-colored glasses fell off and I saw how her mind really worked, it was too late. Debbie was on the way, and I could only hope that motherhood would be a calming influence."

Ben turned back to face her, his eyes burning with pain that she couldn't share or even soothe. "It did only for a short time," he went on. "But she was so emotionally dependent on me that there was little I could do."

He stopped and laughed, but it was a bitter sound. "It was indeed hell, but I don't know that there ever was a time that I can say I really loved her. Not the way love should be between a man and a woman."

Kelly didn't know what to say. She hurt so much for him. Randy had been a bad experience, but a breeze to survive compared to what Ben had gone through. She swallowed hard. "Ben, I never meant to pry. I didn't want to open up old wounds."

"Would you stop apologizing?" he said with an honest laugh. It was a tired sound, but had no hurt or bitterness in it. "We're friends. I thought we established that this afternoon. I needed to tell someone, and you were it. You didn't force any of this out of me."

"How much of it does Debbie know?"

"That her mother was unhappy. Not that I suspect suicide or that I stayed because I loved Debbie."

"Those aren't things any child should know," Kelly agreed.

"And she won't ever find them out, even if I have to move to Timbuktu to prevent it."

The force of Ben's voice surprised her, but so did the words. Was someone threatening to tell Debbie those things? Was that why they moved here? "She's lucky to have you taking care of her," Kelly assured him.

"We're both lucky to have you," he told her, giving her hand a final squeeze before letting her go. "And unless I'm mistaken, this is our pizza on the way."

Kelly looked up to see their waitress coming toward them. "I'll get Debbie."

She hurried over to the video machines, trying to put all of Ben's pain back into hidden corners so she could concentrate on bringing sunshine into their lives. That's what friends were for, after all.


Ben's two girls stepped out of the bathroom. Debbie was all shiny and pink in her summer shorty pj's. Kelly was barefoot, still wearing the shirt over the bathing suit. Her skin had slight pinkish highlights from a day in the sun.

"Kelly said she'd read me a story," Debbie told him.

"I said only if your dad didn't mind," Kelly hastened to add.

Ben slouched down farther in his big overstuffed chair, more relaxed than he had felt in ages. Maybe confession was good for the soul. "Go ahead. I'll stay out here and vegetate awhile."

"Okay." Kelly let herself be dragged into Debbie's room.

Alone, Ben yawned. Today had been marvelous. A day to be put into the memory books. It had been so good to tell Kelly the truth, to open at least some of the doors he'd been hiding behind. It didn't change the fact that he and Debbie had to be careful and always on the alert, but it was awfully nice not to feel so alone. He felt rather than heard Kelly come into the room and looked up.

"All done with the story?"

She nodded.

"I'll go give her a good-night kiss," Ben said, pushing himself out of the chair.

"She's already asleep," Kelly said. "I didn't even get halfway through the story."

Ben laughed. "Boy, you must be one exciting story-teller."

"It's tiring being out on the beach for most of the day," she said. "And you don't look too lively yourself."

"Want to tuck me in, too?" Ben asked before he realized what he was saying. Kelly looked astonished, as well she might. That was some leap. Perhaps being her neighbor and business partner wasn't the type of friendship he had in mind. The fact that his words had mirrored his inner longings was of no importance.

"Nope, don't tell me. I can guess. Only one bedtime story per family per night," he said quickly as he eased by her and went into Debbie's room.

Debbie was all curled up on her stomach. He kissed her on the cheek, then covered her with a sheet. She deserved so much better than she was getting, but he had to be more careful. Just because things felt so comfortable here, he couldn't let himself be lulled into thinking they could ever have a normal life with normal relationships outside of their little duo. Her teddy bear had fallen to the floor, and he picked it up, tucking it into the corner of her bed. Then he crept out of the room, closing the door softly behind him.

Kelly was sitting on the sofa, her bare feet resting on the ottoman in front of her. He sat down by her side.

"Want anything? Lemonade? Iced tea? Soda? Beer? Wine cooler?"

She was lying back, her eyes closed, and just shook her head. "Nope, I'm fine."

"You don't look like you're going to the ball tonight, either," he said with a laugh, though his heart was not playing it light and easy.

She looked so beautiful lying there, her fiery hair aglow in the gentle lamplight. Her slender body woke dreams and desires in him that he'd managed to keep dormant for a long time. But now, here in the stillness of the late evening, he wanted nothing more than to scoop her up in his arms and smother her with his yearning. That wasn't to be, though—he knew that better than anyone. So, instead he stared straight ahead and shared the silence with her.

It had been a beautiful day—he mustn't forget that while fighting the hungers in the air. The three of them had enjoyed the beach and the sunshine. Sharing the physical comfort, the confidences and an overriding spirit of joy. For a time the future had been put on hold with all its dark unknowns.

"What and where is this ball you were talking about?" Kelly asked.

He looked into her beautiful eyes, emeralds of fire. Precious and rare, just as she was. It wouldn't hurt to hold her hand. He reached over and covered it with his. She didn't pull away.

"I think it's the one that's going to be held in my bed," he replied. "It's the Sawing Wood Ball."

"Oh."

The silence stood there like a vacuum waiting to be filled. He'd certainly like to invite Kelly to that ball, but even as he had the thought, he pulled his hand away from hers. That wouldn't be fair or right. He had nothing to offer her. Nothing but pain and trouble.

"I should be getting home," she said. "Gotta be up at the crack of dawn and light up those old ovens."

His tongue seemed frozen. There was so much he wanted to say, so much he wanted to do. Her arms promised so much comfort—promised to lead him to a land of eternal sunshine and sheer happiness.

But what would his arms do for her? Certainly nothing positive. It would be strictly a one-way street. He'd do all the taking, and she'd do all the giving. No matter how much he wanted, he could never be that kind of man.

"Yeah," he agreed. "Debbie and I have an appointment downtown. Real early in the morning."

"You're not going to open for the breakfast crowd?" Kelly asked.

"Just a little late," Ben answered. "I'll still need my breakfast shipment."

"That's going to be some trip downtown and back," she said around a yawn. "If you're still going to serve the breakfast crowd, you're going to have to be up before me."

"We have to meet a friend," Ben said. "He's just passing through, and that's the only time we can meet."

Kelly nodded. "Yeah, that happens sometimes. People passing through on business or vacation. Seems like you have to schedule everything these days."

"Yeah, seems like it."

The comfortable silence was back, and Ben found his hand on Kelly's again. The hand wanted to progress to exploration of other areas, but he firmly held it in control.

"Well, I'd better get going," she said.

"Yeah."

He stood and helped her to her feet. She was as weary as he and Debbie were from the day and paused to rest briefly in his arms, like a migratory bird in flight.

He kissed her. He was no longer able to fight the urge. She was so close, so yielding and so very much a woman. His lips had sought hers without consulting him. There were only needs and hungers. Her in his arms was all that he wanted. Her warmth would rescue him from all the shadows of the night. But she pulled away slightly, and he let her go. She looked vaguely around the room.

"Lose something?" he asked.

"My shoes."

"They're in the kitchen."

"Oh, right."

They walked hand in hand out to his kitchen, where he bent down and retrieved her shoes.

"Thank you."

"You're welcome."

They stared at each other a long moment, then leaned forward to kiss again. It was a light kiss, a gentle brushing of the summer's breeze in the branches of the trees. The peace of the night surrounded him, swallowing him up in its spell. Then it was over, and she left.

Ben watched apprehensively as Kelly took her usual route up on the porch railing and around the post. She might have been tired but navigated the route with no problem, dropping safely down on her side of the latticework.

He really should remove that privacy screen so she didn't have to go climbing all over the place, but, like a lot of other things he wanted to do, he couldn't. He had nothing to offer a woman, so he had no right to pursue her. No right to offer even a hint of his interest. He had to protect Debbie. That was a full-time job that could tolerate no distractions. That lattice screen would stay, and if he was smart he'd build another one around his heart.

## Chapter Seven

Are those people homeless?"

"A lot of them are, honey."

Debbie gripped Ben's hand tighter and squeezed up close as they walked across the waiting room of Chicago's downtown bus terminal. Like bus and train terminals all over America, Chicago's was home to a number of street people. Ben hurried a little faster toward a bank of phones at the far wall.

He found an open one that was relatively clean and pulled Debbie in with him, closing the door after them. After putting a handful of change on the shelf, he dialed the long-distance number.

"Hello?" The voice sounded tired and sleepy, causing Ben to grimace a bit.

"Hi, Mom." He forced an extra dose of joy into his voice. "Happy birthday."

"Ben?" There was a long silence. "You really shouldn't be calling," his mother said in almost a whisper. "They could be tapping our line and be able to trace this call."

"That's okay, Mom," Ben replied. "I'm at a bus terminal. You know, passing through from here to there."

If anyone was listening, that should give them something to think about. Even if they did trace the call, it would just place him at the Chicago bus terminal, from which he could go anywhere in any direction. Looking for them in the city itself would probably be the last thing they'd do.

"I'm sorry to wake you up so early."

His mother chuckled. "You did that once before. Happy birthday to you, too."

Ben tried to force a smile into his voice if not his heart. "So, you having the whole family over as usual? Uncle Leo going to take over the piano until everybody wants to break his fingers?"

"I don't know," his mother said. She sounded more than just sleepy. She sounded tired. "I'm not sure I'm up to it this year."

Their shared birthday had always been a big family occasion. Now it was just something else he'd ruined. "You have to, Mom. You have to celebrate for both of us."

"Cathy wants to have some people over on Sunday. Maybe I'll let her, though it won't be the same."

Nothing would be anymore. A little hand tugged at his pants, and he jumped at the distraction. "Mom, Debbie wants to talk to you."

"Debbie's up this early, too? Let me talk to my little angel."

Ben handed the phone to Debbie and stared out at the barnlike waiting room, trying not to think, not to feel the blame settling on his shoulders for so many sorrows.

"Happy birthday, Grandma. How are you?" A pause. "I'm fine, too. We had a real nice time yesterday. We went to a park and I played on the swings and the teeter-totter and the monkey bars.''

Debbie paused to nod her head.

"I went for a ride on a bus and a train. I'm having a lot of fun.''

Ben's eyes came back to his daughter's bobbing head, and his throat tightened up. Debbie had so wanted to tell his mother stuff, "real stuff," as she put it. She wanted to tell Grandma about the beach, about Kelly and the bakery and about living upstairs above the sandwich shop and helping to fill catsup bottles. About the friends she'd made at the park and her soccer games. But they'd had a talk on the train ride up here. She couldn't give Grandma any details, anything that would tell people where they were. Spies could be listening on the line, then the bad men would find them.

Depression squirmed and settled down uncomfortably onto his shoulders. One little decision, and now his daughter couldn't have a normal conversation with her grandmother. Damn. There were so many ramifications of this thing that he hadn't thought through. But could he have done anything different?

Something bumped his leg. Debbie was holding the receiver out to him.

"Some lady wants more money," she said.

He deposited more coins.

"Can I go outside?" Debbie whispered.

He nodded. It was getting rather close in the booth. "Stay right here, though."

"Ben?"

"Yeah, Mom. I'm on now."

"Things are getting worse back here," his mother said. "Sheila's parents have filed kidnapping charges against you."

"I guess that's their right."

"Ben. That means the FBI will get involved."

"Don't worry, Mom," he assured her. "They have more important things to do than chase a father and his little kid around the country."

"I wish I believed that." She sighed. "So, tell me how you both are, really. Is Debbie getting taller? I bet her hair is long by now. She told me that you're learning how to braid it."

"Yeah," he said with a chuckle. "I'm taking lessons. I'm not too good at it yet, but I can tie up one mean ponytail."

"And what about you? Are you doing okay? Do you need anything?"

"No, I'm fine. Got a good job. Made some good friends." That was one bright spot to report. "Haven't caught a cold, athlete's foot or the bubonic plague."

"I wish there was some way not to worry."

"I know. I ought to be there, helping you take care of your place now that Dad's gone. Cathy's got enough to do with her kids and the new house."

"Hey, I can hire a kid to mow my lawn or shovel the snow. It's more important that you guys take care of yourself."

"Yeah, we are. We love you, Mom. Give my best to everyone."

Ben hung up and sat still for a long moment. He'd handled himself very well. He hadn't broken up or cried or dropped a load on anyone. Once the lump dissolved, he came out of the booth, grabbed Debbie's hand and hurried out of the terminal.

It was only a short walk to the southbound elevated train, and they covered that distance in silence. A few early birds were starting to trickle into the Loop, but the trains going south were relatively empty. He and Debbie maintained their silence on the train as his daughter gazed out at the passing city scene and the traffic-choked expressway. Ben just stared straight ahead.

Run, run, run. That's all that was ahead of them. They wouldn't ever be able to go back for Thanksgiving. They couldn't trade Christmas cards. Debbie wouldn't have anything resembling a normal family.

Their bus was just pulling up to the train station, so they transferred to it and were quickly back in their own neighborhood. Back in the safety of the familiar and the thousand watching eyes. It wasn't a wealthy area, but they had more than money. The people had the care and concern of each of their neighbors. If he couldn't be home, this was the next best thing to it.

Ben opened up the sandwich shop, and Debbie ran next door to get the breakfast goodies. Mike brought them over for her, to Ben's disappointment. But he quickly berated himself for feeling that way. He was already screwing up the life of his daughter and his mother. He wouldn't do the same for Kelly. She ought to find herself some nice guy from the neighborhood, somebody who wouldn't be spending the rest of his life on the run.

Luckily for Ben's growing moodiness, business was good that morning, and he threw himself into activity—serving customers, cleaning up, getting ready for lunch. But he couldn't shake the depression that rode him.

Kidnapping was serious business. His mother was right— the FBI would get involved. Since Ben was Debbie's father, they probably wouldn't assign agents to the case full-time, but they would send circulars to all the field offices as well as local police stations throughout the United States.

Sure, he'd altered his appearance somewhat. Shorter hair and no more beard, but there were some things, like height and weight, that tended to stay the same. And police were trained to recognize things. Hell, it could be one of the beat cops who ate in his place who would eventually turn him in.

Debbie was wiping tables, and Ben could feel the pain in his heart. If she were living with Sheila's parents, she could be lounging by the pool right now. Instead of walking to a little patch of urban green for a pickup soccer game, she could be getting horseback riding lessons.

Ben clenched his fists at his side. Damn it. Sheila had had all of that, and it still hadn't made her into a happy human being. In fact, it had done just the opposite.

He continued watching Debbie, now refilling catsup bottles. Had he taken Debbie for her own good or had he done it for himself? Had Sheila's parents ruined her or had they just been unlucky? Or, given that they had messed up with Sheila, could they have learned their lesson and would now know what love and caring were all about?

A throbbing pain prompted him to go up to the apartment for some aspirin. Damn, he didn't know what was right anymore.


"Kelly," her mother called from the front of the store. "Ben's here."

Clenching and unclenching her jaw, Kelly just stood there in the back, lost in indecision. Ben was just coming for his luncheon rolls—her mother could take care of him. The rolls were all packed on their trays and ready to go. She didn't need to rush out there like a moonstruck junior high kid.

This friendship of theirs had taken strange turns lately. They didn't exactly seem to act like friends anymore. Not that they were acting unfriendly. No, far from it. Maybe too far from it.

She had enjoyed the few moments she'd spent in his arms and had found herself wanting more such moments, longer such moments. But what did Ben want?

"Kelly," her mother called again. This time there was a touch of aggravation in her voice.

Kelly was sure that there weren't any other customers in the store. Why couldn't her mother just give Ben the tray of rolls? Wiping her hands on her apron, she hurried to the front of the store.

Ben was the only customer there. And her mother? Her mother was standing by the cash register counting money. Kelly gave her a frown.

"Oh, there you are, dear," her mother said blandly. "Ben's here for his rolls."

Why couldn't her mother give her a break and realize if Kelly wasn't rushing out here, then something must be wrong? "You mean the tray of rolls right here on the counter?" Kelly asked. "The one that's all wrapped and ready to go?"

"That's right, dear. I'm going to the bank in a few minutes," her mother said. "And I didn't want to stop counting. You know how confused I get if I have to stop and then start something all over."

Her mother had a mind like a computer's data bank—she never forgot anything. But Kelly just said, "Of course, Mother."

She turned to Ben and forced a smile to her lips. "Here you go," she said, pushing the tray toward him.

"Thank you," he murmured.

He had taken in their byplay but hadn't said a word. Kelly thought there was a trace of darkness in his eyes and forgot all about her earlier hesitations. Was something wrong?

"Has Debbie recovered from her outing yet?" she asked.

A smile flickered momentarily and skipped across his lips. "Oh, yeah, she's fine. In fact, she's planning our next one. There was an ad on TV this morning for the Lincoln Park Zoo."

Kelly smiled and nodded. That wasn't the only activity featured on TV that morning. Ben must have missed the announcement about the free concert in Grant Park that evening or else he just didn't care about that kind of thing.

"The zoo's real nice. Dad used to take Mike and me there all the time."

His smile slowly faded away. "Yeah, I'll have to take her one of these days."

A little bunny went hippity-hop in Kelly's stomach. He said "I," not "we," should take her. The quiver continued. Had he been disappointed in their outing? Kelly thought they'd had a nice time. But with her mother standing right there, she didn't feel that she could come out and ask him. If she did that, her mother would start planning the wedding, figuring that Kelly was getting serious.

But this was all ridiculous. She and Ben were just friends. And that's probably what all this was about. There probably wasn't anything wrong—he most likely was just as embarrassed as she about their good-night kiss and was wondering how to get their relationship back on a more platonic basis. Talking about trips he would take Debbie on was his way of putting some distance between them.

Kelly came back to earth to notice that Ben was still standing there. "Everything all there?" she asked brightly, nodding at the tray full of rolls between them.

Ben looked at it briefly. "Looks like it."

The silence pulled and stretched to the very edge of breaking. Should she ask him to the concert in Grant Park this evening? He really didn't look in the mood. Besides, she'd invited him once before—memories of the White Sox tickets danced in her head—and regretted it.

"Well, if you need anything else, just let us know." Kelly was proud how mature and businesslike she was.

"Yeah, I will." Ben reached for the tray, but the welcome tinkle of the front door caused him to pause.

"Hello, Mrs. Koenig," her mother greeted the customer.

"Good morning, ladies." The woman nodded at the two of them, then looked at Ben. "Good morning, Mr. Peterson. And how is your corned beef today?"

"Lean and tasty as always."

Kelly noticed that a bright smile had chased away the cloud of gloom from his eyes. Perhaps his grim expression signified his regret over last night's kiss. He was just trying to discourage any wayward hopes she might be having.

"I'll send my boy over for some sandwiches," Mrs. Koenig said. "Later, when you're not so busy. Save some for me if you can, please."

"I certainly will," Ben assured her.

"What would you like this morning?" Her mother put the money down. "Kelly made some nice potato bread this morning."

Kelly watched as her mother moved farther down the counter. "Maybe you ought to write down where you're at, Mom," she called after her. "I mean, you don't want to have to count the money all over again."

Her mother smiled sweetly at her. "Kelly, be a dear and help Ben with the door."

She put just as much sugar in her own smile. "Certainly, Mother."

"And get his door, too. We don't want the poor man dropping the rolls on the sidewalk."

"Yes, Mother." Kelly opened their door extra wide for Ben.

He smiled as he came out into the morning's heat and murmured a thank you. "You don't have to come along," he said as Kelly shut her door behind her. "Debbie's in the store. She'll get the door for me."

"That's okay," Kelly replied. No need to go quite to that length to put distance between them. "My mother wants me to take good care of our customers."

"She's a very sweet lady."

"Hmm," Kelly replied.

"Well, thanks again," he said as she opened his door.

Oh, what the heck, she thought. They couldn't dance around each other forever. A night out would give them a good chance to talk like adults. He could say the kisses were a mistake, that he'd never meant to take things that far, then she could say that they were sweet and wonderful and she hadn't misinterpreted them. "There's a concert at Grant Park tonight," Kelly said. "Want to go? It's free."

He looked down at Debbie, who had just come to his side. "How about it, kid?" he asked before Kelly could suggest that Debbie stay with Kelly's mother.

Debbie made a face. "Is it a concert where they have noisy music with no words?"

Kelly laughed. "I'm afraid so." Maybe Debbie was going to make it easy for her. "How about if your dad went and you got to stay with my mother and Mike?" Kelly asked.

"Oh, yeah," Debbie exclaimed, her face brightening. "They know how to party. You know, popcorn, ice cream, cartoons, cards."

"Sounds a little wild," Ben said.

"Seven-thirty, okay?" Kelly asked.

He nodded and followed Debbie into the sandwich shop. This friendship would sure run a lot easier if they were adhering to the normal rules, Kelly thought as she walked back to the bakery. One day she knows nothing about Ben, then the next day he confides all sorts of personal things to her. They kiss and feel close, only to be miles apart the third day. Good thing her heart wasn't gearing up for action, Kelly told herself.

"Put another peach in, Kelly," her mother said. "Mr. Zukow said that it's been a good growing season in Michigan this year."

"I already have one for each of us, Mother."

"Maybe Ben likes peaches," her mother protested.

"If he wants another, I'll get him one when we come home."

Her mother frowned a little. "I'd better send some home with Debbie."

Kelly was relieved when her mother left the kitchen. If Kelly didn't get out soon, they wouldn't be able to use a basket for their picnic dinner—they'd need a boxcar. First her mother fussed about the sandwiches, even though Kelly had told her that Ben had insisted on making them. Then Anna'd snuck in an extra couple of bottles of wine cooler, a little bag of cookies and the extra peaches. Her mother believed that the way to a man's heart was through his stomach.

What her mother didn't understand was that Kelly was not looking for the way to Ben's heart. In fact, that was the whole purpose of this outing—to assure him that friends could behave in many different ways, but the common thread was always the no-strings-attached dictum.

There was a rapping at their back door, and her heart gave a skip and a jump. She was looking forward to going out. The Grant Park concerts were always fun, and the weather was beautiful.

"Hi," she said to Ben and Debbie.

"Hi," Ben replied. His lips wore a soft smile, while Debbie's face carried a fierce scowl.

"Something wrong?" Kelly asked.

"He made us come down our stairs and up yours," the girl grumped. "I'll be a gray-haired old lady before I'm allowed to do anything interesting. Where's Mike? He told me he was getting a video."

"He has," Kelly said. "Some movie about a monster eating New York."

"All right," Debbie cried, and dashed into the living room.

Ben just smiled at Kelly, any trace of the morning's gloom now gone. She hadn't imagined the whole thing, but she may have overreacted. His attitude may have had nothing to do with her.

"I guess we might as well go," Ben said.

"I'm not sure anyone cares."

"Debbie, I'm going," Ben called out.

"Have fun," Mrs. Farrell called back.

Kelly and Ben let themselves out, piling their picnic dinner in the back seat of Kelly's car.

"You seem in better spirits this evening," Kelly noted as they drove up toward Grant Park.

"Yeah, my visit this morning wasn't exactly an upper."

Kelly frowned in concentration as she passed a stalled car at the side of the road. "I'd forgotten all about that," she admitted. "I take it that it didn't go well."

Ben shrugged. "As well as can be expected." He seemed to be fascinated by a grocery store parking lot they were passing. "It was just too short, that's all."

No, it wasn't all, but she wasn't going to argue the point. The last thing he needed was a long discussion that would bring his gloom back.

"I thought you were worrying about that good-night kiss last night," she admitted with a laugh.

That brought his eyes back to her, and a smile to his lips. "Why would I worry about that?" he asked. "Or do you think I'm psychotic and worry about the good things in my life?"

It was good to hear that he'd enjoyed their embraces as much as she had, and happiness started to sing in her heart. "I guess I wasn't certain if you viewed it as a 'good thing,'" she said. "After all, neither of us is looking for anything more than a friend."

"And what's your definition of that?"

She pulled onto the expressway and closed her window partway because of the increased breeze. "Someone who likes you and wants to see you happy."

"Who's always there when you need to talk over a problem or share a laugh," Ben added.

"Someone who doesn't pressure you into doing what they want or work on your guilt impulses."

"That all sounds good," Ben said. "Anything else?"

"A friend doesn't put any strings on you."

Ben frowned. "That sounds like a fair-weather friend," he said, and his voice sounded sad. "And that's not what I hope I am."

"That's not what I meant," Kelly said. Traffic was getting heavier as they neared the interchange of the three major expressways just west of the downtown area, and she was silent while she switched lanes. "A good friend is there when times are rough, just as much as when times are good, but because he wants to be, not because he has to be."

"Sometimes a friend wants to be there but can't," Ben said simply. His voice was quiet.

It wasn't just a general comment, Kelly knew somehow. He was telling her that he wouldn't always be there for her, even if he always wanted to be. Clouds seemed to cover the sun, but she forced them away. "Just so long as you're with me tonight to help me eat all the peaches my mother packed."

His laughter sent the last lingering clouds scurrying away, and they talked lightly as she drove the rest of the way. After leaving the car in the underground garage, they walked to the park and spread their blanket out on the grass off to one side of the band shell.

As the orchestra warmed up, she and Ben devoured the roast beef sandwiches he'd brought. She hadn't realized she was so hungry. Maybe it was the cooling breeze off the lake or the strains of music beginning to float through the air. Maybe it was the company. She finished her sandwich and munched on a peach.

"I got an offer today from a video franchise that wants to buy the bakery's location," Kelly told him as she wiped the sticky juice from her fingers. "Actually it's about the fourth offer they've made over the last six months."

"They must want your place pretty badly," he said.

Kelly shrugged. "I guess."

"But you don't want to sell."

She put the napkin in a garbage bag and picked up her bottle of wine cooler. "No."

"Are they offering you a fair price?"

"Money isn't everything," Kelly said.

He looked off into the distance toward Buckingham Fountain, which was sending geysers of water up toward the sky. The music swelled around them, darting and dancing through the evening air. "I guess not."

His reticence surprised her. "Do you think money's the only important thing?" she asked.

"No." He paused a long moment. "But you need a balance. I mean, if you ask a welfare mother, you get one answer. Ask a doctor with a condo in Manhattan and a summer home on Martha's Vineyard, and you get another answer. I guess it all depends on who you are."

"Well," Kelly said. "To me, family is most important. And that includes my father and my grandfather, even though they're both dead."

"So, if you sell the bakery, you're selling your heritage."

"More than that—I'd be selling our way of life."

"Do your mother and brother feel that, too?" Ben asked. "It seems like selling the bakery would replace the money that you lost to Randy."

"But it would also take away our home, where Farrells have always lived."

"Is that really what's stopping you, or is it because you feel you have to earn the money back yourself?"

"That's not fair."

"Isn't it?" He lay on his stomach, propped up on his elbows, and ran his finger lightly over the edge of her shoe in the slow, even pace of the music. "I would think it was pretty normal. You feel you hurt your family, so you don't want to take the easy way and sell the place. You want to earn forgiveness with your sweat and blood."

"All right, that could be a little part of it," she admitted, and rested her chin on her knee. "But it's mostly that I just can't imagine parting with the place. It's been home for so long. It would seem like selling part of myself. Nothing could make me part with it."

Ben grew somber, and the music seemed an echo of the darkness in his eyes. "Don't say 'nothing,'" he said. "Few things are that precious, or should be. When push comes to shove, the bakery's just a building. Everything that makes it special, you carry in your heart and your mind."

Something told her that he wasn't just philosophizing, that his words were coming from his soul and from his past. "Are you saying I should sell?"

He shook his head. "No. Because the time isn't right, and it may never be. But don't be so wedded to things that you can't ever part with them. People are what counts, not things, not places, not money."

"I know that," she said softly. "But you're right about all those other things, too. Thanks."

"That's what friends are for."

It was a time for silence as the sun sank behind the Loop's office towers and dusk settled onto the park. After putting their empty bottles in the basket, Ben stretched out on his side, his head on his left hand. Kelly put her head on Ben's chest and closed her eyes.

She felt Ben's other arm burrow under her head as he bent down to kiss her. Kelly kissed him back. It was all part of the music, the night and their friendship. She was so lucky.

Kelly had a glass of iced tea poured for each of them by the time Ben came back into his kitchen. "She was in dreamland before her head hit the pillow," he said.

"Mike said they had a lot of fun," Kelly said. "He thinks she's a neat kid."

They both took their glasses, but rather than sit down, they stood leaning against the counter. It was so comfortable here, as though it was something he'd always been a part of. He took a long sip of his tea and wondered how to make the magic last, then whether or not he should want it to.

"It was nice out in the park," he said after a time. "That breeze off the lake really cools things."

"Yep." Kelly nodded. "They don't call Lake Michigan Chicago's air conditioner for nothing."

"I guess not."

Sparkling conversation, he told himself. The closeness that they'd achieved that evening seemed in danger of being killed with mundane chitchat—or distance maybe.

"Thanks for cheering me up," he told Kelly.

"You seemed to need it."

He made a slight face and shrugged. "It's my birthday," he admitted. "And I guess I can't help comparing it to past ones."

"Why didn't you tell me?" she cried. "We would have had a party."

"Hey, I thought we did."

Her hair was hanging loose, and there was almost no makeup on her face, which made the freckles across her nose more visible. She looked absolutely, enchantingly beautiful. Ben reached out and took her hand.

"Spending the evening with you was the best birthday I've had in a long time," he told her. "The day started out rotten, but ended up with a smile."

"I see," she said, and moved closer to him.

Holding her hand seemed silly when he could hold all of her. He opened his arms, and she stepped into them, resting her head against his chest. This was the best birthday he'd had in ages. He could stand here, holding her, and close his eyes to shut out the shabby reminders of where he was, of who he was now. Instead he could concentrate on the softness he held, the joy that had come so unexpectedly into his life.

"You know," he said softly, "I was just thinking about our discussion of friendship."

"Oh?"

"In all those descriptions, we never said that friends couldn't kiss."

"No, we didn't," she admitted, a smile creeping into her voice.

He looked down at her, at her eyes so vibrant and inviting. At her hair, glowing with a fire that had to be echoed in her heart. He bent his lips to hers, a sweet and wild touch that brought hope and lightness to his soul.

Everything was magic, just for this moment. Life was a wondrous and special thing to be celebrated. The darkness of the past and the shadows of the future were put on hold as Kelly moved in his arms, pressing against him and bringing back the dreams that life used to hold. Their mouths clung, each drawing strength from the other and giving back sparks of joy to light the dark corners of the night. Then a noise from the alley came in through the open kitchen window—a cat knocking over a garbage can probably—but the spell had been broken.

Kelly pulled away from him. "Well, I guess I'd better get back home."

"I guess."

"Happy birthday."

He grinned and let his hand just gently run along her cheek. "Thanks," he said. "Thanks for everything."

## Chapter Eight

Debbie gazed longingly at the railing as they stepped out of their apartment onto the porch.

"We use the steps," Ben said firmly, and pointing downward.

His daughter grimaced but followed obediently after him. "I don't know what we should do," she said as they climbed down their steps.

"About what?"

"I mean what show should we go see," Debbie said. "Both of them sounded funny in the ads on television."

Ben shrugged as they started up the Farrell's steps. Kelly was going with them to the movies over in Hyde Park, by the University of Chicago, and two comedies were playing. Both looked like they would appeal to adults and kids, and both had been heavily publicized.

"Let's make Kelly decide," Ben said.

"Okay." Debbie knocked on the door.

Mrs. Farrell hurried over to let them in. "Kelly's down in the bakery," she said.

"Is she still working?" Ben asked. Sometimes that woman really took too much on herself. Didn't anybody but him see that she was trying to make a martyr of herself?

"It's those old ovens," Mrs. Farrell said.

"I take it something is wrong with them," Ben said.

The older woman nodded. "Some rush orders came in this afternoon. She got them out fine, but then the ovens quit. I told her she should look at them tomorrow morning."

"I'll go down and see what's happening," Ben said.

Mrs. Farrell and Debbie followed him down. For once the warm fragrant smells of the bread and pies didn't seem welcoming. Thoughts turned to Kelly's self-imposed loyalty to the old business. Ben was all for family, but maybe one had to separate family from the past. Selling this place might be the best thing for her and her family. They found her kneeling on the floor in front of the ovens, digging through a toolbox.

She turned and saw them. "I'm sorry," she said. "We were supposed to be leaving now, weren't we?"

"It's not your fault," Ben replied.

Her shoulders slumped, and she had the look of someone who'd been taking a pounding all day. He wanted to gather her up into his arms and kiss her weariness away, but pushed that idea away. What she really needed was for the ovens to get fixed. A hug and a kiss wouldn't do that.

"Why don't you leave it go for now, dear?" Mrs. Farrell said.

"Mom." He could see Kelly take a deep breath and let it out again. "If I don't get it fixed tonight, I'm nowhere tomorrow morning. There'll be nothing on our shelves."

"Maybe Mike can take a look at it."

"Mike's an engineering student, Mom. Not a technician."

"Maybe I can take a look at it," Ben said. "Do you have any idea what's wrong?"

"I'm sure it's something with the thermostats," Kelly said. "The ovens are old, and a lot of the sensors are corroded." She shrugged. "It's stuff that's expensive to replace."

"I've done odd jobs with stuff like that over the years," he said. "Let me take a look at it."

Kelly hesitated.

"I promise not to break anything," Ben said. "I've repaired other industrial-type equipment."

A mule-headed stubbornness seemed to settle on her shoulders. "You and Debbie are supposed to be going to a movie and out for pizza."

"The three of us were supposed to go to a movie and out for pizza," he corrected her.

The stubborn look increased tenfold. "Just because I can't go, it doesn't mean your evening should be spoiled."

He wanted to tell her that without her company the evening would be a bust before they ever left the block, for both him and Debbie. They wouldn't enjoy themselves knowing she was back here working. Friendship didn't operate that way.

"Movies and pizza are always around," he said. "We can go some other time." He surprised himself, taking the future for granted like any normal person.

Kelly hesitated, seeming to look to her mother for guidance. "Mike's moping around upstairs," Mrs. Farrell said. "Saying he's got nothing to do. Why don't he and I take Debbie out?"

"You've been doing a lot for Debbie," Ben said. "I don't—"

"Hey," Mrs. Farrell said with a laugh, "going out to the movies and pizza isn't exactly my idea of hardship."

Ben had to laugh with her, but there seemed to be a tender spot in his heart. He wished he could do even half as much for the Farrells as they were willing to do for him. Their acceptance of him and Debbie, their willingness to share their home and their lives with the two of them, the way they asked no questions but respected his reticence. If he could just get Kelly to stop punishing herself for the past, he'd repay some of his debt. And the first step was to get the ovens running.

"I'll treat them to the movies, Daddy," Debbie said, apparently reading his silence as hesitation. "I got money saved up."

"You don't have to do that," he said. "I can—"

"You certainly don't," Mrs. Farrell protested. "I've got so much money, it's burning a hole in my purse."

"Really?" Debbie's look was skeptical.

"Almost," Mrs. Farrell said with a broad wink. "Come on. Let's go get Mike."

Ben stared at their retreating backs.

"I presume you know what movie you want to see," Mrs. Farrell said.

"Well, actually there's two."

He didn't hear the rest of the conversation as Debbie's voice disappeared upstairs.

"Did I say it was okay for her to go?" Ben asked.

"I'm sure you must have. I probably blinked and missed it," Kelly said.

"Yeah, I'm sure I did," Ben said. "My little girl wouldn't just walk out and leave me here to work."

They both started to laugh, a tender sound that wound around them, binding them together. This place was such a treasure, and Kelly was such a joy. He'd never expected to find such happiness in his flight and never would again, he was certain. The thought of the future was cold water thrown on the fire of his laughter.

"Well now," he said, "what's with these beasts of yours?"

Kelly sat down on the floor. "You'll have to lay down here and look up to see most of the workings."

"Okay," Ben said, and let himself down, squirming under the partial panel on the front of the ovens.

Kelly leaned in across him, her breast brushing his arm. "Comfy?" she asked.

And to think she thought he had to go to the movies and for pizza to enjoy himself. "Almost," he answered.

"I don't think I'll ask what could make it more comfortable for you."

"Too bad."

She looked at him, straight on and bold, and the ovens were forgotten.

"One never knows where one little question can lead one," he said softly.

"One certainly doesn't," she agreed. "And one might prefer it that way."

"The path avoided can be joy denied." He paused a moment to let the silence settle. "Forever."

She chose not to answer to that. "So, see anything that looks like trouble?" she asked.

What he could really see was a well muscled, shapely female arm and its well muscled, shapely connection to the rest of her well muscled, shapely body. But he turned his eyes to the electro-mechanical junk and nodded.

"It all looks pretty corroded. Must be years of buildup on some of this stuff."

"Most of it probably should be replaced," she said. "But it's really expensive."

He grunted in understanding. "Probably would make more sense to replace the ovens."

"I know," Kelly said. "Something bigger with better temperature control and more automation."

"You'd be able to control the quality of your product better and have less waste," Ben said.

"Yep," she agreed.

"But right now you need these things functioning so you can bake tomorrow morning."

"Yep," she agreed again.

"You have some solvent that might dissolve some of this gunk so I can see what I'm doing?"

"I think so."

"Guess you'd better get it."

Kelly pushed herself out, and he saw her ankles, at the end of two well muscled, shapely legs, disappear. He hoped that she wouldn't squeeze herself back in with him when she came back. Well, he wasn't really opposed to that kind of thing. It's just if she wanted the gunk cleaned off the controls, then she'd better not squeeze in with him. On the other hand, if she had other things in mind—

He shut his eyes tight. Oh, Lord, he prayed. Why couldn't Kelly be a hundred fifty-seven years old with no teeth?

"Ben." Emerald-green eyes, flecked with concern, were staring at him. "You're not sleeping, are you?"

"I'm praying."

"Praying?"

"Yeah. You close your eyes and concentrate your mental energy on the evil obstructing your path to wisdom and truth."

Her concern turned to skepticism. "I have the solvent and some rags."

He took them from her. "The longest journey begins with a single, inconspicuous step."

Did he dare hope that he and Debbie could be safe here forever?

"Boy, I really owe you one," Kelly said as she watched the oven thermostat rise. "You're a magician."

"Nah, I just know my way around machines a bit," Ben said. He was in the tiny bathroom off the workroom, the door open as he scrubbed his hands. "Some of those wires seemed to be held together by the layers of buildup, though. Now that it's cleaned off, they may decide to give up the ghost completely."

"They wouldn't dare."

Kelly put the toolbox back into the storage closet and glanced up at the clock. It was past eight. Ben had put in almost two hours of labor on those ovens.

"How about some dinner?" she asked. "It's the least I can do."

Ben was frowning at himself in the mirror. "I wouldn't mind something light, but can it be at my place? I'd sure like a shower."

"Your wish is my command," Kelly said with a slight bow.

They went up the back stairs to his apartment. Ben disappeared down the bedroom hall while Kelly stayed in the kitchen. What would Ben consider light? She peered into the refrigerator.

"How about an omelet?" she called down toward the bathroom.

"Sounds great," he called back.

Kelly turned the radio on, finding a station playing slow music and setting the volume down low. Just loud enough to set a mood.

And what mood do you want to set? a little voice asked her. To be perfectly honest, she hadn't thought about it. But now, with the soft music weaving dreams for her, the idea of being here alone with Ben was intriguing. She felt a smile grow on her lips and her heart begin to race. She was suddenly a schoolgirl in the springtime.

She beat the eggs with some milk, then chopped up a green pepper, diced some ham and grated up a chunk of cheddar cheese. Not much else she could do until Ben came out. She set the table, but that only took about two seconds, or so it seemed. She found some candles in a cabinet, not fancy ones but fancy enough. She put them on the table, then frowned. Was a romantic candlelit dinner what she wanted? Maybe she should have suggested they go out for fast food.

"Did I take too long?" Ben asked as he came into the room.

It was too late to remove the candles, and she turned slowly. Ben was wearing running shorts and a T-shirt, more than he'd worn at the beach, but her face flushed at the sight of him. At the sight of those arms that could hold so tightly and so sweetly. At the sight of those lips that sang delicious songs to her heart.

Lord, what was the matter with her? she asked herself. Had those few kisses they'd shared totally disconnected her circuits? She busied herself arranging the green peppers into a neat little pile. They definitely should have chosen fast food.

"What'll you have to drink?" she asked. "I've got some of those wine coolers left from the concert."

"I hate to send you back to your place," he said. "There's got to be something liquid here."

"Hey, I don't mind," she assured him. "It'll only take a minute."

And the fresh air would be good for her. Before he could protest anymore, she was out on the porch and around the lattice screen. She was losing her mind, she told herself as she unlocked the back door. Or else the little people had spiked her iced tea at lunch. That must be it. They'd put in a love potion, but she'd fight it. She grabbed two wine coolers from the refrigerator, then two more just in case they were really thirsty, then sped back. Now that she was onto the little people's scheme, she would be immune to Ben's charms.

Ben had finished setting the table and was just lighting the candles when she came back in. Her mouth went dry. She didn't know if she was ready for this jump in their relationship.

"I just put them out in case the electricity died," she said. Her voice sounded strained and her excuse idiotic.

"I thought it was a great idea. I can hide my gray hairs," he teased.

Joking didn't make a bit of difference, Kelly discovered. Neither did knowing the little people's schemes. Her heart was still doing back flips, and her mouth had an urge to hum a love song.

"So, shall I start the omelet?" she asked.

"Either that or watch me starve to death. I'll open the wine coolers, all right?"

"Sure." But did he need to stand so close to her? So what if the kitchen wasn't all that large to begin with and seemed to be rapidly shrinking—there was always the living room or the porch. Why couldn't he go out on the porch to open the bottles? He handed her a glass of wine cooler.

"Here's to your ovens," he said, raising his own glass in a toast. "May the temperatures be always on the rise."

Like hers was right now? She gulped at her cooler, hoping it would live up to its name. It was wonderfully cold and wet, but somehow hadn't successfully extinguished her fires.

"Actually I don't want the oven temperatures to keep rising," she pointed out. "Things would get a little crisp that way."

"True."

His smile seemed to rock her foundations, so she turned the heat on under the frying pan and watched the pat of butter melt. Swell, just what she needed—more heat. She took a deep breath.

"So, what sign are you? Oh, that's a silly question. It was just your birthday. You're a Leo."

"The lion," he said. "And what are you?"

"Libra." She poured the egg into the pan.

"I should have known. The scales of justice."

She frowned at him. "What's that supposed to mean?"

"Nothing bad. Just that I would bet you aren't inclined to look the other way when something is unfair."

"No." She shook the pan to keep the egg from sticking.

"That makes you special."

"No, that just makes me a Libra. Do you want anything with your omelet? Toast or anything?"

"No, the omelet's enough."

He came to stand next to the stove, watching her work. She had trouble catching her breath. Thankfully the stupid eggs were just about cooked. She sprinkled the green peppers, ham and cheese onto the omelet and folded it over.

"So, are you a faithful horoscope reader?" Ben asked.

"Not really. Just sometimes for laughs." She cut the omelet in half, then slid half onto each plate. "Take your pick."

"Both look perfect." He took the plate from her right hand and left a feather-light kiss on her lips in return.

Kelly wasn't quite certain how she found her way to the table, but a few moments later they were seated and eating. Kelly ate about half of her omelet before she found she had strength to speak.

"Anything worth seeing on television tonight?" she asked.

"Is there ever?"

"My gracious. What a pessimist! How did Debbie get to be so cheerful hanging around you?"

He finished the last of his omelet. "I'll have you know, deep down I'm an incurable optimist. My soul is filled with sunshine and happiness at all times."

"It just doesn't extend to television shows," she finished for him. "I think I'll check out the TV book for myself." It seemed important to have the evening planned out, not to just leave things to chance. She ate the last of her omelet.

Ben got to his feet and pulled the dirty dishes over toward him. "Check out all you like. You cooked, so I'm washing the dishes."

"I can dry," she offered.

"You can read us the television offerings," he said. "The paper's in the living room."

As Ben started the dishes, Kelly brought the newspaper into the kitchen. Candlelight wasn't the best for reading, though, and she had an excuse to turn the lights back on. That only made it easier to see Ben, to see the way his shirt was stretched over his broad shoulders and the way his hair fell into soft waves that her fingers longed to touch. She opened the paper to the TV listings.

"Well, we've got some big choices to make," she said. "We can watch some summer comedy specials—"

"Always real winners. That's why they're shown when everyone is away on vacation."

"Or we can learn how to install a Jacuzzi in one corner of our basement."

"If we had a basement."

"Or we can find out about the present state of savings and loans in this company."

"Probably about the same as the state of my finances." He let the water out of the sink, which meant he was almost done and would be ready to retreat to the dimly lighted room soon.

"How about the crossword puzzle?" she suggested quickly. "Let's see if you're as good with words as you are with your hands."

"And how do you know if I'm good with my hands?"

Her cheeks turned to fire, but her voice stayed miraculously calm. "You fixed my ovens, didn't you? All right, what's zero for courtly athletes? Four letters."

He'd picked up a dish towel and was wiping the few dishes, but stopped to frown thoughtfully. "Courtly athletes?" His frown cleared and the sun broke through. "Love."

"Love?" Kelly used his discarded frown.

"Love is zero in tennis."

"Oh," Kelly said, and wrote the word in. Maybe this wasn't a great idea. She looked over the clues carefully. Here was a safe one. "Four and twenty...?"

"Blackbirds."

"Righto." No way to find another meaning there.

But Ben was laughing as he came to sit next to her. "Okay, tell me the truth. Are you making these up?"

"What?" she cried. "All I'm doing is reading what's here."

"Okay, then this was written by the little old ladies in this neighborhood. Love and birds in a pie? It's a strange combination."

"It's the little people," Kelly said with a sigh. He was altogether too close to her. "They're always out for mischief."

He put his arm around her shoulder, a friendly gesture that awoke warmer than friendly feelings in her. She ought to move away just a little, just enough to break that spell that he seemed to weave around her, but that might seem rude or unfriendly. And to be perfectly honest, she wasn't all that certain she wanted to move.

"So, how do we fight them?" he asked. "I have to admit my little-people experience is pretty scarce."

"Well, there's different theories on that," she said, turning to look up into his face. It was a mistake.

With him so close and her heart so shaky, whatever she'd been planning to say just melted in the fire of his eyes. So he wasn't as unaffected by her presence as he'd seemed, she realized. She traced the line of jaw with her fingers, then slid her hand around to the back of his head to pull him closer. Their lips touched.

Joy and delight danced together for a wild moment as their world slipped away. The past and the future had no meaning; the only thing that mattered was this moment of hungers and all-consuming fires. Her arms went around him even as his embrace grew tighter, stronger. It was as if their hearts were beating as one, were actually one.

When breath could be denied no longer, they pulled apart. Ben pushed a curl from her forehead. His touch was as gentle as a leaf drifting through the air, yet sent tremors down into her soul. She'd never felt such longing, such need to be with another. To be held, to be touched became her life and her desire.

"So, how do we fight the little people?" he asked even as his fingers ran lightly over her cheeks.

"Some say you can't fight them," Kelly whispered. His caress was mesmerizing, magical. There was no way to fight it.

"You mean whatever they plan, we do?"

The touch of his hands wasn't enough. His lips took their place, raining delicate little kisses along her cheek, over to her ear and down her neck. Her stomach tensed, and a searing heat seemed to spread out from the very core of her, weakening her limbs and her resolve.

"If we don't obey them, we'll be sorry," Kelly murmured.

"I can see that."

The little people making her braver, Kelly slid her hands under Ben's T-shirt and over his chest. It was as solid and strong as she'd thought it would be. The hair was soft, tickling her hands and her heart, but making her whole body more alive, more aware even as Ben's lips took her mouth again.

There was something in his touch, something in the way his arms surrounded her that drove fears and worries into oblivion. The sweet tension in her heart spread, and like a coil winding tighter and tighter, she took joy in every slight touch. His breath against her cheek, the beat of his heart so close to hers, the scent of the soap he showered with. Her every sense seemed attuned to a higher pitch, a deeper song. She shifted her position, and suddenly her world teetered and rocked, quite literally.

"I'm not certain these chairs were meant for this kind of activity," Kelly said.

Ben's eyes were smoky. "We can move," he said. "Or we can change activities."

It was a time for pulling back, if pulling back was what she wanted. She got to her feet. "The little people wouldn't like that," she said.

"I'm up to bucking their wishes, if that's what you want," Ben told her.

"I don't want to be alone," she said softly, and melted back into his arms. "I don't want to stop feeling your hands on me."

"Kelly," he murmured into her lips, and it was the sweetest of all songs.

For a long moment, they stood locked in each other's arms. Sunshine in the middle of a storm. There was nowhere quite so delicious anywhere else on earth. Then Ben swept her up in his arms and carried her down the hall to his bedroom.

The room was bathed in moonlight, and they needed nothing else. Their hands seemed to know the way, as if they'd practiced all their lives for this moment. Ben's hands helped free her from her blouse and bra, then his lips danced kisses along her breasts. Heat seemed to surround her, engulf her. Fires consumed her as all she wanted, all she knew, were Ben's hands, Ben's lips on her.

The rest of their clothing was bothersome and easily abandoned, then arms and bodies entwined and they kissed again and again. Deeper into their souls they delved, and the chains that bound them tightened ever tighter. She touched him, running her hands over his chest, hard muscles under thick hair. Her hands went lower, over his narrow waist and down to the strength of his manhood. Her touch was light, teasing, and he groaned from the ecstasy of it.

"Kelly, Kelly, Kelly," he whispered, then rolled her over on her back for his own explorations.

His lips danced with hers in a slow, sensuous waltz while his hands brought shivers of desire from her breasts, from her thighs and from the very heart of her love. His hands weren't enough; his touch was too shallow. She needed more, hungered for more.

"Love me, Ben," she breathed into his heart. She had to feel his weight on her, had to hold him within her and be one with him. For that endlessly brief moment, she had to belong to him, and him to her in that timeless bonding.

He moved her over as she parted her legs to take his love into her, then they were one. The skies fell around them, and the stars exploded as they flew in silent union over the heavens. Higher and higher they went, and she clung to him, pulling him closer, feeling their hearts beating together. The rhythms, the stars, the fires swallowed them up. Life, love and Ben were all one, exploding together in joyous delight.

Then Ben held her, and gentleness became her pillow and soft sighs her bed. The silence of night was no longer watching and waiting, but at peace. She lay at his side and closed her eyes, rejoicing as much in his quiet, even breathing as she had in his heated passions. They were still one in their souls.

## Chapter Nine

Ben awoke with a start, suffering a momentary state of panic when he saw that he was alone in bed. Where was Kelly? Had all that just been a dream? His nose twitched. No, it wasn't a dream. The scent of her womanliness still lingered on his sheets.

He forced himself to sit up. His muscles were sluggish, and his eyelids felt heavy. Damn, he had to get up. Debbie would be getting home soon. He was pulling his shorts back on when he heard voices out in the living room. Debbie must be home already. Who was she talking to? Kelly must still be here.

Then Mrs. Farrell's voice intruded on the sluggish confines of his consciousness. Whoops. He hurried back from the bedroom door, putting on a sweatshirt and slipping his feet into a pair of sports shoes. A comb didn't improve his hair much, but slightly tousled was better than totally disheveled. He rubbed his eyeballs to get rid of his sleepy stare, then stepped out of his bedroom. Debbie was giving

Mrs. Farrell a kiss. Behind them stood Kelly, dressed and looking unaffected by the evening's passion.

"Hi, Daddy." Debbie was already in her pj's. "We had a great time, and Kelly's helping me get ready for bed."

"That's good, honey. I'll be in in a little bit."

Debbie bounced off into her room with Kelly laughing and hurrying after her. Well, maybe not unaffected. There was a definite glow in her cheeks, making them the gentle, rosy color of dawn. A fire sparkled in her eyes, maybe only embers now, but he could see the warmth that still lingered. Could everyone? He stole a quick glance at Mrs. Farrell's calm, smiling face. Apparently not.

"Did you two get the ovens fixed?" Mrs. Farrell asked.

Ben nodded. "Yeah. Took some doing, but we got them running."

"That's good."

He found himself swallowing hard. "It was a dirty job."

"Yes, it would have been."

It seemed a tad warm in the room. He'd probably need to turn the air conditioning on. "I had to change my shirt," Ben told her. "That's why I was in the bedroom. I was changing my shirt."

"It's uncomfortable wearing a sweaty, dirty shirt."

"It sure is."

He couldn't think of anything else to say and they waited in silence. What was taking so long? Was Kelly reading Debbie a story? She couldn't be. It was late. He rubbed his eyes a bit. At least, he thought it was late.

Kelly stepped out of Debbie's room, and Ben could feel his heart pause. How in the world could she appear so cool, calm and collected? Maybe he had dreamed it all.

"She wanted a story," Kelly said. "But I told her it was late."

"Kelly," her mother protested. "A child should always have a bedtime story."

"I made up a short one," Kelly replied. "Just like you used to do for us when we were getting to bed late."

Mrs. Farrell smiled her approval. "Oh, that's okay, then."

The three of them stood there and stared at each other for a long moment before Mrs. Farrell finally broke the silence.

"I'll go make sure Mike has the porch light on," she said. "I don't want my daughter breaking her neck, climbing around like some kind of monkey in the dark."

"She's giving Debbie a very bad example," Ben said.

Mrs. Farrell looked heavenward and sighed. "I know. I know. And I keep telling her to quit playing gymnast, but she's been doing it for years."

"It's all Jackie Sirocco's fault," Kelly said.

"They used to live in this apartment when Kelly and Mike were small," Mrs. Farrell explained.

"Jackie was a year older," Kelly said. The glow in her cheeks deepened when she looked right at him. "And she started me on climbing around on the porch."

"You're old enough to know better now," her mother admonished her.

"I've been doing it for a long time now."

Mrs. Farrell's eyes floated heavenward for a moment, then she smiled and gave Ben a small wave. "I'll see you tomorrow. God willing."

"Good night, Mrs. Farrell."

He and Kelly stood in the doorway like two awkward teenagers wanting to bid a passionate good-night while Daddy waited in the car with the motor running. He didn't know what to say to her as she stood there in front of him looking beautiful enough to break his heart. He wanted to tell her that he wished the night would never end, that she had brought such unexpected, such wonderful joy into his life and that he would surely drown in her beauty if she kept looking at him like that.

Finally words spilled out of his mouth. The only ones possible. "Good night, Kelly."

She smiled softly and moved closer to him. Her fingers teased his hair as she moved into his arms and took his lips gently and softly, like a mother kissing a newborn baby.

"Good night, Ben." Her lips lingered and played a moment longer. "See you tomorrow?"

His arms went around her. His mind told him not to do it, but his body, regressing to the stage of a rebellious teenager, went its own way. He pulled her to him and hungrily took her lips in a wild bid to prolong the sweetness of the evening, of this time here with her.

When they finally parted, both gasping for breath, Kelly laughed. "A simple yes would have been sufficient."

Then she was gone into the night. Floating like a firefly, out through black space and onto her porch. He stood there staring a long moment, long after Kelly's lightly slamming screen door announced her safe arrival home.

Shaking his head to clear the clouds, Ben went inside. He checked on Debbie, but she was sound asleep. He kissed her lightly on the cheek. Her breath was a mixture of toothpaste and pizza. He tiptoed out of her room.

By the time Ben reached the kitchen, depression had completely taken over. The crossword puzzle that had started their high jinks stared up at him from his kitchen table. Angrily he threw it down on the floor.

Damn. Damn. Damn. What in the hell was wrong with him? he berated himself. He couldn't afford to get involved. Certainly not now. Not when he was a fugitive.

What did he have to offer anybody? Nothing but pain. Deep in his heart, he knew that Sheila's parents would find him one of these days, and then he and Debbie would have to hit the road again.

But he certainly couldn't ask Kelly to come with him. She had family here and all the love and obligations that her life involved. If she grew too close to him, then he would leave her pain when they left. But if she came along, he'd still give her pain, the pain of leaving people she cared about and the feeling that she was running out on her obligations. And the pain of sharing his fugitive life.

He rubbed wearily at his eyes. Maybe he should just get up and start running right now. He was going to have to do it soon, anyway. Maybe he should just do it now.

Sighing, he got up and turned the lights off in the kitchen, wandering into his bedroom. Up to now, he had been running from something that he couldn't fight. If he ran because of getting involved with Kelly, then he would truly be a coward, for he'd be running away from himself and his own weaknesses.

He took his clothes off and threw them on the floor, then flopped into bed. It was up to him to be a man. He had to put the incident with Kelly behind him and be strong enough to resist temptation. He was acting like some high school sophomore.

Staring up at the ceiling, Ben tried to push all thoughts of Kelly out of his mind. But it wasn't easy. Not with her scent still lingering in the sheets.


"You got a bee in your bonnet, dear?"

"No, Mom," Kelly insisted for about the eight millionth time. "I just have a lot to do today."

"Are the ovens acting up again?" her mother asked.

"No, everything is working ginger-peachy keen." Kelly put a tray of rye bread loaves onto the shelf and then dashed into the back room. She looked sharply around, but unfortunately nothing called out for her attention. The second round of pies were baking, the cakes were cooling and the cookies were all done. That left all too much room for her concerns and worries to begin crowding in again.

Last night had been a mistake. It had definitely not been her wisest moment. It wasn't as if she and Ben were serious about each other. They cared about each other, but only as friends cared. Worry squeezed at Kelly's stomach. At least, she hoped that was the extent of Ben's feelings for her. She had certainly told him often enough that she didn't have the energy for a full-time commitment. She had other responsibilities and needs that had to be taken care of first.

Ben had claimed some of the same barriers—he wasn't alone in the world, since he had Debbie. But that didn't necessarily rule out commitment, Kelly knew. Even though his mouth might be saying he wasn't ready for a relationship, his heart could change his mind very quickly. And when it did, he would need someone who was willing to really be there for him. Someone who'd jump right in and be a wife and mother. And that someone wasn't Kelly, not right now.

She checked the oven temperatures and dusted off some of the tables. It used up all of ten minutes. Another two hours to go until lunchtime, then she could stew over a sandwich instead of icing cakes.

But why stew at all? she asked herself. Ben was mature. He would understand. They just needed to sit down and talk things out, make sure he wasn't assuming something she couldn't give.

"Kelly," her mother called back to her. "Aren't you going to deliver Ben's order?"

Kelly hurried up front. The tray of Ben's luncheon rolls still sat on the counter. Mike had taken over the sweet rolls this morning before he went to his landscaping job, and Kelly had just assumed that he had included the sandwich rolls, too.

"Has Ben called about it?" Kelly asked.

"No, he hasn't," her mother replied. "But I'm sure he's expecting it."

Kelly picked up the tray and hurried out the door with it. She couldn't stay and talk, so she hoped Ben wouldn't expect it. The pies still had another half hour to go, but she needed to be there. Sometimes they needed turning and there was the possibility that the ovens could be on the fritz again.

"Hi," she called over to Ben, who was serving someone at a far table. She set the tray down as he turned toward her. "Can't stay. I'm really busy. See you later."

He said nothing as the door shut behind her, or at least she heard nothing. She hurried back to the bakery. He was probably busy, too.

"Back so soon, dear?" her mother said.

Kelly moved quickly to the back room to check on the pies. "He was busy." Maybe she could start icing some cakes, too. "I'm busy. We're both very busy."

Her mother said something, but the words sounded scrambled to Kelly as she hurried along. The pies were browning nicely, although that one in the back did need turning. Lucky she'd come back when she did.

"I have to go to the bank, dear," her mother said, stepping into the back room. "Would you keep an eye on things here until I get back?"

"Yes, Mother."

Her mother made a bit of a face. "Now I'm your mother."

Of course she was her mother, Kelly thought, but then decided not to question the remark. Her mother seemed out of sorts today. Maybe her arthritis was acting up again, or the heat could be getting to her. When her mother was in one of her moods, it was just best to leave her alone.

The tinkling of the front door alerted Kelly as she was about to start icing a chocolate layer cake. She put down her spatula and hurried out front. A gray-haired lady was peering at the tray of cookies.

"Hello, Mrs. Johnson," Kelly said.

"How are you feeling?" the woman asked, looking sharply at her over the tops of her rimless glasses.

Kelly frowned just slightly. "I'm fine," she said. "Why?"

"I met your mother on my way over," Mrs. Johnson said. "She said you were out of sorts."

"I'm not out of sorts," Kelly pointed out. "She is."

Mrs. Johnson was now checking the pound cakes. "Easy for a woman like you to get out of sorts," Mrs. Johnson said as if Kelly hadn't spoken. "Well past your teens and with no man or children in your life."

"I'm feeling perfectly fine," Kelly insisted.

"Nothing like a man and children," the woman said. "Give you so much aggravation, you don't have time to think about yourself."

"Can I help you with anything?" Kelly asked.

Mrs. Johnson had started looking at the pies, but stopped to frown over at Kelly. "Been ten years since I lost my George," Mrs. Johnson said. Her eyes seemed to cloud over. "He wasn't much for talking but he sure knew how to keep the bed warm."

The eyes dimmed, and Mrs. Johnson fell silent. Kelly bit her lip. She felt for Mrs. Johnson's loneliness and wished there was something she could say that would ease the woman's obvious pain. But still, Kelly wasn't looking for someone like George Johnson.

"The peach pie is delicious," Kelly said gently after a moment. "Made it with fresh peaches this morning."

Mrs. Johnson nodded and glanced out the wide windows at the sun-kissed street scene. "You should check out that man next door," she said. "The one that runs the sandwich shop."

"Check out?"

"Looks like he's got a child and no woman."

Kelly stayed silent with difficulty.

"Not bad looking, either," the woman continued. "And those rangy ones tend to last over the long haul. Too skinny, and they ain't got no spunk. Get them too heavy, and they keel over on you before you know it." She nodded for emphasis. "Yes, sirree. Them rangy ones are best. They'll last you. Wear real well, too."

Kelly said nothing. If she opened her mouth and tried, she wasn't certain just what might come out. Mrs. Johnson meant well—Kelly knew she did. The woman just didn't know anything about Kelly's situation.

"You use fresh peaches in that there pie?" Mrs. Johnson asked.

Blinking rapidly, Kelly forced herself back to the task at hand. "Yes, ma'am. Peeled the peaches and baked the pie this morning."

"I'll have one, please. That there one. Second from the back."

Kelly picked out the pie as directed and put it into a box. She took Mrs. Johnson's money and counted out her change. "Thank you," Kelly said. "Come again."

"If I live, I'll be here tomorrow as usual," the woman said roughly.

Kelly had no sooner stepped into the back and brought her blood pressure back down near normal when the front-door chimes announced another visitor. Kelly stepped out. It was just her mother returning from the bank.

"I hear you're telling the neighbors that I'm getting grumpy and horny in my old age," Kelly said.

Her mother looked blandly at her. "I wouldn't say a thing like that, dear."

"Mrs. Johnson said you told her that I was grouchy."

Her mother shrugged.

"And she gave me a lecture about getting a man and children of my own."

Anna shrugged again. "I don't know anything about that, dear. I said you were feeling bad because the White Sox were doing so poorly this year. And I told her that you said they needed another pitcher."

Kelly gave her mother a hard stare, but it seemed not to have any effect on her. She came up to Kelly and patted her arm.

"You know how that poor woman's ears are. She really should get a hearing aid." Anna went over to the cash register and put in a stack of small bills. "Besides, I'm sure you're right."

"Right?"

Her mother rolled her eyes heavenward. "Where is your mind these days, dear? I'm talking about the pitcher. I agree with you. The White Sox need another pitcher."

"Oh?"

"Probably a left-hander."

Kelly felt a little dizzy as she made her way back to her cakes and the bowl of icing. Pitchers? Men? Children? She shook her head.

She and Ben just needed to get together and talk things out. They were both in the same situation. Their lives were full; he had Debbie, and she had her mother and her brother. They were really in no shape for any other commitments at this point in time.

But there were times when they needed a little companionship. They were mature adults, with very full and active lives, who at times needed the company of the opposite sex. Needed to sit down, talk a bit, laugh a bit. And if it came up—she shrugged—be nice to each other. She and Ben should really talk about it. The question was when.

"I'm a touch hungry, Kelly."

Kelly started at her mother's voice and turned to see her looking quizzically at her.

"Do you want to go to lunch first or can I?"

"You go, Mother. I've got to get these cakes iced."

"I'll bring you something, dear. Ham and cheese okay?"

Kelly nodded as she spread the thick chocolate icing over the first cake. Maybe she was just hungry. A nice lunch would probably go a long way toward settling her overactive mind.

But lunch came and went, and though Kelly no longer felt hungry, neither did she feel settled. She kept herself busy most of the afternoon, though, and away from her mother, since the woman was getting such strange notions about things. It was a relief when Debbie came over for a visit later that afternoon. Someone who wouldn't keep accusing her of being grumpy.

"Hi, Kelly," the girl said. "Hi, Mrs. Farrell."

Kelly's mother smiled and, after hugging the girl, gave her a brownie. "Be careful with Kelly," she warned. "She's got a real grump on today."

"Mother," Kelly said through clenched teeth.

"Oh, yeah?" Debbie paused in her eating to examine Kelly's face. "My father is real grumpy, too. He's been that way all day."

"Oh?" Her mother raised an eyebrow at Kelly, who considered throwing a cream pie at her. "It must be something in the air."

"They're probably working too hard," Debbie said.

Kelly stuck her tongue out at her mother. From the mouths of babes came wisdom. "Or it could be something in the air," she agreed. "It's been so hot that it's causing you all to hallucinate about my behavior."

"Hot temperatures, hot tempers," Mrs. Farrell said under her breath. "Or maybe hot times."

"I think we should all go to the water slide tonight," Debbie said. "You know, to cool off."

"That sounds like fun," Mrs. Farrell agreed.

"It does?" Kelly just stared at her mother. Somehow she couldn't picture the woman on a water slide.

"Not for me," Anna said with a dismissive wave. "For the young people." She turned to Debbie. "You go tell your daddy that Kelly'll be happy to go to the water slide with you both. She'll be ready about seven."

"Mom! I can make my own arrangements." Which might or might not include going to the water slide with Ben.

"Well, you weren't saying anything," Anna noted. "I thought maybe your brain had gotten melted. You know, all these hot temperatures," she said in an aside to Debbie.

The little girl giggled, her hand over her mouth as if to keep the laughter from slipping out.

"As a matter of fact, I had already made tentative plans to go shopping with Moira." Actually she'd seen Moira yesterday, and the young woman had said they should do something sometime, and Kelly had replied maybe they could go shopping one of these days. But today was one of these days, wasn't it?

"And keep this poor little baby from going to the water slide?" Anna asked, her voice and face both in proper scolding mode.

"She can go with her father," Kelly pointed out.

"And what if she has to go to the bathroom? She needs a woman along to take her into the bathrooms. You can't be too careful these days."

"That's right," Debbie agreed wisely.

Kelly was about to point out that one stayed at water slides about an hour or so. That was a relatively short entertainment event that Debbie ought to be able to make it through without any urgent calls of nature. But what was the big fuss?

"I'll cancel with Moira," Kelly said. "And we can go."

"All right!" Debbie cried. "I'll go tell Daddy we're going."

Kelly avoided her mother's eyes and began to clean out the crumbs from the slicing machine. Maybe she did need some cooling off.

* * *

"Did your Daddy bring you here when you were a little girl?" Debbie asked as they pulled into the parking lot for the water slide park.

"No," Kelly said with a chuckle. "This park wasn't built when I was a little girl."

"This is a new park, honey," Ben said. "It was a while ago since Kelly was a little girl."

"Right, back in the time of the dinosaurs," Kelly said.

She and Ben each took one of the girl's hands and walked in silence to the entry gate. There they paid their fee, getting their hands stamped before being let into the Kingdom of Splash. Kelly and Debbie went into the girls' locker room to change. A few minutes later, their T-shirts and shoes deposited in a locker, they met Ben at the foot of the stairs leading up to the slides.

There was no reason for Kelly to feel self-conscious. Ben had already seen her in her bathing suit, and in a lot less, a little voice reminded her. That was a sure way to increase the density of her sunburn. A blush began in her cheeks and threatened to spread. She looked away from Ben, seemingly absorbed in the fascinating Kingdom of Splash.

"So, what do we do?" she asked.

"Go down the slides," Debbie answered, her voice seasoned with a deserving dose of scorn.

"I take it you've never been to one of these before," Ben said. "We just each grab one of those inner tubes and slide down on it."

Debbie had already grabbed an inner tube from the pile and was starting up the long stairway. Kelly and Ben, inner tubes in hand, followed along after her.

"Busy day?" Ben asked her as they reached the first landing.

"Real busy," Kelly said. "How about you?"

"Seemed my busiest ever."

They climbed the remaining stairs in silence, having run out of things to say before they'd even hit the second landing. This was silly, Kelly told herself as she approached the third landing. They were friends. Friends had things to talk about. But the fourth landing came and went without a topic coming to mind, except for a discussion of last night. And how did one lead into that? The fifth landing came before an answer did, and they had to choose which slides they were going down.

"Let's go on Superkids," Debbie said, choosing the steepest and wildest available.

"We should start with the Kiddie slide," Ben argued.

Debbie's face eloquently expressed what she thought of that suggestion. "Why not try Just Kids?" Kelly suggested, pointing to the medium-sized slide.

Neither Ben nor Debbie looked convinced, but Debbie put her inner tube in place and started down. Kelly told Ben to go next, then she followed along after him. The ride was steeper and faster than she expected, but it was exhilarating, too. Her body slid along the curves and twists too fast to hold onto her worries and concerns. By the time Kelly reached the wading pool at the bottom, she'd collided with Ben. All she could do was laugh.

Sopping wet and laughing too hard to stand, she found herself clinging to him for support. And support he provided. His arms caught at hers, and his chest was there for the leaning. She looked up into his eyes and felt the earth move. The heaven she had visited last night was temptingly close. All it would take was a slight sway.

"Hey, you guys, come on," Debbie cried as she grabbed at their inner tubes.

Another slider splashed into the wading pool, creating a huge wave. The undulating current lapped at Kelly and Ben, awakening her from her trancelike state. "That was great," Kelly said. She took Ben's hand as they climbed from the pool and started for the stairs again.

The night was hot, the rides were fun and the water was cool and soothing. It was just what Kelly needed. After a while, she and Ben just sat by the edge of the pool, watching Debbie and the others come hurtling down, screaming into the pool.

"I enjoy the slides," Kelly said. "But it doesn't take long for those steps to get to me."

"Right." Ben snickered. "They ought to install an elevator for us old folks."

Kelly gave him a sharp elbow to the ribs.

"Hey," he protested. "I said us old folks. I wasn't singling anybody out."

"I didn't give you permission to speak for me," Kelly said.

"Geez, what a grump."

"Sorry," she said. "I've received a lot of grump accusations today."

"I've had a few myself."

They sat in silence, Kelly kicking lightly at the water. Debbie came shooting out of the slide, having gone down on her stomach.

"She sure enjoys living on the edge," Kelly said.

"Yeah," Ben agreed. "She's a pretty exuberant sort." He paused a moment and then quietly added, "and tough."

The silence returned, and they watched more children dropping into the pool. Kelly was comfortable and relaxed, the tensions of the day slipping slowly away. Yet there was a sense of waiting and watchfulness in the air.

Ben suddenly cleared his throat. "I don't know how to start," he said.

Kelly looked at him, but he was staring straight ahead. She doubted somehow, though, that he was watching the children romping in the water. But Kelly knew what he was talking about. Hadn't she been waiting for the right time to say something to him?

"Things sort of got out of hand last night," she said.

Ben's eyes caressed her. "Don't get me wrong. It was wonderful. It's just that—"

"It's just that that wasn't the type of relationship we thought we had," Kelly said softly.

His shoulders seemed to slump. "I can't give a woman anything," he said. "Not at the moment."

Kelly put a hand on his arm, running her fingers lightly over the mat of hair. This was a talk she wanted, but not with so somber a tone. She had this sudden fear that she was going to lose him.

"You've given me a great deal," she said. "Laughter and understanding. Companionship. A new outlet for my baked goods," she added with a grin.

His smile was a half-hearted attempt. "I can't offer you anything permanent."

"Good, because I couldn't take anything permanent now. I've got debts to pay before I can pursue any of my personal goals."

A weight seemed to slip off Ben's shoulders. "You don't know how glad I am to hear you say that."

Kelly swung her foot sideways, splashing him. "I don't know why. It seems like we've discussed this about ten million times."

"But yesterday could have changed our relationship."

"Yesterday did change it. But not in the direction you feared."

Ben reached out for her hand and took it gently. His touch was soft, as if he'd captured something rare and delicate in his hands. "'Feared' is the wrong word," he said. "It's not that I don't want to give you all the things you deserve out of life, but I can't. I just can't."

"So, we don't worry about it, then. We can continue to do things together."

"But if someone else comes along," Ben said. "Then I don't want you worrying about me."

"No one else is going to come along," Kelly said.

"I just don't want you to feel obligated."

"You shouldn't either."

They were close, so it was perfectly natural that they should lean forward just a tiny bit and kiss. There wasn't anything serious to it. It was just two friends sealing an agreement. Some people shook hands, but a lot of people kissed instead.

"Hey, you guys. People are supposed to slide here, not go mushy-mushy."

Kelly jerked away from Ben to see Debbie wading across the pool, smiling wickedly at them, along with what seemed to be three million other people.

"Then go slide, why don't you?" Ben shouted.

She dashed off, and fortunately the other people found something else to entertain their nosy interests. Ben held out his hand and helped her to her feet.

"Want to go down as a double?" Ben asked. "Both of us on one inner tube?"

"Sounds wild." Sounded wonderful.

## Chapter Ten

August yielded some of the hottest weather they'd had in years, but Kelly barely noticed. Between Ben and the bakery, her life was too full to worry about another ninety-degree day. Evenings were spent at the park or watching television together. Weekends, they took to exploring the city. The Natural History Museum, the Shedd Aquarium, the Chicago Historical Society—all were studied with rapt attention by Debbie, relaxed interest by Ben and ever-widening joy by Kelly. It was such fun to share her city with them, to share her time with them.

Labor Day weekend, St. Bridgit's Hospital sponsored its annual carnival and, of course, it was an event not to be missed. Kelly and Ben took Debbie over to the grounds Friday evening.

"I start school on Tuesday," Debbie announced as they neared the park.

"I bet you're not excited, though, are you?" Kelly teased.

"No, not a bit," Ben agreed.

Debbie had been hopping up and down, swinging on their arms and just generally burning up excess energy since they'd left their apartment, but a slight shadow lingered in the little girl's eyes.

"A new school is exciting, but it can be a little scary, too," Kelly said.

Debbie nodded. "A lot of the kids from my day camp will be there, but school's not the same as a park."

"No, but it can be even better," Ben said.

They turned the corner, and the park came into view. Carnival music and the smell of popcorn and cotton candy drifted over to them.

"They got a merry-go-round," Debbie said, jumping up and down in excitement. "I hear the music." She began to skip ahead of them.

Ben reached over to take Kelly's hand. His touch was warm and welcoming and wonderfully comfortable.

"She sounds a bit worried about school," Kelly noted.

Ben nodded. "She makes friends easily, and is a good student—I'm sure she'll do fine. But until classes actually start, all she's got to do is worry."

"Poor little kid. She's been through a lot lately."

Ben just looked off into the distance, and something in the air seemed to rapidly change. She could sense a sudden tension, a stillness in his heart that had no place in their evening together.

"I know," Kelly gently teased. "You're a poor little boy, too. I need to save some of my sympathy for you."

Ben seemed to pull himself back from some dark cavern and forced a semismile onto his face. "You better believe it. You give all your sympathy to that little kid, and you're in deep trouble."

"Promises, promises," she said with a laugh, and let go of his hand to slip her arm through his.

Ben's eyes darkened like the coming of night, fires flickering far in their depths. Stars in the velvety blackness of midnight seemed to foretell what lay ahead—cheerful days, warm nights and glorious mornings.

"Come on, guys," Debbie called. "You keep walking like this, and the carnival will be all gone before we get there."

They both laughed, linking their arms even tighter as they hurried their pace. There was time enough later for keeping promises, Kelly knew, and just being with Ben, wherever they went, was enough to keep her heart soaring. They entered the midway with its glittery lights and dizzying rides. Kelly just smiled to herself. She had her own source of glitter and needed only a squeeze of Ben's hand on hers to feel dizzy.

"Let's go on the Tilt-a-Whirl," Debbie suggested.

"How about the merry-go-round instead?" Ben said.

Debbie's shoulders slumped. "Daddy," she whispered loudly. "Are you going to be a wimp tummy again?"

Kelly raised an eyebrow. "Wimp tummy?"

"Hey, I never said I was a fighter pilot."

"He likes the merry-go-round a whole lot," Debbie confided sarcastically.

Kelly's lips twitched even as her heart sighed with delight. She had never known how special just little shared jokes could be. "Does he cry if you take him on anything else?" she asked.

Debbie shook her head. "No, but he gets kinda sweaty and he won't talk."

Kelly patted Ben on the arm. "Poor baby. How about something slow and easy, like the Ferris wheel?"

"I'm not a rides person."

"You know what he said once?" Debbie, hands at her mouth, was giggling uncontrollably. "He said—" Debbie had to pause again for another stream of giggles. "He said that when he's way up high on top of the Ferris wheel he feels like a bird.''

"Oh?" Kelly said.

"Yeah, really," Debbie said. "And he thinks if he jumped off, he could fly." Her last words were a little hard to understand since they were drowning in her giggles.

"It's not an uncommon condition," Ben said stiffly. "I'm okay as long as I don't climb up high or walk on the edge of a cliff."

"I guess we'd better keep you safely on the ground," Kelly said, desperately trying to control her lips. "What can you do at a carnival?"

"I'm good at the games."

"That's something," she said.

Ben's eyes were narrow as he looked from Kelly to Debbie. "I win fantastic prizes, so you guys better be nice to me."

Kelly cleared her throat. "Okay, Debbie, you and I will do the rides. And your Dad will do the games."

Debbie looked over at her father, but her eyes were not filled with pity.

"No more 'wimp tummy' remarks, either," Kelly warned her. "Or no rides."

"I wasn't saying anything." The child's lips were twitching suspiciously.

"Promise?" Kelly said.

"All right, already. I'm promising, I'm promising."

"Want to try the Tilt-a-Whirl first?" Kelly asked.

"Yeah," Debbie exclaimed, then turned to her father. "You just sit here and wait for us, Daddy."

"Sure," Ben replied, dropping himself onto a bench. "I'll just sit here and wait for my girls to get back."

Debbie was already running toward the ride, but Kelly found her eyes reluctant to leave Ben. "His girls." That had such a nice ring—and it gave her such a belonging feeling. For the time being, they could belong to each other. Their hopes and happiness could be shared, as well as their time. Kelly smiled at Ben, and the smile he gave in return stayed with her all through the Tilt-a-Whirl ride and something called an octopus.

Once they got off, they collected Ben and headed for the Ferris wheel. Debbie was small enough to let the three of them share a seat.

"You're not going to try to fly, are you?" Kelly asked as they waited in line.

Ben shrugged. "You never can tell with us birdmen. Maybe you'd better hold me tight."

"What a line," Kelly just said.

But Debbie made Ben sit in the middle when they were helped into a gondola, and grabbed his hand.

"Come on, Kelly," she said. "Grab him someplace and hold on."

Kelly slid over and put her arm around his waist. "No flying," she told him. "I'm keeping you right here next to me. I'm not letting go."

Ben's eyes seemed to turn sad, or maybe it was just the shadowy light. Before Kelly could make a comment, the ride began. Their gondola swung and swayed as it climbed higher. Debbie was squealing in delight and Ben was laughing. Whatever ghosts Kelly thought she'd seen must have been in her imagination.

After the Ferris wheel ride, they pigged out on hot dogs and cotton candy, then Kelly suggested they walk through the game section.

"Let's see some of your expertise," Kelly said.

Ben brought her hand up to his lips. "I thought you already had," he said softly.

The wild carnival lights were no match for the soaring of Kelly's heart. She tucked her hand into his, and they walked through the rides to the games. At a ringtoss game, Ben won a small panda, and at the baseball toss, he won an instant camera. Debbie was delighted with it.

"Now I can take pictures of everybody," she said. "I can start a scrapbook."

Ben just ruffled the girl's hair lightly. "Memories are even more special that way."

For some reason, the night seemed cooler, and the stars didn't seem to shine as brightly. This wasn't how the evening was supposed to go for her buddies. Kelly poked at Ben and pointed over to a target rifle booth.

"Let's see how good you are at that," she said.

"No problem." The gloomy overcast blew away from their hearts as Ben won two games in a row, getting him a giant koala bear.

"Want me to carry it for you?" Kelly asked Debbie.

"Okay," she replied.

Then, as they were walking along, Debbie asked, "Do you have many stuffed animals?"

"Not anymore," Kelly replied.

"Then why don't you let the bear stay at your house for a while? My room is all crowded right now."

"Sure," Kelly said.

A silence settled over them as they walked around the area. The games all seemed repeats of ones Ben had already won, and the lines for the rides were long. They settled on ice-cream cones and sat at a picnic table to savor the flavored ices.

"How did you become so good at the games?" Kelly asked Ben.

"I led a rather dissolute youth," he replied. "Spent my summers traveling up and down the eastern seaboard playing carnie games."

"I'm shocked," Kelly said.

"You should be. I'm the kind of guy your mother always warned you against."

Kelly just laughed and held on to him tightly as they got up and started back home. Was Ben telling the truth about his youth, or was that just another story? It seemed whenever she asked him something about his background, she got a flippant remark. There were so many things that she wanted to know. Were his parents alive? Did he have any brothers or sisters? Did he grow up rich or poor or just in between?

She shook her head. It was really none of her business—whatever Ben chose to tell her was fine. It was just that she felt there was so much about him she didn't know. So much that made him who he was, that was out of her reach. They cleared the edge of the park, and the carnival sounds faded away.

Ben spent Saturday morning doing laundry, but no matter how hard he tried, he couldn't completely rid himself of the worries that the call to his mother had awakened. He kept busy enough during the day, but the night held more voices than he wanted to hear. Yesterday evening at the carnival with Kelly, everything began to weigh down on him. Who was that couple in line behind them? And who were those two guys leaning on the baseball toss booth?

He had to find out what was going on back home, and once all the laundry was done, he took Debbie over to the bakery.

"Hi," Kelly greeted him, then she frowned a bit. "You don't need anything, do you? I thought you said you would be closed today because of the Labor Day weekend."

"I am closed," Ben replied. "I was just wondering if you could watch Debbie for a bit. I have to go downtown and meet with my insurance agent."

Kelly gave him a quizzical look. "Sure. We'd be glad to have her with us."

"Thanks."

Ben didn't stay to chat or start drifting in those deep green eyes, but caught the bus to the rapid transit line and then boarded a northbound train. The cars were pretty empty, and he took a seat by a window, staring out at the expressway alongside the tracks but not seeing anything.

That excuse about visiting his insurance agent was pretty lame. Who conducted business on the Saturday of a three-day weekend? But it had been the best he could think of, and Kelly had been too nice to question it.

Taking the train through the Loop, Ben exited at Division Street and made his way to the Rush Street area. It was the heart of one of Chicago's entertainment districts, but on the Saturday afternoon of a holiday weekend, it was rather dead. He went into a small bar, ordered a draft and then went in back to the public phone. The noise from the bar's jukebox was enough to provide some background but not enough to make a phone conversation hard to hear.

After putting a handful of change on the shelf before him, Ben dialed a number in Los Angeles. "Hi, Gary. This is Ben." He had reached Gary Dowd, his roommate from his early days at M.I.T., at his L.A. apartment. "I need to talk to my mother."

"Gotcha."

After Ben had recited the number on the pay phone, he hung up and waited. He'd already discussed this operation with Gary. His friend would call Ben's mother and then, using his conference call facility, would call Ben back. Any tracing would only identify that his mother had received a call from Los Angeles. The phone rang, and Ben snatched it up.

"Ben?" his mother said. "Isn't this too risky?"

"It's under control, Mom. Don't worry."

He could hear his mother sigh. "I don't know, Bennie."

His stomach took a painful twist. Mom was calling him what she did when he was a little kid. That meant she was very worried.

"We're okay, Mom," he assured her. "Honest. Everything's fine. Anything new happening there?"

"Sheila's parents are spending all kinds of money on private investigators. They want to find you and prosecute you."

"Yeah, I know. But they won't find me."

"You're losing so much, Bennie. All those years of school, learning to be a mechanical engineer, and I'm sure that you're not doing that now. Why don't you come back, Bennie?"

"Mom," he said gently. "You know I can't. If I do, those barracudas will snatch Debbie from me."

"I've been talking to Mr. Rogovitch about all this, and he says you have a good chance of retaining custody."

Ben just clenched his jaw. Sam Rogovitch was an old lawyer from the neighborhood who had served their family for years. He was a nice guy and a decent lawyer, Ben guessed, but it was hard to put any stock in his assurances. After a lifetime of dealing with real estate closings and simple wills, what did he know of dealing with people like Sheila's parents?

"Mr. Rogovitch says all we need is someone Sheila had talked to. Someone she would have told that you are Debbie's father. And then we need another person to testify how mixed up she was about both you and her parents."

Suddenly feeling very tired, Ben put his hand up to rub his face. "I can't take any chances, Mom. After Sheila died, I talked this whole thing over with Barry, and I need to stick to his advice."

"Barry Newhouse? How long has it been since he got his law degree? Five years? Seven, at most. How can he know more about these things than Mr. Rogovitch?"

"Mom, Barry specializes in divorce and custody cases. Mr. Rogovitch doesn't. This is a bit different than closing a house sale."

"You can't run all your life," his mother argued. "I have some money put aside. Why don't I hire a private detective and have him find some people like Mr. Rogovitch wants?"

"Mom, it wouldn't make any difference. Sheila's parents would just buy off anybody we found."

"Bennie, that doesn't have to be so. There are a lot of good people in this world."

"Right, Mom." He forced a lilt into his voice. "Well, I should be going. Say hello to everyone for me."

"And I'll say a prayer for you and Debbie. I do every day."

"Thanks, Mom."

Ben hung up and stared for a long time at the wall in front of him, scribbled with names, numbers and messages. His mother was right—he couldn't run forever, but then that had never been part of the plan. Only until Debbie was eighteen and allowed to decide who she would live with and where. Of course, he could still be prosecuted then, but she would be grown when that happened. Just about an adult, with an adult's understanding of the world and relationships. She wouldn't be an emotional cripple, as Sheila had been, using people to get at others. No, the years of running were an easy price to pay to be certain that his daughter grew up emotionally strong. He stood up and, leaving his barely touched beer by the phone, walked out of the bar.

Outside, a shiver ran through his body, even though it was a warm summer's afternoon. He was going to miss this city when they left. He would miss it more than he could ever say.

"All set for school, honey?" Mrs. Farrell asked Debbie as Kelly brought a high stool from the back room for the girl.

"Yes, I am," Debbie replied, nodding vigorously. Kelly put the stool by the cash register so Debbie could help take care of customers.

"Did you get a new outfit for the first day of school?" Mrs. Farrell asked.

Suddenly the child looked uncomfortable. "We didn't have time to go shopping."

Kelly and her mother exchanged glances. Poor Ben. Being a single parent was hard. He probably hadn't even thought of the importance of a new school outfit for a little girl. Well, what were friends for?

"Why don't we go over to your place and check your stuff out?" Kelly said. "Then if you need anything, we can run out and get it."

Debbie looked uncertainly from one to the other.

"That's okay, honey," Mrs. Farrell said with a wave of her hand. "You go with Kelly. Mike and I can handle things here. It'll be a little slow because of the holiday weekend, anyway."

"Okay." Debbie hopped down from her stool and, taking Kelly's hand, went out the back of the bakery. "Why don't we go up your stairs and then—"

"No way, José," Kelly said.

"But—"

"I promised your father that I wouldn't let you walk on the porch railing."

"Gee whiz," Debbie said, depression forcing her into a slouch. "I never get to do anything."

Kelly struggled mightily and finally succeeded in suppressing her smile. "When you're older," she told the girl.

"Oh, yeah." Debbie's voice was filled with a wisdom far beyond her years. "And when I'm older, people will tell me I'm too old to do that kind of stuff."

The smile broke through on Kelly's lips, and she put an arm around the girl's shoulders as they walked up the stairs. "One advantage of being older is that you don't always have to listen to what someone else says."

"Good," Debbie said, snapping out the single word over tight lips.

Debbie opened the back door, and they went straight into her room. Digging through the closet and drawers, they pulled out clothes for Debbie to try on, mixing and matching different outfits. Soon there were piles all over the room. Some of her garments were too small, and others needed cleaning and mending.

"You're in pretty good shape with clothes," Kelly said. "At least until spring, when you'll probably outgrow a lot of these. So, what would you like to wear on Tuesday?"

Debbie shrugged.

"Isn't there anything here that's really your favorite?"

Debbie shook her head.

"Well, you've got to like something a little better than everything else."

"I wish I had some long shorts," Debbie said. "You know, those kind that are real tight around your legs and go almost to your knees."

Kelly nodded, remembering the bicycle shorts that appeared to be popular with the younger set this summer. She and Debbie could probably run out to Ford City and buy some.

"Want to go out shopping for some?" Kelly asked. "My mom won't mind if we leave her at the bakery for a while."

"You're really lucky," Debbie pointed out. "'Cause you got a real nice mommy."

The look in Debbie's eyes pinched at Kelly's heart, and she vowed that the two of them would have a wild time "malling." After checking back in with her mother and Mike, Kelly drove Debbie to Ford City, a shopping center in an old Ford stamping plant. With Debbie skipping along at her side, Kelly felt on top of the world as they entered the shopping center.

She decided to do the shopping properly, so they took their time. First they went through all the stores and gave them a once-over, checking the shops that offered the best selection in Debbie's size. Then they went back again and tried on colors that the girl liked. Once she'd picked out some shorts, it was obvious that she needed shirts to match.

Then she needed a pair of white-and-blue athletic shoes with knee socks. And to top it all off, she had to have some braided bracelets. When they were finally done, they collapsed on a bench out in the mall's open area.

"You know what?" Kelly said. "Shopping makes me real hungry. How about a super-duper giant sundae with hot fudge sauce and cherries and nuts?"

"Okay."

They found a restaurant in the mall, and within minutes Debbie was industriously digging into her tall sundae creation.

"Thank you for bringing me shopping," she said between mouthfuls.

"Thank you for allowing me the pleasure of your company," Kelly replied. "I had a good time."

Debbie nodded and then resumed eating her ice cream, although at a slower pace. "My mother never took me shopping," she said after a minute.

Kelly kept her head down and concentrated on her sundae. How sad for Debbie. From her perspective, she'd believed her mother hadn't cared to do things with her. Ben was right—it was better to be honest with kids than to let them put their own interpretation on things.

"My daddy always took me places," Debbie said.

"Sometimes mommies are busy. That's why it's nice to have two parents."

"My mommy used to sit around and talk on the telephone and watch TV a lot."

This conversation was heading in a direction where Kelly didn't think she belonged. "Well, it was nice that your dad could take you."

Debbie had finished her sundae and was licking the remains off her lips. "Daddy would always say she could come along, but she never did." Debbie checked the bottom of her glass to see what morsels remained. "Sometimes I thought she hated Daddy."

Kelly swallowed hard. "She couldn't have," Kelly said quietly. "After all, they had you, and you must have been made from a lot of love."

Debbie's uncertainty drained from her eyes, and a slow light began to flicker in its place. "You know what, Kelly? I wish you were my mom."

Kelly didn't know what to say, but couldn't have spoken even if someone handed her a script. She just reached over and hugged the little girl tightly. If she ever had a daughter, she wanted her to be just like Debbie. Did that mean having Ben for her children's father?

"Boy, oh boy," Ben said as Debbie twirled in front of him, displaying the last of her ensembles as Kelly watched from the doorway. "I don't know what I'm going to do."

Debbie stopped and looked at him. "About what?" she asked.

"About all the boys that are going to be following you home."

She went up to her father and hugged him hard. "Don't worry, Daddy. You're always going to be my favorite."

Ben just gathered Debbie into his arms. Love filled his face, love and happiness at the little girl's joy. But when he released her, the same sadness that had been in his eyes since he got home tugged at the edges. It seemed that Ben's "insurance man" hadn't had good news for him.

"Hey, guys," Kelly said, stepping into the room. "You know what I'd really like to do? I want to make dinner for us all tonight."

"You've done enough already," Ben said. "Why don't I take you out?"

And share all her favorite people with strangers? "No," Kelly said. "It's getting late, and restaurants are so crowded on Saturday nights."

"I thought at least half the people would have left the city for the Labor Day weekend," Ben said.

"Yeah," Kelly said. "And most of them are restaurant workers. Come on, what have you got in the old fridge?"

Ben shrugged.

"Hamburger?"

"Always," he replied.

Kelly moved toward the kitchen cabinets. "Where are your canned goods?"

Debbie ran over and opened an end cabinet.

"Ah," Kelly said, "you have plenty of canned tomatoes. Great." She nodded and then looked up at Ben. "You got any green peppers, onions?"

"You really don't have to—"

"We have onions," Debbie answered. "But no green peppers."

Kelly stood up. "Okay, are you willing to be my chief assistant?"

"Yes." Debbie nodded vigorously.

"First thing, make your father sit down and get him something cool to drink."

Serious, with just a touch of power shining through, Debbie pulled her father to a chair at the kitchen table. Then, after pouring him a glass of lemonade from a pitcher in the refrigerator, she stood ready for her next set of instructions.

"Go get my mother and Mike and tell them I'm making dinner for everybody here at your house."

Debbie ran to the door.

"And tell my mother to bring over two green peppers."

"Okay." Debbie zipped out the door but, before it slammed, Kelly was there.

"Use the steps," she shouted, then breathed a sigh of relief to see the girl already halfway down the steps.

"Kind of bossy, aren't you?"

Kelly smiled at Ben. "It's genetic," she replied. "Bossy is a gift bestowed upon every first-born girl."

Ben nodded. "I noticed that with Debbie. And she's got no one to boss but me."

"That's a shame."

Kelly started browning the meat, working easily even though the kitchen was unfamiliar to her. Spring flowers were blooming in her heart. No, that was wrong. It wasn't spring. What was a late-summer image? How about apples ripening in her heart? She grinned into the frying pan.

"What's so funny?" Ben asked.

Kelly tried to look serious. "Nothing," she said. "Just thinking about our shopping trip. We had fun."

"It was really great of you to do it," he said, his voice about three levels lower than the basement. "I don't know how, but I just forgot about new clothes for school. I—"

"You have enough on your mind. I got as much fun out of the outing as Debbie did."

"Still, what do I owe you?"

The meat browned, and she poured the grease off. "Nothing," she said. "I can manage a few shirts, since they weren't expensive."

"No," Ben said. "We're not poor. I didn't not get her things because I couldn't afford it. I just forgot about it."

His voice, his eyes, everything about him this evening seemed so miserable. He was putting on a brave front, but something was obviously wrong. Kelly turned off the frying pan and sank down into the chair across from Ben. She took his hands in hers, but before she could speak, his eyes grew more shuttered, denying her access to his feelings of apprehension and self-doubt.

"Ben, I had more fun shopping with Debbie this afternoon than I've had shopping in ages," she said, though it was far from what she had wanted to say. What's wrong? She shot him an inquiring look.

"But I insist that you be reimbursed for what you bought her," he said. He returned the gaze as if insisting nothing was wrong.

"Considering what you've spent on movies and pizzas for me, not to mention the carnival last night, I think we're even," Kelly said. Don't shut me out—let me help.

But those walls were too high and too well built to let her cross. "You've donated your share to those outings," he insisted.

"Fine." She sighed and withdrew her hands as she heard footsteps on the porch outside. "Twenty should cover it."

Another moment, and her mother and Mike were there. Glad of the excuse to be busy, Kelly put them to work slicing the celery and onions for the hash and making the salad. Debbie set the table with Ben's help.

Unwilling to fall into the blue funk that was tempting her, Kelly managed the dinner conversation, making sure that everything was kept in a light vein. She was happy to see Ben chuckling several times. If he wouldn't confide in her, she could still do her best to cheer him up.

Mike insisted on cleaning up after the meal, but everyone pitched in. It was just as well, for it was fairly late when everything was put away. Debbie was unsuccessfully suppressing huge yawns.

Kelly was tired herself. Trying to fight the evil knights of Ben's depression had been more wearying than she had expected. She was tempted to stay after her mother and Mike went back home. Ben seemed tired, and maybe his defenses would be down and he'd confide in her. But that seemed unfair. Their friendship called for better than that. If he wanted to lean on her, he knew where she was. When her mother and Mike were leaving, she bid Ben and Debbie good-night, also.

Was she really so tired physically, or was it an emotional weariness? Kelly asked herself as she went down the stairs with her mother. Had to be physical. But she wasn't ready for sleep. Her mind was still raring to go, as were her emotions.

"Your young man is very nice," Mrs. Farrell said as they climbed the stairs behind Mike. "I couldn't have picked a better one for you myself."

"Mom," Kelly protested, "Ben doesn't belong to anybody."

They stopped at the door, and her mother smiled at her. "Kelly, sometimes for someone so smart, you are so dumb."

Her mother went into the house, leaving Kelly alone in the darkness. For a long moment, she stared up at the full moon lighting up their backyards. There was such peace and familiarity in the setting, the pale light bathing her world. But it wasn't quite perfect.

Last year she might have said such a moonlit setting would be perfect if only the sycamore tree in the backyard was pruned. Last month she would have said that streetlight shone into their back windows too brightly to enjoy the glow of the moon. But now, this very minute, she knew none of those things were what was really missing. It was just Ben. She wasn't complete, wasn't alive, wasn't whole without him at her side.

Oh, Lordy. Her mother was right. She was in love with Ben. Now what?

## Chapter Eleven

Hah, you blinked first," Kelly whispered to her clock, then rolled over.

Lord, things were really getting bad. Here she was having a staredown with her clock and gloating in victory. But since it was now one-twelve in the morning, she wasn't sure that victory was a thing to rejoice over. She was lucky tomorrow was Sunday and the bakery was closed. She hadn't slept a wink, and it didn't look like she was going to catch a single z tonight.

She sat up in bed and looked around her darkened room. Should she get up and read? Making a face, she just sat there. She didn't want to wake anyone up. Having to explain why sleep wouldn't come was the last thing in the world she needed. Gee Mom, I can't sleep because I just realized I'm in love with Ben. Groaning again, Kelly flopped back down on her pillow.

The night-light in the hallway suddenly seemed the source of her problems, and she glared at it, sending wicked malevolent thoughts through her open bedroom door. It would be easier to just get up and close the door. More considerate, too. Her mother was a light sleeper, with her arthritis, and all Kelly's groaning and bouncing around was enough to wake everybody up in the neighborhood.

This was going to be a great night, super, even. She had another three hours to lie awake and think of how stupidly she'd acted. All those idiotic speeches she'd made about being friends were coming back to haunt her. She could almost see them floating around above the bed, ready to pounce on her, one at a time, until she begged for mercy. But love gave no quarter. She'd learned that the hard way.

Tired of her thoughts, Kelly rose and crept over to shut the door. Then it was even darker in the room. Too dark for her memories to find her? Maybe she should turn her light on and read. But if her mother should get up and see the light under the door, it would be question-and-answer time. And Kelly wasn't in any shape to come up with quick and clever retorts.

Of course, the full moon and the streetlight in the alley almost gave Kelly enough light to read by, but what book was engrossing enough to distract her from her thoughts? So she just flopped down in bed, sitting partially up, to stare at the far confines of her room. Shadows from the old sycamore tree in back formed an intriguing silhouette on the wall.

Did sycamore leaves have the same power as tea leaves? If she studied the shadows carefully, would she be able to see her future?

She stared at the shadows dancing on her wall, and surprisingly they metamorphosed into some intriguing, almost discernible configurations. There was a large one. Big and protective. Like a husband and father. There were a number of smaller ones. Could they be children?

"Oh, fudge," she whispered to the walls.

What in the world had she done to her life? She had so many obligations and responsibilities, but she had to go ahead and fall in love. And fall in love with a widower who wasn't ready for another relationship. What in the world was wrong with her?

Kelly sat up on the edge of the bed, her bare feet caressing the carpet on the floor. Instead of blurred conformations dancing on the walls, the leaf shadows now transformed into a more defined sculpture—much like long fingers intent on grabbing her. It was positively eerie. She had to get out of the room. The walls were closing in on her.

She was wearing only a short nightgown, but didn't bother with a robe before she eased her door open. The night was still warm, and nobody else in the world would still be awake. Carefully she slid out into the hall, over to the kitchen and out on the porch, making a minimum of noise. She was about to sit down when she noticed that a light was on in Ben's kitchen. Was something wrong?

Taking her usual porch railing route, Kelly found herself at Ben's door, gently knocking, before she had time to think about it. The porch light went on, and Ben's face appeared at the edge of the curtains on the back-door window. He quickly opened his door.

"Hi," Kelly said. "It's me."

A half smile turned his lips. "I'm glad to see that," he said. "When I heard the tap-tap-tapping at my window, I was afraid that it was the Raven."

Kelly tried to frown at him, but it would have taken more strength than her newly damaged heart possessed. Joy and laughter kept wanting to spring out. "See if I'll nevermore worry about you."

He groaned and pulled her into his arms for a kiss that would have knocked her socks off, had she been wearing any. His lips whispered sweet love songs to her heart, his arms enclosed her in the only place she ever wanted to be. There was hunger in his touch, but strength, too, and Kelly was ready to light up the night with a celebration of her love. Here, in his embrace, it didn't seem such a frightening thing.

He loosened his hold, and she pulled away, sitting down at his kitchen table. "Actually I came because I was concerned," she told him. "I saw your light still on and I wondered if Debbie was sick or something."

"Nope." Ben shook his head. "Debbie's fine. I've just got an acute case of insomnia."

Was it contagious, or did this just prove that they were in sync? "Me, too."

Ben closed the door behind him. "You think insomnia is one of those things that you enjoy more if you share it?"

"Probably."

"Want anything to drink? Iced tea?"

She shook her head. "Too much caffeine."

"Lemonade?"

She shook her head again, so he sat down across from her. It was crazy of her to come here. She should have made herself a cup of warm milk and gone back to bed. Her own bed. She cleared her throat and looked around Ben's kitchen, anywhere to avoid his eyes.

"It's still warm out," she said after what seemed to be an interminable silence.

Ben nodded.

"Won't be for long, though," she went on. "Another few weeks, and the nights will be getting cool."

Again he nodded.

"It'll be fall before we know it."

This time he smiled. "Have you ever considered being a TV weather person?"

He was laughing at her. She was a nervous wreck, hardly able to carry on a sensible conversation, with her heart doing somersaults every half second, and he was laughing at her. She knew she probably sounded like a fool, but she couldn't think what to say to him, not after discovering less than five hours ago that she'd fallen in love with him. She did the only thing left to preserve her dignity—she got angry.

"My, aren't we humorous," she snapped. "I didn't notice you carrying your load of the conversation."

"It's not like I invited you over."

"I told you, I thought something was wrong." Her voice was rising to match her temper. Somewhere a shred of common sense was trying to call her back, warning her that she'd regret pushing them into an argument, but Kelly didn't have time to listen to reason. Not when her heart was on the line. "I don't remember holding a gun to your head and forcing you to let me in."

There was another long moment of silence, during which Kelly's heart kicked and stomped in protest—in simulcast with her self-congratulatory plaudit for being strong. But then Ben reached over and took her two hands in his.

"I'm sorry," he said. "I've been in a lousy mood all day. I guess I ran out of antigrump pills."

Kelly melted into a pool of remorse. "It was my fault. I snapped at you because I feel silly for rushing over here like I did." She tried for a lighthearted grin, but didn't even want to think how far from the mark she'd fallen. "I imagine there are lights on all over the city, yet I didn't worry that anything was wrong anyplace else."

Rather than laugh at her silliness, Ben seemed to sink back into the gloom that had surrounded him all evening. "We've really been a pain in the neck for you, haven't we? Nothing but trouble."

This trouble was one she brought on herself, she wanted to tell him but didn't. "Ben, what's wrong? You've been upset about something ever since you got back from your trip downtown. What happened? Did you get bad news?"

Kelly looked into his eyes, trying to will trust and hope into those blue depths, but he looked away from her. "Nothing's wrong," he said. "Well, nothing any of us can do anything about. I just got some bad news. My mom's not feeling very well, but she'll be okay.''

Kelly didn't remind him that he was supposed to have seen his insurance agent that afternoon. When had he talked to his mother? "I'd like to help you if I can," she just said.

"You've already done more than could be expected."

The silence claimed them again, and Kelly was ready to let it win. She slowly got to her feet. Staying here with Ben when he was depressed yet silent wasn't accomplishing anything, except accentuating the barriers between them.

"Don't stay up all night," she said. She touched his cheek gently, unable to go without some contact with him, running her hand along his jawline. "Going without sleep won't make anything better. It just makes you less able to cope."

He caught her hand and held it against his face, then turned enough to kiss her fingertips. "It was good of you to come check on us."

She just smiled into his eyes. How could she have stayed away? This is where she wanted to be.

He got to his feet, still holding her hand. Neither of them seemed interested in breaking the contact, the lifeline to the other's heart. The night closed in, the quiet now a blanket that caressed even as it wrapped around them. She took a step closer to Ben, drawn by some hunger in him that was echoed in her soul.

"Do you have to go?" he whispered, then shook his head slowly. "No, of course you do. I shouldn't be asking you to stay."

"I want to." She moved into his arms that opened like a smile to welcome her home.

"Maybe for just a little while," he said.

"Right, just a little while."

She reached up for his lips, meeting them with a raging need that came over her without warning. This was why she hadn't been able to sleep, why her thoughts had danced around Ben all night. Even though her mind was having trouble recognizing her need of him, her heart knew. Her heart had known all along.

Without words they went into Ben's bedroom, closing and locking the door so as not to disturb Debbie. Then their passion took over, touching, kissing, loving the other. Really loving, this time, Kelly knew. And the knowledge made the touching all the sweeter.

Ben could bring her to such happiness, up to touch the leaves of those trees and beyond to the sky. She clung to him, whispered silent words of love through her hands and moved to his rhythms. It was wonder and joy—it was heaven, and it was forever. Her body leaped in delight at his every touch, and even his breath on her skin drove her heart into shivers of ecstasy.

This time she explored him with her lips. She tasted the salty sweetness of his chest and tickled him with her tongue. But his quiet laughter ceased when she took him in her mouth, her tongue weaving a spell over him. She wanted to bring him to the edge of control, to hold a power over him like he held over her. She wanted to be his forever, not just in her mind and heart, but in reality.

She moved onto him, letting her body hug and tease him. They were one now, afire, together—forever. He whispered her name and reached for her even as their hearts exploded in rapture. Peace surrounded them and washed tensions away. The night claimed them once more in its cool and forgiving arms.

Smoke hung heavy over the park, billowing up from the grills loaded with bratwurst and hamburger. This Labor Day picnic had been a tradition for as long as Kelly could remember. She used to come here, riding on her father's shoulders. Now she was bringing Ben and Debbie to share in the neighborhood's tradition.

Saturday night in Ben's arms had done wonders for her emotional state. She could now look at herself in the mirror and admit that she loved him. The timing was off and the circumstances less than perfect, but for Kelly there was no turning back. She loved Ben and would make the best of it, sticking to the rules they'd set up along the way. And maybe, with a little luck and the help of the little people, he'd come to love her someday. It had taken all of Sunday to come to that acceptance, but Monday found her happy as a chocoholic in Holland, knowing that she was going to spend the afternoon with Ben and Debbie.

Neighbors greeted them as they entered the park, but Debbie soon skipped away to join some friends. Kelly and Ben were about to stake out a picnic table when a group of elderly ladies bore down on them.

"Where's your mother and Mike?" a woman asked.

"Mom went over to get Mrs. Johnson," Kelly answered. "And Mike went to pick up Madie Cleary."

"Oh, the Cleary girls. They're a good-looking lot."

"That Michael, he's a handsome lad, too."

"It's just a date," Kelly said laughingly. "Nothing serious."

The women exchanged nods and knowing looks. "One never knows."

"The fates beckon, and man obeys."

Ben just cleared his throat to camouflage his overwhelming urge to laugh. "Would anyone care for something to drink?" he asked.

Kelly nodded. "A soda or lemonade will be fine."

Ben looked at the elderly women. "Ladies?"

"Oh, no," they chorused, waving paper cups at him. "We're fine, thank you."

"Be right back," Ben promised, and hurried toward the concession stand dispensing the drinks.

Five pairs of eyes followed Ben on his trek, then turned back toward Kelly, glittering with an obvious interest in her and her affairs. "He's a fine young man, that one."

"Strong."

"Hardworking."

"And that child's such a lovely little thing."

Kelly could feel her neck warm under her hair. "Yes, they're both very nice."

"Your mother is quite happy for you."

"Oh, yes. Poor soul. She's been worrying so."

Kelly burst into an exaggerated peal of laughter. "This is just a little date, too," she told them. "Just like Mike."

The women continued smiling. "It's nice to start with a ready-made family."

"Helps you settle down. You don't waste your time gallivanting about."

"Yes, a family does settle a woman."

"Makes her content."

Kelly gave up. Time, tides and matchmaking old Irish ladies were no match for any man or woman. Ben was on his way back and maybe he would provide her escape.

"Did I miss anything?" Ben asked, handing her her drink.

Kelly gulped at the soda. "Oh, no. Nothing at all," she replied. "Why don't we walk around a bit?"

"Okay." He nodded at the women. "A pleasure seeing you ladies again."

They nodded as Kelly and Ben turned away.

"Oh, Kelly," one of the women called after them. "Take Ben down by the lagoon. It's quiet down there."

"More private," another added.

Kelly tried to hide her amusement. Ben, too, seemed to be suffering from some sort of inner rumbling himself. She didn't dare look at him, though, not while they were still in viewing distance of the old ladies. After a moment, though, Ben stopped.

her heart strength. Her love was too new and fragile to weather a storm right now.

The rains came early and stayed late, spreading not the promise of renewed growth, but of gloom and misery. Kelly tried to laugh it off, but her smiles never penetrated the surface. The rain and her depression were still in full force Tuesday morning when she crept down to the bakery in her stocking feet—as she always did and as her father had before her—so as not to wake anybody up.

She was up a bit earlier than she had to be, but she couldn't shake the feeling that it wasn't just storm clouds hanging over their heads. There was a growing sense of foreboding sprouting from the very depth of her being, that something or someone lay waiting to tear her life apart.

She knew she was just being silly and decided not to waste any more time in bed brooding. It was just the curse of being Irish, these premonitions. And, of course, they were always of looming disaster. She never woke up certain that she was going to win the lottery.

But today would be a good day. Debbie was starting school, in the height of fashion and French braids. Kelly had to get the bread started first, then she could go over and help her little buddy get ready.

With a cup of coffee to fortify her, Kelly got the bread dough made and rising. Then, after turning the ovens on, she started on cakes. The bakery was practically empty after the long weekend, and everything needed to be restocked. It was likely to be a long day.

Suddenly she frowned. The only sound she heard was the low rumble of thunder. No reassuring little noises of ovens getting hot. She went over and opened a door. Damn. They were barely warm. She turned the thermostat way up and set a timer for ten minutes, but when it sounded, there was little change.

"Damn," she exclaimed.

Then she slouched back against the table and fought back the tears. So the ovens weren't working. It had happened before and would happen again. It was hardly a reason to cry. Except suddenly she was so frightened. Everything in her life seemed to be precariously balanced. She was walking a tightrope, blindfolded and in a high wind.

## Chapter Twelve

Well, Matt," Kelly said to the stocky, gray-haired man wiping his hands on the side of his serviceman's coveralls. "What's the verdict?"

"Stone-cold dead."

Kelly paused to swallow the lump that filled her throat. "You mean I'm out of business for today?"

"I can patch it for today, Kelly. But I don't know how long it will last. It might be a week. It might not even be ten minutes."

"Just get me through the day."

"You ought to dump these old dinosaurs," Matt said. "They ain't doin' you no good."

Kelly, staring at the ovens, did not respond.

"I mean, you're working yourself half to death and got nothin' to show for it. You could use one of those new jobbers with a little conveyor belt and everything. Put your stuff in one end, and you get everything all nice and toasty brown out the other end."

"I know how the new stuff works, Matt. I just can't afford it."

He dropped his eyes, and the silence almost became uncomfortable. "I'll do my best, kid," he murmured. "My father took care of these babies for your father and I'll—" Matt shrugged, but his face was not hopeful. "I'll do my best."

"I can't ask for anything more," Kelly said.

She walked out to the front of the store, leaving Matt to his work. Her mother looked up but said nothing. The answer to her question was obviously written across Kelly's despondent features.

"Everything gets old, Kelly," her mother said.

"But why did they have to quit now?" Kelly asked. "Why couldn't they wait for a few years?"

"What is meant to be, is meant to be," her mother replied.

"Mother, we don't have the money for new ovens." How could her mother be so philosophical about it all? "I'm not even sure we have the money for Mike's tuition for this semester."

"Things will work out the way they were meant to."

Kelly didn't believe that there was some grand scheme and that somehow her ovens were part of it, but wasn't going to stand there and argue the point with her mother.

"I'm going next door, Mom. I promised Debbie I'd French braid her hair for school. Matt's going to be a while in there."

"I'll see what stock we have in the freezers that can be sold."

Kelly just nodded and went next door. Maybe the demise of the ovens was the tragedy she'd sensed was hanging over her, waiting to happen. She guessed that as disasters went, it could be worse, though she was having trouble seeing how. Without ovens, she didn't have much of a bakery. Debbie was waiting for her in the kitchen, dressed in her new bicycle shorts and a red shirt. She was bouncing around with excitement, like popcorn about to pop.

"Hi, Deb. Where's your dad?"

"Downstairs. Getting things ready for the breakfast crowd." Debbie ran and got her brush from the bathroom.

Great. Another person inconvenienced because of her ovens. Kelly'd better warn him that he wouldn't be serving any fresh sweet rolls today. Debbie stopped in front of her, eyeing Kelly with a frown.

"You all ready for school?" Kelly asked, and turned Debbie around as she took her brush from her.

The girl nodded, but then peeked over her shoulder at Kelly. "Don't you feel good?" she asked.

Kelly began to brush Debbie's hair. Lord, was her mood so obvious? "My ovens are on the blink again," she admitted. "I've got tons of bread dough in the refrigerator to keep it from rising too fast and about a dozen cakes waiting to be made."

"You could use our oven up here," Debbie offered. "No one ever uses it during the day."

"Thanks, sugar," Kelly said with the wearying realization that she might just have to resort to that. What a day that would be, running from their apartment to Ben's, checking on the things as they baked. She didn't want to contemplate the possibility.

"So, who do you know who's going into third grade around here?" she asked Debbie.

"Paco and Billy from the soccer games and three girls from day camp. I really like Julie, so I hope I'm in her class," Debbie confided.

"I'll bet there's going to be a whole bunch of really nice kids in your class that you don't know yet," Kelly told her.

"I know. That's what Daddy says, too."

"Well, daddies know about these things."

Once Debbie's hair was done, Kelly went downstairs with the girl. Ben was waiting to fix Debbie's breakfast, so the little girl settled at the place he'd set for her at the counter. A few other people were scattered about the room, eating breakfast.

"Howdy, beautiful," Ben said to Kelly. "Can I fix you some breakfast, too?"

Kelly just sank onto a stool next to Debbie. "You might not want to when you hear the news," she said. "My ovens are out again, and I won't have any sweet rolls for you."

He smiled at her, a ray of light that vaporized the clouds over her head. "Hey, that's a shame, but not reason enough for me to hate you." He gave her hand a squeeze in passing. "Flapjacks for both my girls?"

"All right," Debbie cried, then turned to Kelly. "They're really good the way he makes them. You'll feel lots better."

Kelly started on her orange juice while Debbie told Ben how she'd offered their oven to Kelly, and by the time a plate of pancakes were placed in front of her, Kelly was feeling better. There wasn't any magic in the orange juice or the fragrance of the pancakes as they cooked, but in the warmth and joy surrounding her here. Oven problems weren't the end of the world.

"So, want me to look at the ovens again?" Ben asked once she and Debbie were eating.

"I have the serviceman in." Kelly looked at her watch. "In fact, he should be done about now, and I should be back baking."

"I take it he's recommending that you replace them."

Kelly nodded.

"I thought as much," he said. "I noticed a lot of corrosion and even pitting when I looked at them."

"Yeah." Kelly sighed. "Their demise certainly isn't unexpected. After all, my father put them in when he was on

world into complacency before they threw the evils of winter upon them. She shook her head. Where was all this gloom and doom coming from? Was it the subliminal result of realizing her love for Ben? Most likely. She doubted that she'd suddenly become psychic. The only time she'd accurately predicted the future was in second grade, when she'd told her mother she was going to fail a spelling test. And even then it was hardly the result of any mystical powers, just the plain fact that she couldn't tell "there," "their" and "they're" apart, or "to," "two" and "too."

What would go into a business plan? Her knowledge of that kind of thing was general, at best. The bakery was reasonably profitable, but she wasn't sure of the extent of that profitability. They didn't owe money or anything. All they had was their raw-material costs, utilities and small salaries to herself, mother and brother. At the end of the month, they put a little bit away in the bank. That was it.

Instead of returning directly to the bakery, Kelly headed for the sandwich shop. Ben would let her lean on him.

The lunch crowd was gone, and only a few stragglers were left. Kelly waved feebly over at Ben and sat down at the end of the counter. He gave a customer change, then brought a glass of iced tea down for her.

"It didn't go?" Ben asked.

She took a long drink of the tea. It was cool and life-giving, just as his smile. Buck up, she scolded herself. This was a temporary setback, that was all. Ben would advise her, and everything would be fine.

"They had some questions," Kelly said.

"They wanted a business plan."

She nodded. "I generally know what one is," she said. "But I don't know how to put one together. I never took any business courses in school."

He poured himself a glass of tea, also, and came around to sit at her side. "It's not that hard to draw one up. I'll help you."

"Did you take some business courses?" she asked.

He didn't seem to hear her and pulled out his order pad, ripping off the top sheet and turning it over to write on. "I presume you can come up with an annual sales figure for your shop," he said.

Kelly nodded. "I need that to figure how much sales tax I owe the state."

He wrote "annual sales figure" down. "And how about costs?"

"Mom has a ledger where she records how much we pay for material."

"Good." He nodded and jotted some more down. "And utilities? Do you have one utility meter for your store and apartment?"

Kelly shook her head. "No, we have separate ones for each."

"That's good." He took a sip of his tea. "How about waste? Don't those old ovens cause you to spoil some runs?"

"Plenty," Kelly replied with a short laugh.

"Good, that's a saving for those new ovens."

Kelly just shook her head. "You make it all sound so easy."

"It is. Sometimes things are hard only because we're afraid of them."

Another customer finished his lunch and took the bill up to the register in front. Kelly watched as Ben joked with the man, ringing up the total and making change. Ben was right—the plan had seemed hard because she was afraid of all the business terms, certain that she couldn't understand. She'd been afraid of love for the same reasons. But this time it felt different. It wasn't hard and scary—it was wonderful. It was the song in her day, the heat in her oven and the plan in her business. She had a smile ready for Ben when he got back to her side.

"Shouldn't you be picking up Debbie soon?"

He glanced at the clock. "She'll be getting out in a little bit, but I hadn't promised to meet her at school." He gazed around the sandwich shop at the few remaining souls. "Can't exactly throw everybody out, you know."

"You don't have to," she said. "You've got a ready-made shop sitter right here."

"Shop sitter?"

"You know, like a baby-sitter, but instead of watching the baby, I'll watch the shop." She traced over the hairs on the back of his hand. "I think Debbie would really like having you go meet her—to hear how her day went, without the interruptions of greeting customers and preparing orders."

"I'm sure she would." He glanced up at the clock. "Tell you what. If you can get those figures for me, I'll work on your business plan once I get back."

Kelly leaned up and kissed him full on the lips. "Yes, master," she said.

His eyes caught fire, and the kiss was returned, harder, deeper and longer. "Don't go away," he growled.

"Yes, master," she repeated.

"Are you asking for it?"

"Maybe."

Kelly watched him hurry down the street. The glowing embers in her heart had nothing to do with the afternoon sun bathing the street, although the beautiful late-summer day certainly added to the magic. She turned and went over to phone. Her mother should be able to find all those figures Ben needed. They'd start on that plan as soon as he got back. Well, maybe not right away. Debbie would surely have lots to tell about her day, and first things had to come first.

It was well beyond the lunch hour crush, so Kelly wasn't expecting much in the way of business. The two customers still there when Ben left paid for their meals and left themselves as Kelly's mother brought over a stack of file folders and ledgers.

"I think I've got everything you asked for," she told Kelly. "You think the bank'll change its mind?"

"Ben thinks so." Kelly began thumbing through the papers, looking for the figures Ben had listed for her. "He's going to help me put together a business plan, and knowing him, it'll probably knock everybody's socks off."

Mrs. Farrell patted Kelly's shoulder. "He's a good man, Kelly. You really are lucky."

For once Kelly didn't argue. She covered her mother's hand with her own. "I know, Mom. Believe me, I know."

Mrs. Farrell went back to the bakery, and Kelly began putting some numbers together. On some things, such as the raw-material costs and the utilities, they had very accurate data. On others, like the waste due to the old ovens, close to nothing had been recorded. She'd have to make some educated guess. Closing her eyes, Kelly tried to calculate how much business they lost today because of the late start in baking.

The bell on the door tinkled a welcome, and Kelly opened her eyes, expecting to see Ben and Debbie. "Boy, you sure got—"

It wasn't Ben and Debbie. There, at the entrance, stood two men. Strangers. One was tall with gray hair, and the other was shorter, stockier, with very dark hair and bushy eyebrows. Both were dressed in expensive business suits and had razor-cut hairstyles. They certainly weren't neighborhood people.

"Can I help you?" she asked the men, who were still standing inside the door looking around. Most people just took a seat when they came in.

"You work here?" the bushy-eyebrowed one asked.

What kind of a question was that?

"Ma'am," the taller one said. "Do you work here?"

A distant alarm clock sounded in her mind. Their accent—that was what set them apart. It had a definite East Coast cadence to it, probably Maine or Massachusetts. The same as Ben's. The hackles on her South Side Irish back rose.

"Why do you want to know?" she asked.

They both stared at her a moment before the taller one spoke again. "We were just wondering if you know the guy who runs this place?"

She nodded carefully. "Yes, I do."

The short one pulled two photographs from his pocket. "Is this him?"

Kelly didn't touch the photo, but just stared down at it. She had no idea what was going on, but she felt as if someone had punched her in the stomach. Her breath caught, and for a long moment stillness covered the world—buses outside stalled, the whirr of the cola wall clock was silent and even her heart stopped beating. The man in the picture was definitely Ben. Even though he was bearded, she recognized him. She frowned to cover her exploding fears. The other picture was of Debbie with shorter hair and a slightly younger face.

"The man's wanted for kidnapping in Massachusetts," the taller one said.

"Kidnapping?" Her heart would never start again. "Who did he kidnap?"

"The little girl," Mr. Bushy Brows said, pointing to the picture of Debbie.

Kelly stared at the two pictures. To her the family resemblance was more than coincidental, and she had to speak. "He looks like her father," she said.

The tall man shrugged. "The girl was born to a single mother," he said. "I suppose he could be the kid's father, but the mother never acknowledged him."

"Does the mother want the child back?" Kelly thought the quaver in her voice would alert them to her fears, but their eyes didn't change.

"The mother's dead," Bushy Brows replied.

"The grandparents have custody of the kid," the taller one added.

Kelly continued to stare at the two pictures, trying to jump start her brain. So this was it, the reason for all Ben's secrecy. He had told her the truth, not all of it, but what he told her had been the truth. Debbie's mother was dead, and his life was centered on making a new life for his daughter. Had he known someone was after him? Kelly thought back to the haunted look that she'd seen in his eyes in those unguarded moments. Yes, he must have known, must have feared they were on his trail. And this was probably not the first time the detectives had come close.

Obviously Ben was not willing to let Debbie's grandparents have her. Debbie's little slips came back to Kelly, about the unbending strictness of her grandparents, about her mother acting like she hated Ben. The walls of justice keeping Ben from Debbie must have been so tremendously insurmountable that he'd been compelled to take his child and run. And that's what he'd have to do again. The pain that tore at her and threatened to rip her apart was unimportant, something private to be endured later. Once Ben and Debbie were safe, and Kelly was alone again.

"Ma'am."

She looked back up to find the men were staring at her.

"Have you ever seen the man in the picture?"

What was she to do? Kelly took a deep breath. First of all, she had to get them out of here. That shouldn't be a hard task for someone who once convinced Sean O'Malley that she'd seen the little people carrying a pot of gold up Halstead Street. Of course, the prize that day had been the kitten they'd found in the alley. Today a bit more was at stake. Still, she could do it. Business plans had never been her area of expertise, but acting in the face of a crisis had been.

"Are you police of some sort?" Kelly asked, the essence of courtesy with just a touch of fear. "May I see some identification, please?"

Bushy Brows grimaced slightly, but both pulled ID from their pockets. They were private investigators, not police. A big difference.

"Have you ever seen the man in the picture or the child?" Both of them were frowning at her now.

"We understand that the man is running a sandwich shop in this area. And that he and his child also live nearby."

They certainly hadn't got that information from anyone in the neighborhood. Canaryville took care of its own, and the townspeople had taken Ben and Debbie as one of their own.

"I'm not really sure," Kelly said, shaking her head. Her frown was sincere, but puzzled.

"Not really sure of what, ma'am? That you've seen him?"

Kelly nodded her head. "I'm a baker," she said. "I see a lot of people over time."

"But you might have seen him?"

Kelly was silent, then tapped the picture with her finger as if lightning had just struck. "You know, there's a guy that runs a place over in the Bridgeport neighborhood," she said. "Sometimes he buys sandwich rolls from me."

"This guy?" Bushy Brows asked, pointing at the picture of Ben.

Kelly just shook her head slowly. "I'm not absolutely sure, but it could be."

"Where's his place?" the taller one asked.

"A couple miles north on Halstead," Kelly replied. Near where the little people buried that gold. "I'm not sure what the name of the place is. Has a red-and-white sign with black letters in front." As did about ninety-nine percent of the businesses in the area.

The men looked at each other, and Bushy Brows returned the pictures to his pocket. "Thanks for your help, ma'am," he said, handing Kelly a business card. "If you see him, give us a call. We'll make it worth your while."

Her eyes lit up with interest. "Yes, sir. I certainly will."

Kelly followed the two men to the door and kept the smile on her face until they drove away, then she raced back to the table and threw her papers into a big envelope. The clock was ticking away, the minute hand inching past the hour. Please God, make those two go north on Halstead as she had directed them, not south in the direction of Debbie's school.

She had to warn Ben about the detectives. No one in the neighborhood would deliberately turn them in even though persistence and money could chip away at the most loyal and upright citizens. It was only a matter of time before someone inadvertently gave Ben away. A truck driver, a cabdriver who frequented Ben's sandwich shop, someone who wouldn't realize what havoc he was causing. Sooner or later someone would recognize the pictures. Sending the detectives off toward Bridgeport would only delay them, not throw them completely off the track.

## Chapter Thirteen

The children came spilling out of the school like puppies out of a pen, pushing, shoving and tumbling over one another, ebbing and flowing around islands of teachers. Ben smiled a bit, refusing to let his resident depression settle in on him again.

He'd had fun growing up. High school hadn't been any piece of cake, but his early years had been a happy, carefree time. That's what childhood should be and what he wanted for Debbie. There'd been an awful lot of pain in her past, and that was why he was so glad that there was so much happiness for her in the present. He knew the future held nothing but uncertainty, but for now they had paradise. And that was due entirely to a redheaded beauty named Kelly. He had never considered himself particularly lucky, but somewhere in the heavens there must have been a god who liked him. Or else the little people were the ones to thank.

"Hey, big Daddy," Debbie called out.

She was standing at the top of the steps, waving her arms wildly at him. Two girls stood next to her, jumping up and down and giggling. Her joy gladdened his heart beyond belief. The worries about being found still lingered in the corners of his thoughts, but the very back corners. No use borrowing trouble to darken a sunny day.

He returned her wave, and she came bounding down the steps toward him. At the same time, she was waving and shouting goodbye to her friends, pushing a boy who had said something to her, clutching her books and brushing back some strands of hair that had escaped Kelly's French braiding efforts.

"Hi, Daddy." She ran into his arms and gave him a big hug.

"How was school?"

"It was great," Debbie enthused. "I got two teachers. Mrs. Matson is like my regular teacher and she has me in the morning and she's real nice. Then Mrs. Wille is my reading and math teacher. She has me in the afternoon and she's almost regular, too, because I have her every day in the afternoon."

Debbie paused, her face glowing with excitement, to draw in a lungful of air. "And I'm in the middle reading group, but both Mrs. Matson and Mrs. Wille say that I should probably be in the higher reading group, and they're going to move me when they know me better."

Ben just nodded, hoping they would get into periods and commas soon. He didn't think he had the stamina to handle this fire-hose stream of information for long.

"Julie and Sammi are in the higher group," Debbie went on. "And they're my very best friends in the whole world. So I hope that I get put there soon. They said they'd wait for me and not get too far ahead. Sammi is a girl. You know that because she spells her name with an *i*."

"Sounds like you had a slow day," Ben said.

"It's only the first day of school, Dad. Like, what do you expect, huh?"

Ben just looked at her glowing face and sparkling eyes. In his day, sophisticated humor for an eight-year-old was the screwball antics of a clown with a rubber ball and bat. "You look sharp in your new duds."

"Yeah. And everybody liked them. Sammi said my shorts were really radical."

"Radical. You mean different?"

"No, Daddy. You know, radical like rad."

Ben stared and he could see clouds of concern gathering in Debbie's eyes. Was eight too young to find out your father was like really dumb? He took her hand and started down the sidewalk.

"Oh, look," Debbie said, pointing ahead of them down the street. "There's Kelly."

Kelly? She was looking after the sandwich shop. He followed Debbie's pointing finger, and there Kelly was, driving toward them in her little coupé. Ben's stomach sank. Something had to be wrong. Oh, God.

He took a deep breath. Maybe it wasn't what he thought. Maybe Kelly decided they should take Debbie out for ice cream even though he had a freezer full of ice cream. He stooped down so he was on the same level as his daughter.

"Debbie, did you get a school calendar?" he asked.

"I don't think so," she said, her frown telling him she was thinking hard.

"Why don't you go in and ask your teacher for one?" He turned her around and gave her a slight push. "I'm sure you should have one."

"I can get it tomorrow."

"But you might forget," he said. "I don't want to be too long without one."

Rolling her eyes, Debbie marched off back into school. Ben walked over to the curb, his stomach twisting and tearing into a knot that he was sure would never unwind. Kelly pulled up next to him.

"What's up?" he asked.

Her eyes told him everything he didn't want to know. Those beautiful green eyes were filled with anguish and pain. "Two men came to the sandwich shop, Ben. They were private detectives from Massachusetts."

What little strength he had left in him rapidly drained away. He turned from Kelly's green pools of concern and looked down the street. Damn. He and Debbie were going to have to hit the road again. The poor kid was just sinking roots, and he was going to have to tear her away from it all again and again and again, forever.

"Debbie's grandparents are charging that you kidnapped her," Kelly said.

Slowly Ben forced his attention back to Kelly. Debbie wasn't the only one that had been putting down roots. "Yeah, I know," he murmured. "My mother told me."

"I sent them off into Bridgeport," Kelly said. "But I'm sure they'll be back."

"There's no doubt about it." Ben felt so tired. "They will be."

"They offered me money if I turned you in," Kelly said.

"Sheila's parents have a lot of that," Ben said.

"That's not at the top of my list."

Her green eyes shone bright with so many promises. Promises that he couldn't ask for, promises that he couldn't even think about now.

"They'd probably buy you all the new ovens you needed and then some," he said roughly.

All Kelly did was take his hand. "Ben," she said softly.

Luckily Debbie came bouncing down the sidewalk at that moment. "I asked Mrs. Matson," she called out. "And she said we'd get the school calendar tomorrow."

Ben stood there. His eyes locked on his daughter, his hand trapped by Kelly's and his heart securely nestled between the two of them.

"We're going to have to go, Debbie."

His baby's bouncy good cheer vanished in a split second. All at once the joys of being a little kid, bursting with joy and energy, were rapidly replaced with the old strain of being a child-fugitive. These months on the run were aging her way beyond her years. He didn't have to say anything; she read the bad news in his eyes and just nodded her head. No tears came, but her chin wasn't any too steady as they climbed into Kelly's car.

Kelly drove them to a small motel near Midway airport. "Mike's got a buddy who works part-time here," she said. "Wait here in the car, and I'll see if he's on duty."

She left the keys in the car in case Ben and Debbie had to take off, then hurried into the motel's front office. Lennie was at the desk.

"Hey, Kelly. How you be?"

"Lennie," Kelly said, "I need a room, please."

"What's the matter?" the young man said with a laugh. "You can't stand Mike and your mother anymore?"

"Yeah, but no questions. A lot's riding on this."

Lennie sobered and ran his finger down a row of keys hanging on the wall behind him. "You want one toward the back?"

"That would be great."

He pushed the registration card toward her, and Kelly registered a Mr. and Mrs. Jones, paying cash for one night. Lennie made some notations and handed her a receipt and a key.

"You need anything, I'm on duty until midnight," he told her.

"Thanks." She sped back out to her car and drove it around to the back. The paint was peeling on the back wall, and a laundry cart was down at the far end. "I registered us as Mr. and Mrs. Jones and didn't mention Debbie."

"Wasn't the clerk suspicious?" Ben asked.

"He's from Canaryville and he's my brother's friend. We can trust him."

Ben looked out the window. "Are you so sure he wouldn't like a couple of thousand extra in his pocket?"

"Loyalty is more important than money in Canaryville," Kelly said as she parked in front of their room. "We take care of each other there. We all grew up as one big family. Sure, we squabble among ourselves, but let an outsider come in, and we close ranks."

"I'm an outsider," Ben pointed out.

Kelly leaned over and kissed him, a solid, loving kiss. "Not since I snagged you, buddy. Then you became one of us."

They got out of the car and walked in silence to the room, Kelly holding Debbie's hand. The poor kid, Kelly thought. So much life had drained from her face that she looked like a little old lady.

The room was drab and chilly, with functional furnishings and an air conditioner that ran only on high. Kelly went around turning on lights, hoping to make the room feel warmer and more cheerful. She chose not to judge whether or not it was working.

"Would you like a snack or anything?" she asked. "I can run down the street and pick up something."

"We can go out if we want anything," Ben said. "We're not criminals, you know."

She swallowed the lump in her throat and nodded. "I know you're not criminals, but those private detectives will be back real quick once they find out I've given them a bum steer." She pushed her hair away from her face, trying to force her mind back to the details she had worked through on her drive to the school. "I thought I would pack up your stuff and bring it to you here. No sense in risking a trip back to the apartment."

Debbie just sat in a chair looking wide-eyed at the two of them while Ben nodded. Kelly had a million questions she wanted to ask and a million things she wanted to say to him, but now seemed neither the time nor the place.

"I don't know what to do about any money you might have in the bank," Kelly said. "Maybe you could fill out a withdrawal slip for me and I'll—"

"I don't have anything in the bank," Ben replied. "All my extra money is in traveler's checks. They're in a pouch in my upper left bureau drawer."

She'd forgotten he must have done this before. He would know what to do. "Do you have enough?" Kelly said.

"It doesn't take that much to relocate. I've gotten proficient at unearthing jobs that come with an apartment." His eyes were bleak though—dim pools of lifeless blue. He walked to the window and parted the drapes slightly to gaze out at the parking lot. "There are some suitcases in the hall closet. If you'd fill them with the essentials. The rest of the stuff will have to be left behind. He who travels light, travels fastest."

She cleared her throat as if to fight back the raw pain that had been in his voice. She had no time for her own hurt. "Anything special I should pack?"

"Just some clothes and toiletries." Ben left the window and sank into the easy chair by the window. "And there's a packet of letters and papers in the nightstand drawer."

Kelly nodded as if it wasn't killing her to see their lives reduced to this. She willed her tears away and smiled at Debbie. "How about you, honey? Anything special I should pack up?"

Debbie raised her eyes, still wide and appearing dazed. "Could I have the koala bear Daddy won at the carnival? I know I said you could have it, but—" Her voice was so quiet, almost a whisper.

Kelly grabbed the child into her embrace and held her tightly for a moment. "You got it, kid," Kelly said. Don't break down, Kelly ordered herself. She had to be strong and get them through this. No thinking about tomorrow or the day after. She picked up her purse and started for the door.

"Hey." Ben's voice stopped her. "What was that pile of papers in your back seat, the cost figures from the bakery? Why don't you let me look at them while you're gone? I don't have anything to do except watch television."

Kelly wanted to tell him that her business plan hardly mattered now. Then it occurred to her that maybe he needed to be busy. Sitting here in this dismal motel room, waiting for the sky to fall wouldn't be any picnic. She hurried out and brought back the pile of papers, but she didn't trust herself to speak, so just dropped the papers on the bed. Without a word, she was back outside.

Tears slowly straggled down her cheek as she drove north on Cicero Avenue, and she was glad of every red light she hit, giving her the chance to blow her nose. Was running really the only answer? What kind of a life was this for Ben or Debbie? Yet she trusted Ben. Would he subject Debbie to a life of endless running if a compromise could be worked out with the grandparents? Ben wasn't the type to sacrifice a child for his own ego.

The detectives had said that Debbie's mother had never acknowledged Ben as the father, so maybe he didn't have a legal leg to stand on. As the mother's blood relatives, maybe the grandparents would take Debbie so that Ben would never see her again, not until she was an adult. By then she might not even remember him.

Kelly parked the car in the alley behind the stores and walked around the block so that she could check out the area in front. She stood in the entryway of the hardware store, looking up and down the street. There didn't appear to be any well-dressed strangers on the sidewalk, nor did she see the rental car they had been driving.

The scene blurred even as she watched, a weariness settling on her shoulders. Ben was leaving. In a few hours he and Debbie would be gone. Out of her life forever. All the happiness that had been hers the past two months would be gone, leaving only emptiness in its place.

She stared at the bakery. Farrell and Sons Bakery, the sign above their store proclaimed. Her grandfather had put that up, but where were the sons now? Mike was going to be an engineer, had always wanted to be one. That sign had once been the harbinger to the future, but now stood as a monument to the past.

Why was she bothering to hang on to the old place? She'd been telling herself that it was all for her mother and brother, but the money that the video chain was offering was more than enough for all of them. Mike's education would be paid for, and her mother wouldn't have to worry about anything for the rest of her life. But Kelly had no dreams invested in her own share of the money, and maybe that was why she'd always refused to sell.

Her own share. Kelly felt a certainty growing in her. Her share wouldn't be enormous in terms of starting a new business or buying a condo on Lake Shore Drive, but maybe it could make a difference. What if Ben were running with Debbie because he didn't have the money to stay and fight? Maybe the money from the sale of the bakery would give him the chance to stop running.

She ran across the street, down the alley and climbed the stairs to Ben's apartment. She found the suitcases where Ben had said they would be and began to pack as much as she could into them. She put the koala bear in for Debbie, and the two dolls that were on the girl's bed, promising herself that somehow she would send the rest of their belongings on to them once they were settled in their new place. Maybe she could even bring them herself. There were no more tears as Kelly drove back to the motel. She had a purpose now.

Ben opened the door and let Kelly in, even though he was on the phone, making a reservation for the final leg of a trip to California. Debbie was curled up on the far bed, asleep.

After hanging up, Ben said nothing, just looked at Kelly for the longest time, then he took her in his arms. For an endless moment that was all too short, he just held her. She could feel his weariness and his pain, for they matched her own. But she could also feel his strength that lay beneath the surface. A strength that would enable him to carry on, to protect Debbie as best he could. When he let go of her, she sat down on the edge of the bed, keeping a hold of his hand as she settled next to him.

"I'm going to sell the bakery," Kelly told him. "I'm tired of fighting those old ovens. And Mom's arthritis really acts up in the cold weather. She should be in Florida with her friends. Mike's so smart he should get his doctorate. He's always wanted to be a college professor. That old sign on the front says Farrell and Sons Bakery. That's been a lie for years. Mike's never wanted the bakery."

Ben shook his head as if to clear it. "You don't really want to sell. You love the place."

"Not as much as I love you."

Ben stared at her with a pained expression. "Don't," he said, putting his hand gently on her arm. "There's too much hurt in this thing as it is."

"But there doesn't have to be," she said. "Let me help you. If I sell the bakery, I'll get my share of the money. Maybe it'll be enough to take Debbie's grandparents to court and win."

Ben sighed and stared down at their hands, still intertwined. "I can't take your money," he told her. "And don't decide that I'm just being noble. If money was the issue, my family would have mortgaged their lives to the hilt to give it to me. This whole mess is a result of Sheila's last will and testament, clearly giving custody of Debbie to her parents.

I have no rights. Sheila and I were never married. I'm not even named on Debbie's birth certificate.''

"Why not?"

He shrugged. "Why not? How can I explain Sheila to you in ten words or less?"

"Debbie says her mother hated you."

Ben's grimace was of pain mixed with humor. "She both hated me and couldn't live without me. It was a trap that there was no escape from, at least not for me. Leaving would have meant abandoning Debbie—staying meant having to deal with Sheila's phobias and insecurities."

Kelly couldn't imagine such a life. There was no way to deal with the hurt and anguish, except to go past it, to focus on the problems that they could solve. "But anyone can see you're Debbie's father. She looks just like you."

"She looks even more like my sister when Cathy was a kid," Ben said, glancing over his shoulder at Debbie. Her thumb was in her mouth. "Things have been rough on her."

"It isn't doing you any good, either," Kelly pointed out.

"Ah, I'm an adult," he replied with a wave of his hand. "She's just a little kid." He shook his head as he stared over at Debbie. The love on his face was so strong, so deep that it hurt Kelly just looking at him.

"You should have seen her when I picked her up from school." His voice was soft but raw. A wound that wouldn't stop bleeding. "She was on top of her world. She'd made some new friends and had some teachers that she felt really liked her."

He turned away and got to his feet. "And now what is she going to have?" He shook his head again, as if making his voice strong once more. "Damn if I know. That's the whole thing. She has no certainty in her life."

"She's got you."

"She needs a family, friends. She needs stability in her life."

"Let me come along."

That stopped him. He turned and just stared at her. His eyes were deep and stormy, but Kelly couldn't read their message. Or maybe she was afraid to read it.

"Let me come with you," she repeated. "I told you I love you. Well, that includes Debbie. I know your life isn't any bed of roses, but let me share it."

"Maybe a bed of roses is a good description of it," he said, and turned to look again through the drapes at the parking lot. "There are a lot of thorns everywhere you move." He was stiff and unbending, as if his role had been written ages ago and he couldn't budge from it.

Kelly got to her feet. She had to make him see. "But there'd also be good times, sweet moments when the running is forgotten."

Ben just shook his head, not even looking at her. "You have no idea what my life is like. I can't just call up my family any time I choose. I can't go back and visit on Thanksgiving. Hell, I can't even send them a Christmas card for fear the postmark might get traced. I won't do that to you."

She went to his side, touching his arm and, through the sheer power of her love, forcing him to look at her. "Maybe I have the right to choose it for myself."

"No," he said. His eyes were stormy no longer, but icy and cold. "He who travels light, travels fastest," he repeated. "Your place is here with your family, running the bakery and playing matchmaker for your friends." There was no compromise, no mercy in his gaze.

"My family can get along quite well without me." Didn't he see how much she loved him? That her life would be nothing unless it was spent at his side?

"And so can Debbie and I."

His words hung in the air, echoing in her heart until she wanted to cover her ears to keep from hearing their mockery. One thing was more than obvious. Whatever her feelings were for him, Ben did not love her. He'd said often enough that he wanted no strings, but she'd forgotten all that lately, believing her love was so strong that he'd have to share it sooner or later.

"I'm sorry," he said suddenly, and ran his fingers through his hair. "That's not really true. You've been wonderful and we'll miss you. It's just—"

She put her hand on his arm. She didn't want to hear the brutal truth. She couldn't bear for him to actually tell her that he didn't love her. "No, I understand," she said. "It'll be safer for you and Debbie not to have me tagging along. The more people along, the more chances there are of someone making that one mistake that gets you caught."

He nodded, but his face was turned away. It didn't matter. She didn't want to see that cold, forbidding emptiness in his eyes.

"I need your help to get away, though," he said. "We need to impose just a bit longer."

"No problem," she said as if her heart wasn't shattering even as she spoke. "I told you, you were accepted in Canaryville. We take care of our own."

Ben took a deep breath and went over to the dresser. "I've made reservations for Debbie on this flight to Kansas City from O'Hare." He handed her the itinerary detailing the flight information. "If you could take her to the airport and get her on the plane, it would be a lifesaver. Her tickets are under the name Jenny Nolan."

"Sounds easy." Kelly shrugged, but then anything sounded easy compared to leaving her man behind. Just how did one cope with the separation from a loved one?

"Actually I'll be boarding the same flight under a different name, but I don't want anyone to connect us. She knows to ignore me until we're off the plane in Kansas City. From there we'll go to California. It should be safe for us to be seen together once we're out of here."

"Okay." What else was there to say? "We probably should be going. Traffic out that direction can be hectic this time of day, and we don't want to miss our flight."

There would be no words of goodbye, but she didn't move. She just stood there watching him, trying to tell him with her eyes just how much he'd come to mean to her. If only he understood that this wasn't some schoolgirl crush, but the real thing. Something that would last forever. But he just went around her and woke up Debbie.

"Come on, sugar. Kelly's going to take you to the airport like we talked about."

"All right," Debbie said.

She rubbed her eyes, letting her father pick her up and carry her out to Kelly's car. Ben put her in the back seat, where she could lie back down. Staring out the window Kelly searched for a way to tell him he had come to mean her whole life. But maybe there was no way.

Ben walked over to where Kelly stood at the driver's side of the car. Saying nothing at first, he just took her in his arms and held her tightly. For a wonderful magic moment, she thought he had changed his mind. How could he hold her like this if he didn't love her?

"I can't tell you how grateful we are to you," he said as he let her go.

Gratitude wasn't what she wanted. That was what she got from Mrs. O'Brien for saving the biggest apricot danishes for her. "It's no big deal," Kelly said. "Debbie loves you and you love her. You two belong together."

He pushed back an errant curl that had fallen onto her forehead. "Not everybody would go to the extent you have to help us, though."

She shook her head, shook that curl back onto her forehead. She wished he wouldn't touch her. This was agony enough without those little touches that she thought spoke of love. "Maybe more people would than you think."

He opened her car door. Even the densest person would catch on that it was time to go. She gave him her best smile and got in the car. "If for some reason we miss that plane, I'll put her on the next flight to Kansas City, even if it means staying at a motel near the airport until tomorrow morning."

He nodded, then closed her door for her. Stay cool, stay in control, her mind ordered. She took a deep breath and was about to start the engine when he leaned in through the open window and kissed her.

This was the last time she'd feel his lips on hers, the last time her heart would sing to his. Tears burned at her eyes, but she just clung to his lips and prayed that the moment would never end. He pulled away slightly, but stooped down so that he looked straight into the window.

"You know, I never understood that crazy nursery rhyme about the four-and-twenty blackbirds baked in a pie," he said. "But somehow since that night we worked the crossword puzzle, I always connected it with you."

Where was this all going? she wondered. Why didn't he let her leave so that her heart could shatter in peace?

"But now I've got it figured out."

"That's good."

"Sometimes you get something attractive, meet someone attractive, and expect the filling or the inner person to be attractive, too. But when you get to know the person, and they're more special, more generous than you ever expected—it just sort of blows your mind." He looked away for a moment, staring at the gate to the swimming pool swinging in the breeze.

"That probably came out incoherently," he went on. "I can't seem to get the words right. But what I meant was that I knew from the start you were nice, but I never dreamed how good you'd be to us and how much we'd owe you. You've given us both a really special time that we'll always remember."

He reached into the car, pushing that stupid curl back again, and Kelly could have sworn his eyes were swimming with tears. Or maybe it was just that hers were and she couldn't see clearly.

"I hope someday you meet someone who can give you even half as much as you've given us," he said softly. "You deserve nothing less than the best."

And that was what she wanted, for she knew the best was him. "Ben—"

But he put his fingers over her lips and got to his feet. "Have a good life, Kelly Farrell," he said. "I hope that someday you find blackbirds in your pie."

Then he turned and went back into the motel room. Kelly started the car and drove slowly, leaving her heart behind.

## Chapter Fourteen

Kelly was wiping down the worktables the next morning when she heard the front doorbell give its soft welcome. Mike was out front and could help any customer who dropped in. Work seemed the only way to keep from going crazy, to keep the paralyzing pain at bay.

"Hi, there."

Freezing in mid-motion, Kelly caught her breath as the voice floated in from the front. Those private detectives were back.

"Hey, guys. What'll you have?" Mike's South Side tough guy accent was out in full bloom. His antennae must have warned him that these men were not friends.

"You got a young gal working here, fella? About five foot three or so. Reddish hair, green eyes. Nice looking."

"We sell cakes, doughnuts, pies, that kind of stuff, fella." Mike put a sneer on the last word. "We don't sell what you seem to be looking for. If you want any baked goods, then go ahead and buy. Otherwise, beat it."

"You're sounding like a hard case, kid."

"You're welcome to see if I'm for real." There was a dangerous undertone in her brother's voice.

Kelly threw down her cleaning rag and hurried out. Starting a fight wasn't going to help anything. "What is it you gentlemen want?" she asked.

"Don't worry about it, sis," Mike replied. "Just a couple of bums playing at tough."

Both men cast baleful glances at Mike, but the taller returned his attention to Kelly. "Good morning, ma'am," he said.

Kelly nodded, watching out of the corner of her eye as Mike slipped out the front door.

"The sandwich shop next door appears to be closed," the tall man said.

"I know," Kelly said with a shrug. "The owner hasn't been in to pick up his order yet."

"Looks empty in the apartment above the shop."

"I guess he's not around, then," Kelly said.

"I don't suppose you know where he and the kid went, do you?" The smirk on the man's face indicated that he didn't expect a truthful answer.

Kelly fulfilled his expectations and just shook her head.

"Do you expect him back?"

Kelly shrugged. "Unless he gets here by noon, I'm stuck with a bunch of pastries. Would you like some? I'll give you a discount. By tonight no one will want them."

Bushy Brows moved toward her—the counter was still between them. "Look, lady," he growled. "We ain't much for waltzing. So why don't we just—"

The front door tinkled as eight young men marched in with Mike.

"Donnie," the tall man murmured to his partner under his breath.

Bushy Brows stepped back, his hand going under his coat.

"Let me repeat my offer, gentlemen," Mike said as his friends spread out, surrounding the detectives. "You want some sweet rolls, then buy. If not, beat it. Now."

Kelly could feel her temper near to boiling over, but fear was also churning along with it. Bushy Brows wasn't scratching his belly—he was probably armed, and anyone getting hurt was the last thing she wanted. Kelly was just reaching for the phone when flashing blue lights outside stopped her. The blue-and-white squad car drove right up on the sidewalk and a black patrolwoman and a redhaired patrolman burst into the store. The men at the door parted to let them through.

"What's the problem?" the policewoman asked.

"No problem," the tall detective said, putting an ingratiating smile on his face. "We were just chatting with the lady, and the young man misunderstood things."

"They were trying some James Cagney imitations on us," Mike said.

"Do you want to file charges?" the policeman asked Kelly.

She was hesitating as another patrol car stopped in the street. A slender, gray-haired policeman got out, his blue sergeant's stripes visible on his white shirt.

"It's Morgan," someone in Mike's group said.

Sergeant Morgan nodded as he came in, and everyone quieted down. "What's the problem?" he asked, directing the question to anyone but looking at his two beat officers.

"Mike says they were threatening," the policewoman said, nodding toward the two detectives. "They say they were just talking."

"He's packing a piece, Sarge," Mike said, pointing at Bushy Brows.

"Look, Sarge," the taller detective said. "We apologize for any misunderstanding."

"Search 'em," Morgan snapped.

The policeman searched both and pulled an automatic pistol from Bushy Brows's belt. A wave of dizziness threatened to drown Kelly, and she clenched her hands at her side to fight it back. Suspecting Bushy Brows had a gun and actually seeing it were two different things. Just what had he planned to do with it when, and if, he found Ben and Debbie? Take Debbie by force?

"Sir," the tall detective said. "We're private investigators. My ID is in my inside coat pocket. And my friend here has a permit to carry that piece."

"In Illinois?" Morgan asked. "Have you registered with the proper authorities, stating the purpose of your visit?"

"Ah, Sergeant," the tall detective said quietly. "Can't we discuss this?"

Sergeant Morgan smiled. "Sure. At the station." He nodded to the beat cops. "Book them for conducting investigative activities in the State of Illinois without proper authorization and that one for carrying a concealed weapon without the proper permit from the authorities in our fair state."

Within minutes the store was clear, and Kelly was left alone with Mike. Her knees suddenly seemed ready to give out, and she leaned against the back counter. By now Ben and Debbie were in California, she told herself. They were far away from here and those detectives, and safe. For the time being.

Mike watched until the police cars disappeared down the street, then turned to Kelly. "I don't think those guys will be back again," he said.

"No." Kelly's voice was about as strong as her knees, which meant they had all the power of whipped cream.

Mike came over and put an arm around her shoulder. "Don't worry, sis. They'll be okay. Ben's a pretty sharp guy."

She nodded again, not trusting her voice. But the fear found another avenue of escape, and tears pooled in her eyes. Sure, those detectives wouldn't be back, but that was only because they knew that Ben wasn't here. They, and others like them, would just fan out and broaden their search.

She blinked her eyes, hoping to stem the flow, but it was like holding back the tide. Tears poured down her face, and she hurried into the back room. Ben loved Debbie, and for that he was being chased and hounded like some animal in the wild. And all she could do was watch helplessly.

The front door announced visitors, and Kelly felt her heart jump. A week had passed since those detectives had been sent away, but she couldn't help her reaction. So much fear was resting in her heart for Ben and Debbie that it carried over into every aspect of her day-to-day life.

This set of visitors were hardly threatening, but neither were they customers from the neighborhood. They were an elderly couple, dressed like Kelly'd never seen before except on the nighttime soap operas on television. The man's clothes were cut to fit him, and the woman was loaded with furs and jewels.

"Is there a Kelly Farrell here?" the man asked.

"Who's asking?" Kelly's mother asked in turn.

The man turned his lips upward, but that generated no warmth for his face or his eyes. "I'm sure she wouldn't know us," he said. "We're Mr. and Mrs. Webster."

Kelly stepped forward, uncertainty engulfing her. They didn't look like detectives. Could they somehow have a message for her from Ben?

"I'm Kelly Farrell," she said. "How may I help you?"

"We'd like to talk to you about Ben Patterson," the man answered.

"I believe he used the name Peterson while he was here," the woman corrected.

Kelly looked from one to the other, her flicker of hope dampened by some inner sense that she couldn't put her finger on. They'd brought a chill into the Indian-summer air. Then she knew—they were Debbie's grandparents.

"We were told that he ran the sandwich shop next door," the man said.

A chair scraped the floor—her mother planned to stay. Kelly appreciated the show of support. "You were told," Kelly repeated. "Told by whom? Those two private bozos you hired?"

The man grimaced. Or maybe it was a smile. It didn't seem to matter what he tried—it all looked the same. "I'm sorry about that," he said. "I understand they weren't very diplomatic."

"I don't know about that," Kelly said with a shrug that covered the pain that her numbed heart was beginning to feel. "I do know they were stupid and they were lucky to get out of here in one piece. We don't take to being pushed around down here." Kelly stared at them until both looked away.

The man recovered first. "This Ben Patterson has our granddaughter," he said. "He's kidnapped her."

"She's his daughter," Kelly said.

"That remains to be proven," the man said.

"No one knows who the father is," the woman said, pausing, and her face grew harder. "Our daughter knew many men."

"Maybe if you'd sit down together, things could be worked out," Kelly said. "You could share custody, and everyone, especially the little girl, would benefit."

"He kidnapped our granddaughter," the man repeated, lines of stubbornness streaking his face.

"He took our Sheila from us," the woman said, her voice rising. "And he kept her from us. Now he wants to do the same with our Deborah." Tears glistened in the old woman's eyes, poised to spill over her eyelids and ruin the precise picture-perfect makeup.

Kelly wasn't moved. "But you're also trying to keep his daughter from him," she pointed out.

The woman's eyes grew hard. "Charles," the woman said. "Let's quit this foolishness. There are better things to do in this city than argue with a baker."

He cleared his throat and drew himself up. "Young lady, we are prepared to make it worth your while if you tell us where Mr. Patterson has gone with the child."

Kelly felt sick. The bastards. Not one mention of love or worry. Not one question about how Debbie was, if she was happy or seemed to miss them or if she was well.

"Ten thousand dollars."

Kelly shook her head.

"Fifteen thousand, then," the woman interjected.

"I'm not for sale, ma'am," Kelly said quietly.

The woman looked around the bakery, disdain riding her lips like a lady on a high horse. "I imagine there are any number of things a person like you could do with fifteen thousand dollars." The woman paused to look directly at Kelly. "Cash. Tax-free cash. We're not about to tell anybody who we gave the money to."

"I wouldn't sell one of my doughnuts to someone like you." Kelly spit the words out.

"You drive a hard bargain, young lady," the man said, a smirk growing on his pale face. "All right, I'll go to—"

It was just too much. "Get out," Kelly said in a low tone, a real sign of approaching rage anyone in the neighborhood could have attested to. "Before I dump you out on the street right on your silverplated cans."

The man's mouth opened but quickly shut when Kelly stepped around the counter. "Out," she said, pointing to the door. "While you can still walk."

They left, climbing stiffly into a limousine while a small crowd stopped on the sidewalk to watch. Silence reigned in the bakery until the car had pulled away and a bus filled the street with noise and normality.

"They must know an undertaker," Mrs. Farrell said as they turned away from the window.

Kelly just hugged her mother for a long silent moment, gathering strength and ordering the mistiness from her eyes. She refused to cry anymore. It seemed that was all she'd been doing for the past week and it hadn't changed a thing. Her heart was still broken, Ben and Debbie were still gone and the ovens were still on the verge of collapse.

"At the rate those two were going," her mother said, with a short laugh, "we would have had enough to pay Mike's tuition, buy new ovens and put a down payment on the Sears Tower."

Kelly chuckled, but even that slight laughter died as she watched her mother package up a loaf of bread. Her short, stubby fingers were worn and calloused from a lifetime of work. What was the point of hanging on all this time?

"I should have sold this damn place long ago," Kelly said with sudden vehemence. "It's old and broken-down and outlived its usefulness long ago."

"Honey, honey." Anna took Kelly's hands and steadied her faltering world. "It's supported three generations of Farrells and given good food to our neighbors for all these years."

Her mother didn't understand. Kelly'd built her life around this place the past few years, but it had taken Ben to teach her that people were more important than places or traditions. She'd held on to the bakery without giving much thought to whether her mother or Mike were reaping any benefits from the business.

"Mom," Kelly said, pulling away. "People can get bread in supermarkets."

"Not as good as ours," her mother said. "And we're getting more and more people coming here. And not just neighborhood people. Gold Coast folks are coming here, too. Mr. Arnold said that we should open up an outlet on the Near North Side."

Kelly closed her eyes and took a deep breath. New ovens. Remote outlets. It all took money. And anything they spent kept her mother further and further from that retirement condo in Florida.

"Honey." Her mother took her hand. "You're upset now. Your heart is aching for Ben and Debbie. So don't do anything. Let's just go along like we have been and wait for things to settle down."

"Those ovens are going to break down any minute, Mom."

"Leave them to God's hands."

"How about Mike's tuition?" Kelly asked. "Is God taking care of that?"

Her mother laughed.

"Maybe he is." She hugged Kelly. "Mike got a letter this morning that he was going to surprise you with at dinner. He got a full scholarship for this upcoming year. Tuition, books and lab fees. Your little brother says he's got it made."

Kelly sighed. A little of the pressure was now gone, but Kelly was still facing some tough decisions. And the emptiness of being without Ben.

"Let things float for a while, honey. Things will work out for the best. Remember what Grandma Farrell always said."

Kelly rolled her eyes heavenward. "Mom, I'm too old for fairy tales."

"It's true, it's true. Some Farrell once rescued one of the little people, and they've taken care of us ever since."

"Right, Mom." And they buried a pot of gold over on Halstead Street. She wished she still believed in the little people. "Do you think they might be keeping an eye on Ben and Debbie?" Kelly frowned slightly. "But then I don't think they're Irish."

Her mother's face turned thoughtful. "That Ben's such a nice boy. He's got to have a little Irish in him."

That old Irish philosophy—if you're a quarter-Irish, you're half-Irish, and if you're half-Irish, you're all Irish. Shaking her head, Kelly put her apron back on.

"I guess I'd better get finished in back. Call me if the little people come with a message from Ben."

"If those icicles are still hanging around here for clues, they mustn't have any leads on him," Mrs. Farrell called after Kelly.

That was true, Kelly thought, her heart lightening a touch. She began getting bread pans ready for tomorrow's baking. Good old Mom. She was always there to wipe a tear and kiss a hurt. Except the deepest hurt of missing Ben wasn't ever likely to go away, no matter what her mother did.

A pile of pans toppled over on the table. The little people at work, Kelly thought. That was the excuse she and Mike used whenever something fell when no one was near. Pans never fell because they'd been piled poorly. She stopped and took a deep breath, closing her eyes.

"Instead of knocking over pans, do you think you could be a wee bit more helpful?" she whispered to the air. "Ben and Debbie really need some looking after, and if they aren't exactly Irish themselves, you've got to admit Debbie is a little person herself."

Never hurts to cover all the bases. Any good White Sox fan knew that.

Saturday morning, the mailman brought a large brown envelope for Kelly. Her heart stopped beating—it had to be from Ben. And it was. It was her business plan, all neat and precise and businesslike. She had forgotten all about it, but Ben hadn't.

Along with the plan were the papers she'd given him and a short letter. Everything in their trip went fine. He and Debbie were well and missed her chocolate doughnuts. Kelly should take the plan to the bank and make Farrell and

Sons the best damn bakery in the city. That was it. No words of love, no words of hope. She wanted to sit down and have a good cry, but another one of those and the city would issue flood warnings.

Instead she did exactly what Ben told her to do—she took the plan to the bank first thing Monday morning. By Friday she had her check, the new ovens were on order and Farrell and Sons was alive once more.

Once the new ovens were installed at the end of September, her output doubled. She had to hire two helpers for the baking and found three neighborhood groceries on the North Side that wanted to sell her products. Four more approached her, but she put them on hold for the time being. By the end of October, business was booming. Their savings account was looking healthier—it just didn't seem to matter anymore, because Ben wasn't here to share in her success.

But then nothing seemed to matter as much as it once used to. When Kelly hired the extra help, she'd been elevated to supervisor, but she still put in long hours and threw herself into the work. It filled up her days and made her bone tired, but nothing seemed to be able to help the nights.

As soon as Kelly's head would hit the pillow, her eyes refused to close. She'd lie there staring at the ceiling, and images would float above her. Gentle blue eyes and arms that were a haven of peace. A little girl with French-braided hair trying to play jacks. Sleep would come in fitful snatches, but too much of the night would be spent sitting up in bed, staring into the darkness.

Mrs. Farrell kept telling Kelly she looked terrible, that she needed more sleep, but actually Kelly was more worried about her mother. Mike was all wrapped up in school, using his newfound free time to be the kid he was. But her mother didn't seem to know what to do with herself.

"You ought to take a vacation, Mom," Kelly said one evening just before Halloween.

Her mother looked up from the shawl she was knitting. "I'm not the one working herself almost to death."

"Mom, I'm just keeping busy," Kelly replied. "And that's exactly what I need right now."

Her mother just grunted.

"Anyway," Kelly said after a pause, "you haven't been on vacation for longer than I can remember."

"Your father and I used to go," her mother said.

"Yeah," Kelly said. "You used to go with Mike and me."

"So, that's the kind of family we were back then. Mother, father and two little kids. You want we should have left you in a kennel?"

"Mother, you're being difficult."

"Don't play big executive with me, young lady," her mother said. "Or it's no more chocolate-filled bismarcks in your lunch box."

"Mom."

"So you want to get rid of me."

Kelly sighed. "Mom, the business is making real money. I want to give you something. Something for all that you've done for me."

"Mike's hardly around anymore," her mother said. "And with me out, you'd be all alone. Wouldn't you be lonely?"

Kelly had to look away and stare out the window for a long time. The way things were right now, she'd be lonely at Soldier's Field at a season opener for the Chicago Bears. There was only one person who could solve that problem, and it wasn't her mother or Mike.

"Why don't you go to Florida, Mom? Take a few weeks and check things out. Visit some friends that you haven't seen for ages."

Her mother shrugged. "I suppose I could visit Sara. She's always writing me to come down."

"Sure, Mom. That would be great. I'll bet you'll have a ball."

This time her mother sighed. "Well, if you don't want me."

"Mom, it's either take a vacation or I murder you."

"Maybe I'll go give Sara a call."

Kelly closed her eyes and leaned against the back of the sofa. She could hear her mother's voice in the distance as she talked to Sara, but Kelly was too tired to tune in to the conversation. Actually, once her mother was gone, Kelly would enjoy the solitude. With all the people in the bakery around her all day and her mother in the room next to her at night, Kelly hadn't had time to herself. And she needed it desperately. She hadn't had a good cry for weeks.

## Chapter Fifteen

Want me to come early tonight?'' Mike asked as he picked a doughnut from the shelf, then paused in midbite. "Am I allowed to do this now that Farrell Bakeries is such a hotshot business?''

"No problem.'' Kelly looked up from the cake she was boxing. "I'll have my accountant bill you. But why would I want you to come home early?''

"With Mom gone, you're all alone here now,'' he said. "I thought maybe you'd like some company.''

Kelly gave her brother a quick hug, touched by his concern, but she had been feeling alone for two months now and was getting used to it.

"I'm fine. Really I am,'' she told him. "This is the first time in ages that I've had a chance to get sloppy and sit around all night eating potato chips and cheese puffs. I'm not giving that up for anybody.''

He just stood there and stared at her, disbelief written all over his face.

"Go on," she said. "Get to class before I throw you out."

"Okay. See you later." He grabbed his bag of books and headed out the door.

Kelly watched out the window as he made his way down the street, stopping for a word or two with people along the way. Was it that obvious how lonely she was?

Ben and Debbie still haunted both her dreams and her waking hours, but it was even worse now that Mom was visiting in Florida. The days were too quiet without her mother's chatter about friends, jokes and the passing scene of life. There were no distractions except work, and even that failed to hold her attention for long.

"I'll be in back, Rosita," Kelly told her newly hired chief clerk and went to the corner in the back room that she'd partitioned off into an office.

Piles of paper dominated her desk. She ought to get a small computer now, what with the increased business. But she really had no desire for the extra time a computer would give her. Things were going great guns, and she only wished she could enjoy it a little. But that seemed an empty wish, and she just plowed into her work, frowning in vague annoyance a little while later when she sensed a presence at the door of her office.

"You really ought to get yourself a computer, Kelly," her mother said. "A growing business, and you're still doing some things like your grandfather did."

"Mom!" Kelly flew over to envelop her mother in a hug. "What are you doing here?"

"Standing here and talking to you."

"You're home early," Kelly said. Her mother looked good. She had a light tan and a new gleam in her eyes.

"What's with the 'early'? Was I being punished?"

"Mom, we talked about you staying a month or more."

"We talked about maybe I might want to stay a month or more." Her mother shrugged. "I got down there and decided I didn't want to. I just didn't like it there. Florida isn't for me."

Kelly cleared off a chair for her mother, then pulled her own desk chair around for herself. "I'm sorry to hear that."

"They don't really have fall down there. And with the hot weather and rain, they got bugs you wouldn't believe. As big as cats. And they got alligators."

"Alligators?" Kelly said. "I thought they were in the Everglades."

"They got them everyplace. In ditches and hiding in the backyards. You got a little dog, you can't let it out by itself. Not unless you like feeding alligators." Her mother made a face and shook her head. "Ugly old beasts."

"So how are Sara, Edna and all the others?" Kelly asked.

Her mother shrugged. "Hanging on."

"Sounds exciting."

"Kelly, they live in one of those retirement villages. Places like that don't give you 'exciting.' They give you a lot of old people and protection. Too much protection. No, give me Canaryville any day of the week."

They sat and shared a long moment of silence. She was sorry her mother hadn't had a better time, but it was sure good to have her back.

"Well," her mother said, standing up, "I better get upstairs and see what we'll have for dinner."

"Mom," Kelly protested, "we can go out. It'll give us more of a chance to talk."

"We already talked." Her mother leaned forward on the desk and lowered her voice. "Besides, tonight's the regular senior citizens meeting over at the park. I gotta find out if that nice Mr. Arnold missed me like he said he would.''

Kelly smiled and shook her head. ''I'm sure he did, Mom.''

''If he didn't, I'll smack him a good one.''

By the time Kelly finished her bookkeeping and closed up the bakery, it was almost six-thirty. They had a quick dinner, then her mother left for the senior citizen center and Kelly was alone once more. She washed the dishes, then put a sweater on and went out on the back porch.

The air was nippy but pleasant. She breathed deeply and leaned on the railing. Things were going so well with the bakery. Better than she could have imagined even in her wildest dreams. Soon there'd be enough money to send Mike to graduate school and buy her mother a condo in Florida. Except that with Mike's scholarships and good grades, he didn't need her help anymore. And her mother vetoed the condo in Florida, opting instead to play pinochle with Mr. Arnold here in Canaryville.

Kelly looked off into the darkness. Ben and Debbie might still need her, but where were they? She couldn't even tell them that she was free of her responsibilities here because she didn't know where they were. She shook her head. She'd wanted to do so much for everybody, but now all she had was the bakery.

''Hello, Mrs. Johnson,'' Kelly greeted her customer as the woman stepped in the door, shaking the water from her umbrella. ''How are you today?''

''As well as can be expected,'' Mrs. Johnson grumbled. ''That rain and wind out there chills a body to the bone. I'm supposed to go to Ila's for dinner tomorrow, but I don't think I will if this rain keeps up. I'd rather just stay home where it's warm.''

"Oh, goodness, Agnes," Mrs. Farrell said. "You'll go. Thanksgiving should be spent with your family, not all alone."

Mrs. Johnson just sniffed. "I suppose." She peered into the glass display case. "Have you got any dinner rolls? I told Ila I'd bring some. Don't have any decent bakeries out there in the suburbs."

"Got some just fresh from the oven," Kelly said. "How many can I get you?"

"A dozen should be fine."

Kelly began to pack up the rolls, still warm from the oven.

"Where's that boyfriend of yours?" Mrs. Johnson asked suddenly.

Kelly stopped packing. "Boyfriend?"

"I'm too old for cute, young lady. You know exactly the one I mean. That good-looking fella used to run the sandwich shop next door."

Kelly swallowed back the pain that still rose to the surface at just the thought of Ben. "I don't know where he is," she said.

"They're going to put a video store in next door," Mrs. Johnson said, shooting accusing eyes from Kelly to her mother. "Store's been a sandwich shop since I was a young woman."

"Things change," her mother said.

"Too damn much change, if you ask me." Mrs. Johnson shook her head. "Got to go to Thirty-Ninth and Halstead when I want a corned-beef sandwich now. And it's full of fat. Not nice and lean like that nice young man of yours used to sell." She turned to face Kelly. "Why did you ever let him leave?"

"I didn't—"

Mrs. Johnson turned back to Mrs. Farrell. "Young people these days. Everything's got to be perfect. Got no compromise in them."

Kelly closed up the box of rolls and rang up the order. There was no sense in arguing with Mrs. Johnson, no sense in trying to explain what was really an inexplicable situation.

"Two-fifty," Kelly told the old woman.

She counted out the change. "Got to learn to compromise if you want to hold on to a man," she said.

"I'll try, Mrs. Johnson. Have a nice Thanksgiving."

"Goodbye, Agnes," her mother called after the woman, but the door was already closing and they heard no reply, doubting if there was one, anyway.

Kelly just took a deep breath and ignored the ever-present ache in her heart. She wondered if she should bake another batch of pumpkin pies. They only had two left.

"I'm sure they're all right, honey," Mrs. Farrell said.

Kelly forced a smile for her mother, knowing her mother was discussing Ben and Debbie, not pumpkin pies.

"Ben will find a way to take care of Debbie," her mother added.

Kelly just nodded. For the first month after Ben's departure, everyone asked where they were and when they were coming back. Now everyone was sympathetic. Customers no longer joked with her about settling down, but confined their conversations to the business and how marvelously she was managing. They joked about her owning most of Canaryville someday. Little did they know that she'd jump at the chance to leave all of this if it meant being with Ben and Debbie.

The mailman walked in, and Kelly's heart did its usual somersault. There'd only been that one letter from them, the one that had come with the business plan, but she'd never stopped hoping.

"You got yourself quite a load this morning," the mailman said, and dumped a packet of mail on the counter. "Now my bag's about ten pounds lighter."

"Have a nice holiday, Rob," Kelly called after the man, and began to eagerly page through the mail. The door had barely closed after him when she dumped the mail back down on the counter. "Ad circulars, bills and other assorted junk."

"He's going to be back, Kelly," Mrs. Farrell told Kelly. "By the end of the month. Mark my words. The wee folk are working on it."

"Sure, Mom."

As Kelly began to clear the counter of the stack of envelopes, the UPS truck stopped out front. She watched the driver step out and noticed he was carrying a large package.

"You expecting something?" Mrs. Farrell asked.

Kelly saw the gleam in her mother's eyes. "Parts for the new conveyor, Mom. They should have gotten here yesterday or the day before."

The man came into the bakery and put the large box onto the counter. "Looks like you got an early delivery from Mr. and Mrs. Claus."

Kelly eyed the big box as she signed its receipt. "More like parts for my conveyor."

He shook his head and laughed. "People like you take the romance out of this job."

"Sorry," Kelly said, and left her mother to handle any business that came in, taking the mail and the box back to her office.

The salesman had promised that the conveyor would really streamline business. Production and profits would rise dramatically, though at this moment Kelly was uncertain if any of that mattered. Making forty loaves of rye bread a day instead of twenty did not mean her days would be twice as happy. She set the box on her desk and began to open it.

Whoever had wrapped the item had been very thorough about it, wanting to make sure that the contents were not disturbed in shipment. Kelly was a little surprised. She hadn't thought conveyor parts were that delicate.

As the last of the shredded newspaper fell away, Kelly's surprise turned into amazement. It wasn't an industrial part at all. It was a ceramic pie.

She took it out and set it on her desk. Not just a pie—it was a music box. After winding it up, she flicked the switch. The tune from the nursery rhyme "Four and Twenty Blackbirds" filled the office. As it played, triangular-shaped pieces of the top piecrust opened up and twenty-four little blackbirds appeared underneath.

Oh, Ben. Dear Ben. Tears filled her eyes. There was no note, but she knew who had sent the music box. He hadn't forgotten her.

"Are you sure you don't want to play?" Mrs. Farrell asked Kelly after the dinner dishes were cleared away.

"No, thanks, Mom." She picked up a Scrabble tile that had fallen onto the floor. "You and Mike go ahead. I want to fix my brown skirt so I can wear it tomorrow."

"She's just chicken, Mom," Mike said as he spread the game out on the low table in front of the sofa. "She knows we're too good for her."

"Dream on, little brother, dream on."

Kelly playfully mussed his hair as she passed by. She was not going to be depressed for Thanksgiving; she was not going to let her own unhappiness seep out and touch any-body else. Those were promises she'd made to herself this afternoon, promises she was determined to keep even if she had to recite them every moment of the day. She had no idea what to make of the music box, but Ben had obviously gone out of his way to find it for her. She couldn't have received a more cherished gift—except his ultimate return.

Kelly brought the portable sewing machine into the kitchen and set it up on the table. She'd started this skirt last winter, then got sidetracked. It was about time that she got it done. After threading the machine, Kelly got out her skirt and was about to start sewing when she stopped. She'd heard a noise like hammering coming from outside. There—it came again.

Kelly got to her feet and looked out the back window. The streetlight cast enough of a glow over the porch and yard, but she saw nothing. No movement at all. She was about to sit down when she heard the noise again.

"What the—" She opened the door this time, letting cold, damp air swirl around her.

The hammering was coming from the porch next door. Ben's porch. Except, of course, it wasn't his anymore. But it hadn't been anybody else's either—the apartment had stayed empty since he and Debbie had left. Now Kelly guessed someone had moved in. It was to be expected, she knew, but somehow that knowledge didn't help the sinking in her heart. All traces of Ben and Debbie were being wiped away, and pretty soon only those in her heart would remain.

She turned on the porch light and went out. The light from the neighboring apartment was on, also. Small, diamond-shaped pieces of light fell at her feet as the light came through the latticework privacy screen. There was someone on the other side of the screen, hammering.

"What—" Kelly began, but then the screen wobbled.

Someone was taking the screen down! Were there to be no memories left for her?

"Just a minute here," she called out, but the hammering had started again.

She'd normally swing around to the other side, but with the screen loose, that wasn't safe. She could go down her stairs and up theirs, but the screen was almost down, so she just waited.

This screen was originally erected by her family and former neighbors years ago for privacy. She would tell the new occupants that it could only be taken down with the consent of both apartments. Besides that—

The screen was down, and who should be standing there, smiling at her, but Ben!

"Surprise!" Debbie squealed.

"Ben? Debbie?" Kelly couldn't believe it was really them. This had to be a mirage, a figment of her overworked imagination. She should have listened to her mother and got more sleep, or eaten better breakfasts.

But then Ben was there in front of her, taking her into his arms. "Hi, love," he said, and kissed her.

His lips on hers dispelled any idea that she was dreaming, for her dreams never contained such fire, such hunger, such love. Ben's touch was different this time—stronger, surer, more possessive. Much as she wanted to rest in his arms for eternity, too many questions and too many worries came crowding in between them.

"Ben, you shouldn't be here," she said, pushing him away slightly. "What if we're still being watched?"

"You're not. It's over," he said, and reached for her again.

But Kelly sidestepped his arms and looked at Debbie. The little girl was all smiles and giggles. The haunted look was gone.

"I'm Daddy's now," she said. "We went to court and showed them my Mommy's diaries, and now I get to live with Daddy."

Kelly turned to Ben, her hand groping for his. "Ben?"

"That's about the gist of it," he said, a grin bursting to the surface. "After we left here, I realized I couldn't keep running with Debbie forever. It tore both of us apart to leave here. We had a long talk when we got to California and decided that we had to take the chance."

"I don't understand," Kelly said slowly. "What chance?"

"The chance that we'd lose in court," he said. "You see, neither of us expected things to go the way they had when we were here. We never thought it would be any different than Atlanta had been or D.C. We'd stay here a few months or a year and move on. But it didn't work out like that."

"Why not?"

He pulled on her hand, pulling her back into his arms. "Because of one redheaded young lady who swung into our lives around that privacy screen."

"Daddy said it has to come down because he doesn't want either of us swinging on it anymore," Debbie said.

Either of us? Did that mean they were staying? Kelly was having a hard time believing all of this was real.

"Go on," she said impatiently.

"Both Debbie and I fell in love with you," Ben said, his voice soft and low, as if his words weren't enough to permanently weaken her knees. "And living on the run for the next ten years without you just seemed too much. We decided that we had to go back to Massachusetts, take Sheila's parents to court and win so that we could come back here to you."

"And you did?" Kelly asked. "You've got custody?"

"Forever," Ben said. "I told Debbie what my mother had told me, the advice her lawyer had given her, and Debbie told me about Sheila's diaries. They proved to be the key. We had to subpoena them from Sheila's parents, but they proved I was Debbie's father, her unstable emotional state and the fact that she knew Debbie would be safe with me if anything happened to her.''

"Oh, Ben. It's all so wonderful." Kelly pulled far enough from his embrace to include Debbie. She hugged the little girl and kissed the top of her head. "I don't know what to say."

"Say yes," Debbie cried out with a great fit of giggling.

"Yes to what?"

"That you'll marry him," Debbie said impatiently.

"I'll thank you to let me do my own proposing," Ben said. His voice was rough, but his eyes were gentle. He stooped down to his daughter's level. "Why don't you go in and tell Mrs. Farrell and Mike the good news?" he suggested.

"Okay." Debbie raced over to the Farrell's door, then stopped. "Can I tell them Kelly's going to be my new mom?"

"Yes," Kelly said. "Now, get in there."

"All right!" Debbie was gone in a flash.

"All right!" Ben echoed as he pulled Kelly back into his arms. "Now, you aren't just saying that because you feel sorry for us, are you? I've got a good job at the Acme Machine Tool Company."

"Over by the tracks?"

"The very one. And Debbie's enrolled back in school here, plus we've rented out this apartment for a year."

"I see," Kelly said. "So you don't really need me, is that what you're trying to say?"

"Need you?" His hold on her tightened so that she could barely breathe. "Are you kidding? I need you so badly that it hurts. I've never had someone who understood me the way you do, who I could talk to about anything and know that you cared. Not a day went by when I didn't worry that you'd found someone to put blackbirds in your pie."

She looked up into his eyes. It didn't matter that they were in the shadows—she could still see the love shining through. She hadn't believed that such happiness could be hers.

"I did," she said. "I found him about five months ago, sitting right out here. Even though he didn't know how to play jacks, he made a mean ice-cream cone. Nobody else had a chance. I thought you must have known that when I offered to come with you and Debbie."

"I didn't want to believe it then," Ben admitted. "I didn't want anyone to care that deeply for us. Then, after everything was settled, I was afraid to hope you'd still be here waiting for us."

"Where else would I be?"

She met his lips and melted into them, promising love and forever in a silent song of devotion. They had tomorrow and tomorrow and all the tomorrows after that to touch and love, but somehow the moment was all there was. His lips devoured hers, and she felt herself being consumed by the fires and by his touch. Life was suddenly so sweet.

"I received the music box," Kelly said after a moment. "Where on earth did you find it?"

"Did you like it?" he asked. "I saw it in California, when we were still trying to decide what to do. I had to have it. It was like having you close to me, and it turned out to be our good-luck charm."

"I love it. I love you," she added on a breath.

Suddenly, as they swayed into each other's arms again, the porch lights went off, then the streetlight in the alley went out. Ben paused. "Much as I appreciate the privacy, how did that all happen at the same time?"

Kelly just lay against him, revelling in the solid, safe sound of his heartbeat. "Don't tell me, but you're part Irish, aren't you?"

"Yeah," he said, though clearly puzzled. "On my mother's side. Both her parents were Irish, so I'm half-Irish."

"Half-Irish—you're all Irish," Kelly quoted her mother with a sigh. "It's the little people at work."

"The little people again?"

"If I had known you were Irish before, I would never have worried," Kelly said. "I would have known they would have got us out of that mess. Whatever the little people want, they get."

"Remind me to thank them tomorrow," Ben said as his mouth came down on hers. "Right now I'm sure they have other things they want us to be doing."

Kelly was sure he was right.

## *Epilogue*

I'll take one of those Easter lamb cakes," Mrs. Johnson said. "The third one from the back."

"You having Easter dinner at Ila's?" Kelly asked as she carefully removed the cake from the display case.

The old woman nodded. "I don't know why they can't come here. You can't get a decent ham in the suburbs."

Kelly just nodded as she wrapped up the cake, then carried it and the bread Mrs. Johnson had bought over to the cash register.

"So, when is your baby due?" Mrs. Johnson asked.

Kelly just stopped, staring at the old woman.

Mrs. Johnson shook her head. "I asked your mother, but since she married Tom Arnold, she pretends not to know what's going on here."

Kelly found her voice once more. "She's very happy."

Mrs. Johnson just snorted as she counted out her change. "You never answered my question, young lady."

"Mrs. Johnson, if and when I become pregnant, you'll be one of the first to know," Kelly promised.

The woman just gave Kelly a look as she picked up her purchases. "I know the look," she said. "You've got that glow that comes with being pregnant."

"Maybe it's from the heat of the ovens."

Mrs. Johnson delivered a frown, then carried her bags to the door. "I'd say late November or early December. Too close to Christmas. No child is going to thank you for a birthday like that." The woman's nod punctuated her sentence, then she left.

"Have a nice Easter, Mrs. Johnson," Kelly called after her, then locked the door, switching the sign on the door to read Closed.

A baby. Kelly put her hand over her stomach and felt a secret smile weave its way onto her lips. Did she really have some sort of glow? It was almost too early to tell—she'd only had faint suspicions herself and hadn't even mentioned the possibility to Ben. She flicked off the bakery lights and hurried up the back stairs.

"Hey, everybody, I'm home," she said.

"We're in the kitchen," Debbie called out.

Kelly hurried in. Debbie was doing her homework at the old round table, and Ben was taking dinner out of the oven since he cooked on the days she closed up the bakery. There was so much love in the room that Kelly had to catch her breath. Sometimes she couldn't believe how lucky she was.

"Hi, sweetie," Kelly said, giving Debbie a quick hug. "Get that math done?"

"Almost," the little girl said. "Julie invited me to her birthday party next Saturday. Can I call her and tell her I can go?"

"Sure."

As Debbie raced to the other room, Ben came over to Kelly to encircle her with his arms. "How was your day?"

"You asked me that an hour ago when you stopped in downstairs," she pointed out, and doubled the chain by wrapping her arms around him. He was so good to come home to.

"And has it changed?"

"Well, as a matter of fact, I did have an interesting chat with Mrs. Johnson," Kelly admitted with a smile. "She told me I'm pregnant."

Ben grew still, though his eyes were afire. "She got a side business in obstetrics?"

"She says I have the glow." Kelly snuggled farther into his arms, planting a tiny kiss on his lips. "I don't know about that, but I do know she could be right. My period's almost two weeks late."

"Kelly, love." Ben just held her, his touch gentle, as if he feared she might break. Then he swallowed hard and held her away from him. "Is this something you want? I mean, with the bakery and all."

"Want?" She held him tighter, trying to erase that worry from his eyes. "I want your child more than anything else. I've got good people running the bakery. It doesn't need me full-time. And if it did, it still wouldn't matter. I can't think of anything more exciting than to have your child."

"Oh, Kelly," Ben whispered as he pulled her back into his embrace. "I never dreamed life could be this perfect."

"The little people sure know how to do things right," she said, reaching up to find his lips.

\*　\*　\*　\*　\*

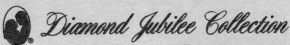
# Diamond Jubilee Collection

## It's our 10th Anniversary... and *you* get a present!

This collection of early Silhouette Romances features novels written by three of your favorite authors:

**ANN MAJOR**—*Wild Lady*
**ANNETTE BROADRICK**—*Circumstantial Evidence*
**DIXIE BROWNING**—*Island on the Hill*

* These Silhouette Romance titles were first published in the early 1980s and have not been available since!

* Beautiful Collector's Edition bound in antique green simulated leather to last a lifetime!

* Embossed in gold on the cover and spine!

This special collection will not be sold in retail stores and is only available through this exclusive offer.
Look for details in all Silhouette series published in June, July and August.

DJC-1

**Double your reading pleasure this fall with two Award of Excellence titles written by two of your favorite authors.**

*Available in September*

DUNCAN'S BRIDE
by Linda Howard
Silhouette Intimate Moments #349

Mail-order bride Madelyn Patterson was nothing like what Reese Duncan expected—and everything he needed.

*Available in October*

THE COWBOY'S LADY
by Debbie Macomber
Silhouette Special Edition #626

The Montana cowboy wanted a little lady at his beck and call—the "lady" in question saw things differently....

These titles have been selected to receive a special laurel—the Award of Excellence. Look for the distinctive emblem on the cover. It lets you know there's something truly wonderful inside!  DUN-1

*Silhouette Special Edition*®

Appearing in October
for a return engagement, Nora Roberts's
bestselling 1988 miniseries featuring

# THE O'HURLEYS!
## Nora Roberts

Book 1 **THE LAST HONEST WOMAN** *Abby's Story*
Book 2 **DANCE TO THE PIPER** *Maddy's Story*
Book 3 **SKIN DEEP** *Chantel's Story*

And making his debut in a brand-new title, a very special
leading man ... Trace O'Hurley!

Book 4 **WITHOUT A TRACE** *Trace's Tale*

In 1988, Nora Roberts introduced THE O'HURLEYS!—a close-knit
family of entertainers whose early travels spanned the country. The
beautiful triplet sisters and their mysterious brother each experience
the triumphant joy and passion only true love can bring, in four books
you will remember long after the last pages are turned.

Don't miss this captivating miniseries in October—a special collector's edition available wherever paperbacks are sold.

OHUR-1

*Silhouette Romance*®

# LONG, TALL TEXANS

**Diana Palmer's fortieth story for Silhouette . . . chosen as an Award of Excellence title!**

## CONNAL
## Diana Palmer

This month, Diana Palmer's bestselling LONG, TALL TEXANS series continues with CONNAL. The skies get cloudy on C. C. Tremayne's home on the range when Penelope Mathews decides to protect him—by marrying him!

One specially selected title receives the Award of Excellence every month. Look for CONNAL this month . . . only from Silhouette Romance.

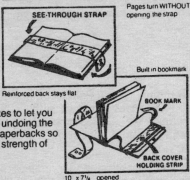